There's Something About You

Yashodhara Lal is a marketing professional and the mother of three children, apart from being a bestselling author. She graduated from IIM Bangalore in 2002 and manages to balance her professional life with her various interests, including fitness, writing and music. She lives in Gurgaon with her rather tolerant husband Vijay and their kids nicknamed Peanut, Pickle and Papad, all of whom never fail to provide her with material for her entertaining blog at yashodharalal.com. Her first book, *Just Married, Please Excuse*, is a hilarious account of marriage. Her second novel, *Sorting Out Sid*, is the story of a man having an early midlife crisis and, consequently, a divorce. *There's Something About You* is Yashodhara's third book.

There's Something About You

Something About You

Yashodhara Lal

SHE WAS IN ENOUGH
TROUBLE BEFORE
HE CAME ALONG...

YASHODHARA LAL

HARLEQUIN INDIA PVT LTD

First published in India in 2015 by Harlequin
An imprint of HarperCollins *Publishers*

Copyright © Yashodhara Lal 2015

P-ISBN: 978-93-5177-199-9
E-ISBN: 978-93-5177-200-2

2 4 6 8 10 9 7 5 3

Yashodhara Lal asserts the moral right
to be identified as the author of this work.

HarperCollins *Publishers*
A-75, Sector 57, Noida, Uttar Pradesh 201301, India
1 London Bridge Street, London, SE1 9GF, United Kingdom
Hazelton Lanes, 55 Avenue Road, Suite 2900, Toronto, Ontario M5R 3L2
and 1995 Markham Road, Scarborough, Ontario M1B 5M8, Canada
25 Ryde Road, Pymble, Sydney, NSW 2073, Australia
195 Broadway, New York, NY 10007, USA

Typeset in 11/14 Adobe Garamond Pro
by Jojy Philip, New Delhi 110 015

Printed and bound at
Thomson Press (India) Ltd.

To my husband, Vijay.
There's something about you.
And one day, I'll figure it out.

Contents

CONTENTS

1

Trish

'Lift, please. Hold ... HOLD!'

Trish reached the elevator just as the doors were closing and, in her desperation, did something she normally never would have done – she thrust one thick denim-clad thigh through the doors, causing them to open again, revealing several faces inside the lift with expressions varying from mild surprise to studied innocence. A few people stepped aside to make way for Trish and she squeezed her heavy frame, still panting, into the already crowded lift.

Trish tried not to meet anyone's eyes as she stepped on multiple sets of toes. She directed a 'Sorry, sorry!' towards the floor. She gave up trying to reach the back of the lift, where she would have felt more comfortable. Inwardly, she was seething at this typical rudeness of the corporate crowd in this building. These people had *seen* her running towards them. The polite thing would have been for someone to reach out and press the button to keep the lift waiting for her. Instead, they appeared to have reached some unspoken collective decision to pretend they had all suddenly lost their respective visions and therefore couldn't see Trish, all seventy kilograms of her, with her curly hair and dark-rimmed glasses, hurtling towards them.

She felt breathless and dizzy now. She had known it would happen. She closed her eyes and waited for it to pass. Trish hated being in crowded lifts. Thankfully, the lift opened on the second floor and four people stepped out, squeezing past Trish, who tried to make herself smaller. She took a couple of awkward steps back, stepping on three more sets of toes in the process, and finally settled into a much more comfortable position at the back of the lift. She had thought at one point that she had a fear of enclosed spaces, but then had noticed she felt this way in the lift only when there were other people around. She hadn't delved further into it; Trish didn't believe in overthinking her feelings.

It helped her to distract herself by discreetly observing the other folks in the lift, and this was partly why she liked to stand at the back. She usually started with the shoes, to see whether she was dealing with a brightly insecure pink-strapped high-heeled junior management professional or a suave, egoistic boss in his smooth, polished-by-someone-else-of-course, stylish, formal shoes. The next clues were the legs and what covered them. Trish noticed that the shape of a woman's ankles was a good indicator as to whether she had yet tried the latest in fitness, whether it was Pilates, kickboxing, power yoga or a healthy combination of all three. It was easier to figure this out in the skirts and annoyingly named 'jeggings' that were so fashionable these days. Formal pants made it tougher.

With men, Trish would have to shift her glance upward, past the crotch – quickly past the crotch! – to check for signs of the potbelly. The potbelly was pretty much a ubiquitous phenomenon amongst these relatively upper-class men in the corporate world. The men didn't seem to really know how to work it off, except the select few who clearly went to the gym with religious fervour. Women who had entered the state of motherhood recently still carried the signs in the belly region. The bright, insecure twenty-somethings, of course, had the tiniest, flattest tummies possible.

Trish made all these observations without judgement. She herself had given up on seeing her toes ages ago. Her weight problem had bothered her a little when she was younger, but now, at twenty-eight, she didn't think she needed to meet anyone else's standards. Her loose, dull, shapeless kurtas hid her shape fairly well, although they added to the bulk.

3

The lift cleared out further by the time it reached the seventh floor. They were now heading straight for the top floor – the tenth – and there were only two other people in the lift, a man and a woman, both from her own office. All three of them exchanged brief smiles and went on to studiously ignore each other. After a second, Trish glanced up again at their faces. The rise of the smartphone and the zombie-like downward gaze of smartphone owners made it easier for her to study faces these days. She thought her female colleague from the marketing department, who nuzzled a cup of takeaway black coffee from the Costa on the ground floor of their building, had partied too hard the previous night, given the tell-tale dark circles under her eyes. She was probably uploading selfies right now. The admin dude on the other hand looked like he might have got lucky last night. Maybe he was texting his wife or girlfriend or whoever right now to say how much he had enjoyed it. That had to be it, she thought. No one could look so happy on a Monday morning, especially not an admin guy. Unfortunately, he looked up at exactly this point to see Trish staring at his face. She blushed. 'Bloody lift, so slow, making us late. It's already ten. Ridiculous.'

He looked like he felt compelled to say something. 'Yes. Very slow lift.'

Trish shifted her weight from one foot to the other and went on: 'And the stupid new swipe card system. If you miss ten o'clock even by a minute, it marks you late. Wonder which idiot came up with it.'

The marketing girl looked up at them now with some interest, while the admin guy froze, appearing affronted. Too late, Trish realized that it was this fellow, Rajiv or Ravi or whatever his name was, who had been lauded for implementing the new swipe-to-enter technology at the last monthly HR announcements meeting – a mind-numbing function where Trish usually zoned out. Well, this was awkward.

The lift door opened. Trish abandoned all pretence of courtesy. Despite the fact that she was farthest from the door, she was the first one to get out of the lift.

❀

Trish waited at the coffee machine while three girls in front of her discussed, in great detail, the movies they had watched over the weekend, all of which had apparently been 'total bore, yaar'. Who were all these bubble-headed pretty young things flooding the office these days, anyway?

Trish figured Akshay had something to do with this. The new boss had arrived on the scene several months ago and had proceeded to throw himself into the heart of the business. Apparently, this didn't include content creation, which was Trish's function. She was the only one of his direct subordinates whom he hadn't bothered to spend any time with. No formal induction session, not even a subsequent review. Which, frankly, suited her just fine – she had already slotted him in as an egoistic slime-ball. Plus, he looked really young, perhaps just a couple of years older than her. This stung her slightly. She had risen to the position of content head after slaving away for years, but Akshay was clearly a corporate dynamo, considering he was already a vice-president.

He was the most visibly successful boss she had ever had: sharply dressed, gel-haired, cleanshaven, fair-skinned, gym-fit and eloquent, amongst other various vaguely annoying qualities. Bloody show-off. She frowned as she made her way to her desk, holding the hot paper cup gingerly out in front of her. She sat down, closed her eyes and took a deep breath. Her coffee smelt delicious. A gentle wisp of steam wafted up to tickle her nostrils as she slowly lifted the cup to her lips for the first glorious sip of the day.

'Trish, can I see you in my office, please?'

Her head snapped up, the coffee halfway to her lips. It had been more a command than a question. Akshay was standing right in front of her desk, one hand resting on the edge of her cubicle. Considering that he barely ever spoke to her, why on earth did he want to see her, of all people, first thing on a busy Monday morning?

'Um, okay, be right there,' she managed to get out. As if she had a choice in the matter. He looked suave as always, and having him in such close proximity made her feel grubbier and even dowdier than usual. She found herself wishing she hadn't worn this old brown kurta again today, comfortable as it was.

'All right.' He glanced down towards her desk and added, 'You might want to ...'

She looked down and saw that the coffee was trickling down one side of the cup on to her desk and the papers on it. She hadn't realized she had been squeezing it so hard. She shifted her grip slightly and managed to get some of the liquid on her fingers. Ouch, it was *hot*. Where were the tissues? Oh, there. Good. By the time she stemmed the flow and placed numerous tissues around the slightly deformed cup of steaming liquid and looked up, Akshay had disappeared.

With her usual vague sense of skepticism mingled now with an uneasy curiosity as to what this was all about, Trish made her way to her boss's office.

6

❀

'Ah, come in, Trish,' Akshay called out as Trish opened the door. She found herself feeling a little irritated by this. He had just invited her into his office but was now acting as though she were asking for his permission to enter. Idiot MBA-type.

She went over and sat down on one of the chairs in front of his desk. She hadn't been in here in ages. The previous boss, Sunil, had been fuzzy-headed but inclusive, prone to calling in people for random brainstorming sessions about various business problems that he seemed unable to solve himself. Trish had often taken part in those sessions which were painfully unproductive but usually involved a round of freshly ordered doughnuts. Sunil had been the grey-haired, mild, absent-minded variety, more suited to being a professor than a business head, but he had been a fundamentally nice person and at least had the decency to look *way* older than his team.

Akshay was now staring with a frown at some sheets of paper. A glistening white bone-china cup, half filled with what looked like green tea, was on the desk in front of him. Green tea! And bone-china cups! What luxury the top brass in this office enjoyed. Oh, well. Trish told herself that she still liked her low-pressure job. She had been the content head for two years already. With each new website that the business added, she got an additional content writer to report to her. So she now had a team of four young people. She had carefully chosen folks who weren't overly enthusiastic in the interviews. Stability, she decided, was the quality she was looking for. People needed to be steady and not rushing off with ambitious dreams every couple of years. Look at her. A total of seven years in this company now, straight out of college, obediently moving from the print department to the new-fangled Internet department five years ago. Sure, some people would have expected her to have a more senior position after all this time, but Trish was satisfied. Content with content, she quipped to herself with an inward smile.

Akshay looked up at Trish, his face impassive. 'So.'

Trish cleared her throat, unsure of what the response to that one was supposed to be. Akshay didn't seem to expect a response though, because he went on.

'I noticed, Trish, that you've come in late several days last month.'

Was that seriously an *attendance sheet* that he had printed out in his hands? Trish felt the colour rise to her cheeks. She could make out what seemed to be people's names in the rows, each followed by a series of numbers. Her mind raced. Maybe it was the admin dude who had gleefully brought Akshay the printout. She tried to stay calm. It wouldn't do to turn into a tomato in front of Mr Perfect. But it was a biological trait she couldn't control, this colouring of her cheeks when she felt bothered or embarrassed. She was both insulted and caught off guard. She was a senior manager – well, relatively senior, anyway, and had been with the company for so long – how could he—

'You're a senior manager – relatively senior, anyway', Akshay went on. What, he was reading her mind now? 'It wouldn't do to set the wrong example for your team and other young people in the office, right?' He leaned back and she noticed for the first time how dark and curly the hairs on his forearms were, even the ones on his wrists. It gave her a bizarre sense of satisfaction to know that there was something imperfect about him. She swallowed and then found her voice.

8

'Akshay.' She spoke deliberately, refusing to call him 'sir' like the others. 'I've been here for years. I've delivered on every single deadline and project that we've got going on, whether it's involved staying late or working over weekends. And I must tell you, I've never been called in for a discussion about coming in late.' She was watching his face closely and noticed something change in his expression. She went on. 'Is there something else you mean to tell me?'

'Well, Trish.' Akshay hesitated only a moment before adopting the smarmy, soothing tone she had distrusted from the beginning. 'Your contribution has of course always been valued here. You've been with the company for ... seven years now? Commendable!' His smile looked more like a smirk to her. 'Not feeling the seven-year itch or anything?'

She sat stiffly at the edge of her seat. What was he on about? The smile dropped off his face.

'Look. I need to bring you onboard with some of the new

thinking we're instilling here. The business is in trouble, and even though the last two quarters have shown some recovery' – the last two quarters since he'd been around of course – 'we've still got a long way to go. I've been thinking of rationalizing the structure, and we've all got to be ready to go with the flow – or find something more suitable.'

Wait, was that a warning? Trish willed herself to stay neutral. 'Could you be more specific?'

Akshay's eloquence came from his ability to spin a yarn around the simplest facts, but even he seemed to struggle a little with the next words. 'It's like this, Trish. You must be aware that we're starting a new fashion-and-lifestyle vertical next month?'

She had heard vague rumours about this a couple of months ago, but had no idea that it was actually planned so soon. She had been waiting for a project brief on this. It had sounded interesting and her assumption had been that, as content head, she would be pulled in naturally for something like this.

'I, um, yes, but … next month?' She stopped and bit her lip as the implication sank in. She had been sidelined.

'We felt …' Akshay hesitated for a second. Trish wasn't sure who the 'we' was here. 'We felt that something like this needs a vibrant new team of fresh, young people. That's why all the design graduates have been hired.'

Ah. *That* explained the pretty young things floating about in their six-inch heels. Wow. A whole new content department had been set up right under her nose and Trish hadn't even seen it. How blind of her. Her approach of keeping her head down and just delivering on her existing projects had done her in.

'As we're shifting resources to the new avenues of growth,

9

we're having serious thoughts about the current structure and whether indeed we're justified in paying out salaries to people who aren't *directly* contributing to the topline.' He went on to use a few more big words, but Trish was barely able to register what he was saying because her mind was racing. She did catch the word 'rationalization' being used more than once as he droned on.

Oh, she knew where this was headed. She could finally see the writing on the wall, although it was too late now. She hadn't demanded raises like the others, even though she was underpaid given her seniority. She hadn't been proactive in asking for new responsibilities, preferring to stay out of people's way. She had set up systems and trained her team well to function independently – in short, making herself redundant. She was dimly aware that Akshay was offering her the option of a month's pay for immediate termination or two months' pay for one more month's work. Her cheeks felt hot. Staying wasn't even an option as far as she was concerned. She couldn't bear to be here a moment longer.

'Trish? Are we on the same page?'

Twenty-eight years old. She couldn't remember the last time she had felt like crying. She certainly wasn't about to cry now. Still, it was through strangely bright eyes that she now looked straight into the face of her smarmy, so-successful boss. She raised her hand and pointed at the attendance sheet on the desk, with its neat rows and columns and names and numbers. She tried to keep her voice steady as she said, 'Are *you* on that page, Akshay?'

He froze for a second and then glanced at the sheet before looking up at her with a confused frown.

'Didn't think so.' She shook her head and added firmly, 'No. We're not on the same page, and we never will be.'

Without another word, she stood up. A part of her badly wanted to tell him that his hairy wrists were terribly unattractive, but she wasn't sure she had it in her to say anything more at this point. She quickly turned, left the room and walked back to her desk, trying to maintain a steady pace.

Her coffee lay there, looking forlorn. It had gone all cold in the blast of the air conditioning. Trish took a small sip from it – it was horrible. She tossed it angrily into her dustbin.

And then, slowly and methodically, she began to clear out her desk.

11

2

Home Sweet Hell

'It's you.'

The words themselves were innocuous, but given that they had come most unexpectedly out of the dark stillness, they made Trish jump. She put her hand on her heart, feeling it beat too quickly. She had just let herself into her apartment and it had been completely quiet, so she had assumed her parents were asleep. She had certainly *hoped* they would be asleep. It was exactly for this reason that she had spent the entire day driving around Mumbai aimlessly, until she had realized that she could ill afford the petrol. So she had parked some distance from her home and spent several hours sitting on a rock at Bandstand, staring out at the sea's grim grey waves. And yet, even though it was now almost midnight, her mother was still pouncing on her like a cat upon a mouse.

Ma was seated at the table in the drawing room that doubled up as the dining room. Trish could just about make out her angular profile in the dim light coming in through the windows. She dropped her purse to the floor with a thud. She'd thought her spontaneous solo tour of Mumbai would have calmed her down, but she felt all her irritation rising to her throat now as she snapped at her mother: 'Of course it's me. You were expecting maybe Shah Rukh?'

It was a standing joke in their otherwise humourless relationship that Trish's mother was a big SRK fan. When both her parents had moved in with Trish two years ago, Ma had been brimming over with excitement at the prospect of seeing Shah Rukh in the flesh, considering that he too lived on Bandstand, albeit in a mansion approximately seventeen times the size of this matchbox apartment which was all that Trish could afford to rent. *Used to be able to afford to rent.* Trish followed, glad that it was too dark for her mother to make out her expression.

'I was worried ...' Ma said, her voice trailing off.

Trish let out an exasperated sigh and lowered herself on to the chair opposite her mother. 'I had called you saying I would be late. And remember the deal, Ma?'

Her mother didn't answer, which Trish took to be a silent confirmation that she did remember. The 'deal' was that, once her parents moved in, no one would stay up waiting for anyone, since *everyone* in the house was an adult now, as Trish had emphasized. She couldn't be made to feel like an errant teenager in her own home or the whole tenuous arrangement would implode. Oh yes, Ma knew the deal and had honoured it all this while. It had been easy, considering this was actually Trish's first really late night in months.

'So.' Ma's voice became brisk, as she made a clear shift from the defensive to the offensive. 'Did you ask about the medical insurance today?'

13

'Oh.' Trish hesitated. 'That.'

'Yes.' Her mother's voice rose plaintively, 'You've been postponing that for *weeks* now. You know how Ba's new medicines are so costly, and you said even this morning that you would check on the company's policy for dependent parents. And you didn't?'

'No,' Trish admitted.

'I knew it.' Her mother fumed, now getting into full form. 'Delay, delay, delay. Just like your father. It's a wonder how anything moves forward in this family with all this procrastination, there's absolutely nothing that anyone ...'

Trish interjected: 'Ma. I got fired today.' She figured it was best to just get it over with.

Ma either hadn't heard or pretended that she hadn't, because she went on railing. 'Even when it was well past the time that we could look after ourselves, your father insisted that we stay in Indore.'

Trish began to worry that she would disturb Ba, sleeping in the other room, but Ma wasn't about to stop.

'No matter how many times I said, "What's the use of having a grownup daughter living in a big city with the best medical facilities if we don't stay with her in our old age?" and ...'

Trish felt herself quivering with anger as her hands clenched and she hissed at her mother: 'Ma! I said I got *fired*.' She glared at her mother. 'Are you even *listening*?'

Ma sure as hell was listening now. Even in the dim light, Trish could make out her shocked expression. Ma blinked hard once and then opened her mouth to speak.

Before she could say anything, another voice floated in. 'Trishna?'

Ba was the only person who ever referred to Trish by her

full name. Both Trish and her mother automatically glanced in the direction of Ba's room. Ba sounded confused and worried. They would have to set their differences aside for now. It was important to keep him calm.

'Trishna?' His voice came again, louder and more urgent this time.

For once, Trish didn't move in response. She just sat stubbornly at the table, staring at her mother, who was looking at her with a mixture of disbelief, panic and, Trish imagined, a hint of disgust.

Finally, her mother rose and hurried out of the room and down the hall to attend to her husband, calling, 'Yes, yes, she's here, she was delayed at work. What is it now, why are you up?' Her voice trailed off as she shut the door behind her.

Trish put her arms on the table and lay her tired head down. She felt overwhelmed by the events of the day. Someone else might have thought it might be better to let it all out with a good cry. But Trish didn't believe in that shit.

15

✿

Redness. Bright, hot, uncomfortable redness.

It was a ray of the morning sun, shining right into Trish's eyes. She blinked awake unwillingly, groaning softly to herself. What time was it? She sat up with a start and then realized it didn't matter anyway. She had lost her job. It hadn't been just a bad dream after all. Damn.

She glanced over at the small clock on her bedside table. Eleven o'clock. Wow. Well, she'd had a bad night, tossing and turning, unable to sleep. There had been sounds from her parents' room, indicating that Ba was giving Ma trouble about something or the other, but she hadn't gone in to investigate and try and calm Ba down. She felt a little guilty because she knew that her mother's ability to handle her father was nowhere near her own, but she just hadn't felt up to it.

The sound of the waves rhythmically crashing upon Bandstand hit her ears. Usually, she loved the fact that she could wake up next to the sea, with what, to her, was the most soothing sound in the world. Right now, though, it only served to remind her that a sea-facing apartment in Mumbai, even one the size of a matchbox, was an indulgence she could no longer afford.

Her throat felt parched and dry and she struggled heavily to her feet to go and fix herself a glass of water. She was wearing her pink flowered night-shirt, one she'd slept in for years. It was her favourite, although it had become rather tatty with use. She was in a loose pair of Winnie-the-Pooh pyjamas. She had no love for Winnie the Pooh, it was just that it wasn't easy to find pyjamas her size. Besides, here at home, there were only Ma and Ba. No one she was trying to impress. Not that it took much to impress Ba these days; Ma, of course, could never be impressed anyway.

She was still rubbing her eyes as she ambled towards the kitchen. She could hear Ma's voice in the drawing room. Who was she talking to on the phone? It wasn't the phone, Trish realized as a high-pitched voice rang out in response, 'So what's she going to do now? Sit around in her pyjamas all day?'

Trish rounded the corner and stood in the doorway, the glass of water and parched throat forgotten. Her friend and neighbour Akanksha sat there in all her petite, coiffed and judgemental glory, across the table from her woebegone mother. Both women registered her presence and glanced up at her with sudden bright smiles that only irritated Trish further.

16

'Good morning, dear,' said Ma, who only used terms of endearment under the pressure of guilt. 'Akku just came two minutes ago ...'

'Took just two minutes for you to tell her?' Trish growled. 'So that both of you could sit there together and judge me for losing my job?'

'Now, Trish,' Akanksha cut in smoothly. 'Don't be silly. Aunty is just worried.'

'"Aunty" is always worried, Akku.' Trish went over and sat down next to her friend. She pointedly ignored her mother, grabbing a bottle of water from the table and glugging the water straight from the bottle, a habit she knew Ma hated. She then picked up the newspaper and made a show of pretending to read the headlines. She looked up for just a second and saw the meaningful glance that her mother and Akanksha were exchanging. She quickly turned back to the paper.

After a few minutes, her mother rose from the chair, saying something along the lines of, 'I suppose I'll see what that lady of yours has made for lunch.'

That lady of hers was Munni the part-timer. She'd been with Trish for five years, and it had taken a lot for Trish to persuade her to continue with the household chores after her parents had moved in. Her mother was of little help in the kitchen but she certainly knew how to hover and make the help's life miserable. So poor Munni, who had become so used to Trish's easygoing ways and lack of interest in household matters, had suddenly found that she no longer ruled the roost. Trish felt a lump rising in her throat. She might even have to let Munni go now; money was going to be tight until she found another job. She didn't even have a resumé ready. Plus, she had chosen not to go in for that damn MBA. Ma's fault – if she hadn't pushed Trish so insistently towards an

MBA, Trish might not have automatically dismissed the suggestion, choosing instead to find work straight out of college. Where had all her hard work and initiative got her anyway?

'Trish.' Akanksha's voice, gentler than before, snapped her out of her reverie. She looked up to see her friend's perfectly made up, pretty, pixie-like face, with its stylish smooth hair framing it, staring at her with concern. 'Tell me, what happened?'

Trish sighed. Akanksha lived in the same building in one of the big, luxurious ground-floor apartments. Trish didn't recall exactly how they had become friends in the first place, especially given how different they were from each other. Akanksha was married; she was a mother; she was rich and beautiful. All the things Trish knew she would never be. It was probably just that they had lived in close proximity for so many years here, occasionally helping each other out with mundane neighbourly matters. Also, Akanksha was usually too self-centred and thick to see through Trish's sarcasm, so Trish had wearied of her usual tactics to fend off potential friends and had accepted that Akanksha was going to hang around.

Akanksha was the persistent sort, so Trish knew she wouldn't give up until she knew the all details. She said reluctantly, 'There's nothing to tell, Akku. My boss called me in yesterday and pretty much said that there was no place for me in the organization any more.' The memory of the humiliating conversation began to fill her with anger again and she continued bitterly. 'There's some new fashion portal that they're launching and I guess he figured I wasn't hip enough to do the content for that.' Her friend's expression flickered for just a second, but Trish caught it. 'What?' she said sharply.

'Nothing,' Akanksha said, just a little too quickly. 'Go on.'

Trish frowned. Akanksha's expression continued to hover between sympathy and impassiveness. Then Trish's frown cleared. 'Ah. Of course. You think he's right.'

Akanksha protested. 'Who? No! You must be crazy.' But Trish saw through it.

'You think he's right!' The full implication hit her. 'It's all about appearances with you people, isn't it? There's no such thing as talent or determination or hard work. It's all to do with style, not substance.'

Akanksha narrowed her eyes. 'Look, sweetie.' Trish was usually tolerant of her friend, but right now the 'sweetie' made her want to strangle Akanksha. Akanksha continued, oblivious to her glowering. 'I won't try and sugarcoat this, okay? I've been telling you for years that you've got to try harder as far as putting yourself together goes ...'

'Not the time, Akku,' Trish said quietly.

'Sure, it's not the time. It's never the time.' Akanksha was undeterred. 'Except that it *is* the time now. Wake up! Smell the coffee. Look at your pyjamas. Look at you!'

'Is this some kind of new-fangled therapy you're suddenly into? It's *not* helping.'

'It isn't any therapy. It's the truth you've been denying.' Trish rolled her eyes but Akanksha went on. 'You haven't bothered to try and stay relevant. You had this new boss who clearly wanted to shake things up, and you never made a single bit of effort to get to know him and align yourself with his agenda. I don't work, but even *I* know that that's how things go in the corporate world.' This got another eye-roll from Trish which Akanksha just ignored again. 'And now that you've gone and messed up your only source of income, you're just taking it out on us.'

'Who the hell is "us"?'

'Your well-wishers. Me and your mom, who only want to help ...'

'Akku, please.' Trish put her face into her hands. 'Can you stop now? You did this when I told Ma to get off my back about finding a man too. I don't know why you always side with her. I don't need the two of you ganging up on me right now, all right? It's my problem. I'll handle it myself. So can you please just drop it?'

There were a few moments of silence. When Trish looked up again, Akanksha was staring at the wall in front of her in silence, biting her lower lip. It struck Trish once again how similar Akanksha and her mother were. They both looked younger than their respective ages, they both didn't seem to want to *act* their age; they had both never had to work a day in their lives to support themselves; and they both were always trying to *solve* Trish – fat, unmarried and now jobless Trish.

But when Akanksha finally spoke again, her voice had more of what seemed like concern. 'How are you on funds? Will you need something for a few months? I can always ask Vinay ...'

Trish shook her head brusquely. 'No. No thanks.' No way, she thought. No loans. Trish had barely said two words to Akanksha's husband over the last few years. He was a perfectly nice, handsome man with a big business of his own. Akanksha always proudly said she had lucked out with her arranged marriage. But there was no question of Trish borrowing money from anyone. 'I'll figure it out,' she added more gently, noting that Akanksha looked disappointed at her response. Her friend was irritating, but at least her heart was in the right place. In approximately the correct region, anyway.

Akanksha's breezy tone was back. 'Well, you're right. You've got substance. You've got some solid experience. You'll be back on your feet soon.'

Trish's head was buzzing and heavy despite the fact that her day had just started, but she tried to end the conversation by making a joke. She rubbed her ample tummy and said, 'Yep. Lots of substance here. Plenty of me to hire. I could offer a BOGO scheme – buy one employee, get one free!'

Akanksha frowned. 'Let's not do the fat jokes.'

'Okay,' Trish agreed, dropping the act. It was draining anyway.

Akanksha smiled at her. 'You'll be okay. You'll get another job in no time.'

'Sure.' Of course. Trish feigned confidence as she returned the smile.

After all, it was a fake-it-till-you-make-it kind of world. Especially if you were a single twenty-eight-year-old woman with two dependent parents and no job in the unforgiving city of Mumbai.

21

3

The Search

'Well, thanks for coming down. We'll get back to you.'

Trish looked up at the beaming face of the HR girl who had been sent to tell her that she was done for the day. The week. The month. Forever. 'We'll get back to you.' Of course they wouldn't. She had learnt to read the signs now. After all, it was the sixth interview she'd had in the last two months, each culminating in that phrase. Never to be actually followed through on.

Trish slowly rose from her seat in the small conference room while the puny HR girl continued to beam in that unnatural fashion so popular with HR people. Oh, well. At least the coffee had been good. The last guy who had interviewed her – who had been so cool and senior that he hadn't bothered to introduce himself, naturally assuming that Trish should recognize him on sight – had clearly been unimpressed with her. They had been the same old painful questions, which she knew indicated that the guy was just going through the motions because his team had falsely led him to believe that this lady was perhaps worth his time. Even though she had tried to answer sincerely, his disdain had made her so uncomfortable that her words had rung false in her own ears and she was just glad it was all over for now.

'What are your strengths and weaknesses?' *Puke.* 'What have been your biggest achievements?' *Gag.* And the most annoying one, which usually set her babbling. 'So. Tell me about yourself.' *Double-puke-gag-slide-under-the-table.*

What Trish really dreaded even more than these questions was the inevitable, 'So why did you leave your last organization?' The honest response, 'They sort of made me,' was always on the tip of her tongue, but she usually ended up with a one-liner about irreconcilable ideological differences, which usually left the interviewer looking unconvinced.

No one actually mentioned it, but she knew it was possibly this lack of clarity on why she was out of work that was doing her in. And also her non-MBA-ness. And her looks. She had tried to make herself presentable for these interactions by taming her thick curls into a ponytail and by not wearing her glasses, but she knew that her plus-size wardrobe, consisting mostly of loose kurtas, didn't make for smart, formal dressing. Akanksha had repeatedly suggested that they go shopping together, but Trish had put her off obstinately, digging out and dusting off a couple of formal trousers and shirts from several years ago. They weren't in the best of shape, and neither was she, so it was a real squeeze getting into them. She had really allowed herself to balloon up over the last few years, she realized. She'd got too comfortable in more ways than one.

She smiled a wan goodbye at the puny HR lady and then walked out past the reception to wait for the elevator. This

23

was just yet another organization that had called her in only to dash her hopes. Well, it wasn't like she had harboured that much hope anyway. After the fourth interview, she was pretty much just going through the motions herself.

Still, it was important for her to get out of the house occasionally and these interviews served as an excuse. It had been bad enough having to deal with her parents in the mornings and evenings while she was working, but being cooped up with them the whole day was too much. Ba had become even clingier and more dependent on her now that he had figured she wasn't leaving for work. And her mother was just being herself, which was enough to drive anyone crazy.

The basement where she had parked was dark and dingy, but she was in no tearing hurry to get back home. She let herself in and sat behind the wheel for a while, doing some mental calculations. She had been avoiding the thought for a couple of weeks, but she knew that her money was running out, and she was going to be in serious trouble. Her assumption that she would have a new job within a few weeks, with at least the same level of pay as her previous job, had proved to be grossly untrue.

Medical bills and treatment for Ba, plus rent for sea-facing matchbox, including the hike of ten per cent due in four months as per the lease, plus regular grocery expenses plus ...

Great. A whopping amount already, and she hadn't even factored in other expenses like the maid's salary, gas, electricity and petrol. She absent-mindedly rubbed the steering wheel. She had bought this Opel Corsa secondhand three years ago largely on the basis of its price and aqua-green colour, and it had served her well, but it sure guzzled up a lot of petrol. She stopped musing when she noticed that a couple of guards were staring at her rather suspiciously. Just as one of them began to approach her, she turned the key and started the car.

She revved up and drove out of the basement, feeling furious with herself. Why on earth hadn't she *invested* in anything? Why hadn't she built up sufficient savings? What had been the point of living just within her salary, assuming that she would continue to earn that much and more forever? She remembered the various times she had turned a deaf ear to her mother's advice about planning for the future. But then her mother was one to talk; she never planned for anything in her life herself, and had always left all important household matters to her husband. Now look at them – her father had been diagnosed with Alzheimer's and couldn't do a thing, slowly losing his memory and his grip on reality, while her mother stood by, watching helplessly and doing the only thing she could now, which was blaming Trish for everything that had gone wrong.

25

Trish had been determined that she would do better than her mother, but it didn't really look like it any more. She barked a short laugh at herself as she waited for the guard at the exit gate to amble over and press the switch to raise the security barrier for her. The bright light of the outside world after the cool darkness of the basement made her blink, and she reached for her sunglasses on the dashboard. She caught a glimpse of herself in the rearview mirror as she headed out on to the main road. Her hair was already loose from the ponytail and some curly locks had stolen out of it to stick out behind her right ear. Her cheeks were chubby and the sunglasses, a purple pair which she had bought on a whim a couple of years ago, looked too small on her face. Ridiculous, actually. She hated them. She tore them off her face and tossed them to the backseat. No. She hated *herself*.

She drove moodily along Marine Drive. This company had its fancy-ass office in Nariman point and now it would be at least an hour's drive before she got home. She soon wouldn't have the luxury of driving in Mumbai. The local train was going to be her only option. The very thought made her feel suffocated. She remembered from years ago what it was like, even in the ladies' compartment, being jammed together like that, like sardines in a can. Even the memory was making her breathless and dizzy now. Whoa. Her head was spinning. She quickly decided it would be better to pull over. She stopped the car on the side of the road adjacent to the beach.

Why was she feeling so dizzy? Hunger. That's what it was. She hadn't eaten all day. First her mother had made some remark about her clothes while she was sitting down to breakfast. It had only been an innocent 'Are you wearing that?' while staring at Trish's tight flowery blouse from the summer of 2009, but the question was loaded with meaning. It had caused Trish to lose her appetite. Her nervousness about the interview and her irritation with her mother caused the toast to turn to cardboard in her mouth and she had gruffly risen from her chair, saying, 'I'm late,' and brushing past Ma's attempt to push one stray curl behind her ear. She hated that about her mother, her ability to make Trish feel like an unkempt teenager ... when, really, she was an unkempt fully-grown woman.

She wished she had packed a salad or something. It was already lunchtime. Her windows were half open since she was trying to cut down on air conditioning in the car, and the inviting, smoky smell hit her nose right on cue. Aaah.

She rolled up the window and got out of the car. The bhutta-waala saw her coming and grinned in welcome. It was a yellow, broken-toothed smile, but it struck her as the most genuine smile she had seen all day, and her mood lifted. She said to him, 'Ek, please,' and then watched him expertly toss the corn on the cob over the hot charcoal. The smell of the nimbu and masala and corn was tantalizing, and her mouth watered in anticipation. She paid the man his fifteen rupees, tossed her purse back into her car and went and sat on the ledge overlooking the rocks leading out to the sea. She took a deep breath and bit into the corn, savouring the spicy taste as she stared out at the waves, which were an attractive shade of blue in the light of the afternoon sun.

That was when she saw it.

She squinted against the glare of the sun on the water. A stick? Or one of those rods implanted in the seabed near the shore as a guide for the fishermen? A wayward branch? But how come it was moving like that? Curiosity compelled her to get up and walk a few steps closer to the ledge.

She strained her eyes again, wishing she had taken her glasses out of her purse after the interview. Her eyes adjusted after a moment or two, and she suddenly realized that what she was currently gazing at looked an awful lot like someone drowning.

'Oye! I mean, hello! Bachao koi isse ...' She reached out and caught hold of the arm of a random passerby. She spun him around and pointed at the drowning man. He peered suspiciously in the general direction Trish was pointing at with her bhutta and then shrugged himself free and walked away. Trish shot him a furious look. Maybe the idiot might have stopped to help if she had been thinner and hotter. But she barely had time to complete the thought because when she looked out into the ocean again, the arm had disappeared.

Had she just imagined it? Her heart was beating fast. She was still disoriented from hunger. Yes, perhaps that was all. Just her imagination.

Shit.

She dropped the bhutta as she climbed over the low boundary wall that separated the road from the shore and then made her way towards the water tenuously. Stupid high heels she had worn in a bid to look taller for the interview. She could barely carry these things off on regular flooring, and these were rocks, slippery and wet. She lost her balance and almost fell. The tide was coming in now, and the dark grey, treacherously smooth rocks were dangerous. People probably drowned here all the time. It was stupid to be doing this. She couldn't even remember the last time she had gone swimming – wasn't it as a kid? Not that she intended to go into the water or anything. She just had to check and make sure it was nothing.

She was dimly aware, from the sound of warning shouts from behind her, that there were a few curious eyes following her progress. But no one seemed willing to step forward and help. She knew she made quite a sight, an overweight woman in a tight flowery blouse and trousers and high heels teetering towards the waves. Yes, she supposed it was all very funny. Trish, the big joke. She slipped again and, with a growl, bent down and whipped off one sandal, then the other. She carried on barefoot, feeling the hardness of the slippery rocks, the lukewarm waves already lapping at her ankles.

Where had it been? Around here? Or a little farther on? Now the water was up to her knees. This was beginning to feel more and more like a fool's errand. There was nothing here. She looked hard at the water around her. She sensed that going any further would be dangerous.

28

A movement that she saw out of the corner of her eye made her whip her head around to the right. And there it was: an arm, a definite arm, full-sleeved. There was a man in the water about fifteen feet ahead of her. He currently didn't seem to mind drowning all that much, given the limpness of that arm and the rest of his body, of which she now caught a sudden glimpse. He wasn't struggling at all, it was more the motion of the water that was throwing him up to the surface. He appeared to be unconscious.

Shit. Shit. And shit.

'Hello, sir? SIR? Listen to me, sir. You have to wake up now and ... SWIM ... I mean ... hello, BOSS!'

There wasn't anyone around who could actually hear her, but Trish's panicked instructions sounded idiotic even to her own ears. She turned around towards the shore and saw that there was now a small crowd watching her. She waved frantically at them and was supremely frustrated when a few of the people automatically waved back at her. Luckily, a few of the more intelligent or foolhardy souls appeared to take it as a call for help and began to slowly advance towards her. Too slow, though.

Trish whirled back around towards the sleeved arm and her heart sank when she saw that it had moved a few feet farther. Oh god. She felt more helpless than she ever had in her whole life. All she could do was stand there and wait and watch. Big, dumb, useless woman waiting on the sidelines.

The water was up to her hips and then her waist. The tide was coming in too fast. She found herself wading towards the man. There was no point to this, of course. Her sandals floated away from her. The people behind her would never make it in time.

Could she swim? She couldn't swim. She was swimming. Oh, good. Swimming was apparently something you never forgot. Like riding a bicycle. Except that her clothes felt like they weighed a ton, which didn't happen on a bicycle. Unless you were cycling in the rain or something. But you'd have to be brainless for that. She was pretty brainless herself, come to think of it.

The water was murky and not as blue as it had looked just a few minutes back. It was brown and dull and dangerous and sucked you in and pulled you down. But she was near the man now. He had two arms, after all, it was just that one of them appeared to be currently wedged in between two rocks. Trish was drowning now. That was what it felt like as she swallowed water while attempting to free him. She tugged at his shirt and managed only to tear it. He was face-down in the water. She caught hold of his hair, gasping and barely managing to keep her own head above the water. A wave came over them and Trish's mouth was filled with some more salty and sandy sea water. It was too much effort to stay afloat now.

'Wonderful,' was her last thought as the blackness closed in around her with another treacherous wave of deathly brown-grey water. A useless life, rounded off nicely with a useless death.

4

Wake-up Call

'Trish?'

The black faded away slowly as Trish blinked into consciousness. This voice was all too familiar, so this was unlikely to be the afterlife. At least she hoped so. The face came into vision, first blurred and then sharp and angular as always, against a backdrop of an unfamiliar sterile-looking white and blue background.

'How are you feeling?' said her mother, her voice anxious.

'I'm okay,' Trish slurred. She made an effort to sit up and then immediately wished she hadn't because the room started to spin. She lowered her head back on to the soft pillow. 'What's going on?'

'What's going *on*?' Ma cried. 'Well, you almost drowned!' Trish was too dazed to react to the accusing tone. Her mother's voice dropped now as she added, almost to herself, 'Trying to save some lunatic.'

'Lunatic?' Trish remembered with a start, and looked around the room. 'How is he? Is he okay?'

'Under observation. By the time they got both of you out, you had swallowed even more water than he had. Must have been the extra weight on you.' Trish frowned, but her mother went on. 'What was the need for the overly heroic act, Trish? You could have been ...' Ma swallowed the word and Trish could see the lump in her throat.

This hint of emotion made her uncomfortable and she cleared her throat and asked Ma, 'Who is the guy anyway? Where is he?'

'Somewhere in the hospital. Special ward. Under police observation.'

'What? Why?'

'Oh.' Her mother waved the question away dismissively. 'They're saying it was attempted suicide. I don't know the details. They said they will have to question you too. Trish, why would you get yourself into this mess? It's not like ...'

'So he's going to be okay, right?' Trish interrupted. The realization was sinking in and she suddenly felt all funny and light inside. The guy was alive. She had done it.

'Yes, but he's just some psycho and you went ahead and ...'

'Oh, just drop it, Ma.' Trish's voice was so angry that, for once, even her mother couldn't ignore it.

'I just meant ...' Ma spoke tentatively, 'He wasn't worth risking your own life for.'

'And how do *you* know that?' Trish growled, her eyes narrowed.

'Because,' her mother hesitated. 'He was trying to commit suicide. It wasn't like it was an accident ... suicide ... it's a sin,' she finished, sounding sanctimonious and lame and aware of it, all at once.

Trish shut her eyes tight, wishing she had the power to make Ma disappear. She decided to go ahead and try getting up. She opened her eyes and raised herself on her elbows, more gingerly than before. She looked down and noted that she was dressed in a striped blue hospital gown that made her feel even more matronly than usual. She ignored her mother's feeble attempts to help her and swung her legs off the bed to put her feet on the ground. Her anger towards her mother had now turned cold. This was nothing new.

She was determined not to talk to her mother at all, but a sudden thought struck her. 'Who's with Ba?'

She could feel her mother's eyes on her. After a second, Ma exhaled softly. 'Akanksha. She wanted to come here when we got the news about you, but I asked her to stay home with him. He would have worked himself up into a fit otherwise.'

'Good,' Trish said gruffly. She almost added, 'You shouldn't have come either,' but she wisely kept the thought to herself. She rose, relieved to find that she was able to stand without support. A wave of nausea overcame her as she remembered the helpless struggle to stay afloat. No, she certainly wasn't going to start swimming for the joy of it any time soon. She closed her eyes to steady herself, swallowing hard. Ah. A little better.

'The doctor said he would have to examine you,' her mother suddenly recalled. 'Wait, let me press the bell for the nurse.'

'Oh god. Ma. I'm fine,' Trish groaned, shaking her head slowly. 'I don't want a fuss, I just want to get out of here and go home.' She looked down at herself again. 'I hate this stupid thing. What did they do with my clothes?' She suddenly had a horrifying realization. 'Wait.' Her voice became shriller. 'Who changed my clothes?'

'I don't know.' Her mother was wide-eyed. 'You were sleeping in this gown by the time I came in.'

Trish cringed, feeling humiliated and furious. Someone had taken the liberty of removing her clothes. They had seen her naked, imperfect, flabby body. How dare they? She knew she was being unreasonable, but it was all too much to take.

Her mother seemed to be trying to appease her now because she pushed forward a bag. 'I got you a fresh set of clothes from home.'

Trish almost snatched the bag from Ma's hands. She tried to make up for it with a gruff 'Thanks', but she said it in such a low voice that she knew her mother wouldn't have heard. She didn't bother to repeat it. She busied herself with stepping out of the ghastly gown and into the underwear, well-worn bra, large jeans and loose kurta that her mother had packed for her. She kept her back to Ma, trying to ignore how uncomfortable it felt to change with someone else in the room, never mind that it was her own mother. She felt better in her own clothes, though. She looked around, frowning. 'Shoes?'

'Oh.' Her mother said delicately. 'I forgot about those. Maybe the ones you were wearing are here? I'll go check.'

'Don't bother.' Trish recalled the sandals floating away. 'I lost them in the sea.'

'What?' Her mother cried. 'That nice new pair of heeled sandals? You lost *them*? They were your best pair!'

Trish was incredulous. 'Yeah, Ma. I'm sorry I didn't save the pretty shoes. I kind of had *other* things on my mind.'

'You can stop with the sarcasm now, Trish.' Her mother spoke coldly. 'It's not as if it's been an easy day for me, having to get a call and hear that my only daughter almost drowned.'

Of course, Ma, it's all about you. Trish tried to tune her out by looking for alternative footwear. What was that? A pair of fuzzy bunny slippers – why did hospitals think they made the most practical accompaniment for people whose only visits were likely to be to wet bathrooms?

'Hello. You're up and awake?' A nurse materialized in front of Trish as she finished struggling her large feet into the tiny bunny slippers. Trish looked at her mother suspiciously. Ma must have pressed the call bell when Trish wasn't looking.

She replied breezily to the nurse. 'Up and awake and ready to leave.'

'Oh no!' The nurse laughed, showing white, even teeth. 'That is not the way. First we make sure you are okay, no?'

'No,' Trish said firmly. 'I'm fine. I didn't admit myself here or sign any consent forms. I feel fine. Thank you. Goodbye.'

The nurse looked past Trish at her mother, and Trish felt a twinge of annoyance. Ma was always exchanging meaningful glances with other people. First Akanksha and now some random nurse.

'I will have to call Doctor-sir, he will see you and then decide on your release.'

'Release?' Trish repeated with a short bark of a laugh. 'This is like a prison cell? Bring on the warden, then. But hurry up, I haven't got all day. I'm a busy person.'

She waited with bated breath for her mother to say one thing, just one thing, to contradict this statement. *Come on, just one remark on how I'm actually jobless and have nothing to do all day, bring it on, Ma.* But her mother stayed quiet. The nurse's teeth shone, but her grin was more uncertain this time. 'I will call Doctor-sir,' she repeated and then turned on her heel and trotted away.

35

✽

'Gone?' Trish repeated, not sure she had heard the doctor right.

He was a friendly, humorous, good-natured fellow, this Dr Behl, and he was doing a lot to cheer her up with his hmm-ing and tch-tch-ing as he examined her. He was one of those doctors with innate natural charm. He looked about fifty-five years old and was treating Trish as if she were an errant, well-meaning teenager. Trish was a tough nut to crack, but he had won her over when he exuberantly congratulated her on her daring escapade, and so she had cooperated with the physical examination that he had promised would take only five minutes 'tops'.

'Oh, yes, the chappie has gone. Vanished without a trace. Vamoosed. Disappeared into thin air.' He removed his stethoscope from Trish's back, appearing satisfied. 'And now, so may you. You're absolutely fine, young lady. Just eat the piping hot nutritious meal we're providing you and then go home.'

'Er, but doc ...' Trish hesitated. 'How did he ... disappear like that? Wasn't he under police observation or something?'

'Gave them the slip,' Dr Behl said breezily. 'Evaded them. Gone in the blink of an eye, while the hardworking fellow on duty took a well deserved nap on the stool outside the room.' He paused, gazing over the top of his glasses at Trish, and said, in a gentler manner, 'I suppose you wanted to see him?'

'See him?' Trish repeated blankly. 'No. Well, yes. I mean. I just wanted to know if he was okay, that's all.' She couldn't fully hide her disappointment. Maybe she had wanted to see the guy after all. Just to talk to him. And find out what the hell he was thinking when he decided to end it all in a watery grave that had almost taken her in with him. Fool. And now he had disappeared.

'Anyway.' She looked up at the doctor. 'Thank you, Dr Behl.'

'Oh! You're welcome, young lady. You did a wonderful thing. Keep it up. Are you a lifeguard by profession?'

'Me?' Trish said automatically before she realized he was joking. He had a dreamy expression on his face as he said to himself, 'I used to love *Baywatch*.'

Her mother was staring at the two of them, unsure as to what was going on. She wasn't used to large, friendly doctors, Trish realized. She had only gone to that one slimy, small family physician neighbour of theirs, who was now approximately a hundred years old, but still practising back in Indore. Trish couldn't help but grin at her puzzled expression. She turned back to the doctor. 'Bye, doc.'

The doctor smiled at her and said, 'Farewell, young Trish.' And with a slight bow towards her mother, he swept out of the room, the young nurse scurrying to keep up with him and get him to sign the discharge papers.

He had convinced Trish that it was in her best interest to eat the meal that had been placed in the room for her. She picked reluctantly at the tray. She then slowly peeled back the silver foil covering the largest dish. Aah. Khichdi and dahi. How annoyingly healthy. Still, it was warm and she realized only after she started eating how famished she really was. Shovelling down a few bites, she finished in a matter of minutes. Another small cup contained some cut melons. She gulped them down too and then sipped from the small juice box that had come with the tray. She wiped her mouth with a napkin, wishing her mother would stop watching her. She could feel her mother's eyes on her even without looking up.

Aware that her mother wouldn't think of doing anything about the formalities required to actually get out of there,

Trish ran her fingers through her curly hair once, gave up trying to look presentable, and stalked out of the hospital room in her newly acquired bunny slippers.

※

They were accosted at the reception by two grim-looking policemen who claimed to have questions about the incident. Trish was loud and insistent that she knew nothing about the fellow, but had simply gone in when she saw he was in trouble. She told them she needed to leave right away and that they could interview her at her home address if they wished. They hovered. Finally, the mustachioed one, who looked more senior, nodded, and they let Trish and her mother walk out of the hospital. Trish trotted ahead of her mother and didn't glance back once, realizing it had been a lot easier to get away from them than she'd thought it would be. She wasn't about to hang around, in case they changed their minds.

They took a taxi from the hospital to Marine Drive. Trish worried that her car would have been stolen by now because she had left it unlocked, but there it was, right where she had parked it on the side of the road. The bhutta-waala grinned in recognition when she got out of the taxi. She approached her car with some trepidation, but it looked fine even though the back window was open. Even her purse still lay in the backseat, untouched. The bhutta-waala called out that he had watched it the whole day, awaiting her return. He exclaimed with admiration, 'Aap to ekdum hero hai, madam!' He proceeded to offer her a free bhutta. She refused the bhutta, but thanked him for his vigilance. She opened the car door and got in, reaching for her purse. Yes. The key was right where she had automatically popped it, front pocket.

Thank god for the bhutta-waala. Ma also got a friendly yellow-toothed grin and an offer of a free bhutta, which she shrank back from suspiciously, and she gingerly made her way around to the passenger seat. Trish revved the car up and took off almost before her mother had closed the door. They drove home in complete silence, her mother only occasionally gasping at Trish's fast turns and tendency to brake hard at the last minute.

The white bunny slippers were dirty by the time Trish and her mother reached home an hour and a half later. She took them off as soon as she entered the house and pushed them to one corner of the hall. It was really late now, but the light in Ba's room was still on. Dropping her keys on the side table and the purse to the floor, she headed straight down the long narrow hall to her parents' bedroom.

'Trish.'

Akanksha stood up rather dramatically and she reached up to envelop her friend in a tight embrace. When she didn't let go, Trish said in embarrassment, 'I'm fine, okay? Don't make a big deal out of it.' She looked over Akanksha's shoulder. 'Not in front of Ba.'

Akanksha's grip loosened and she looked at Trish's face searchingly, concern on her pretty face. Trish gently patted her on the shoulder as she slipped away to go to her father.

'Ba?'

'You've come, finally.' Her father addressed her without turning his head away from the window. He was staring out at the ocean. Trish had given up her bedroom to her parents when they moved in. She knew that her father loved the sea view. He spent most of his day staring at the movement of the waves, watching the sunset and the ebb and flow of the tide like most people watched TV. He didn't remark on the view.

39

Ba rarely talked these days, and even more rarely about his feelings. But Trish instinctively knew what he felt about it.

Trish sat down on the bed next to him. She felt a little guilty and ashamed for having neglected him over the last several weeks. She had been so preoccupied with herself ever since she had lost her job that she hadn't felt up to spending time with him. In the past, even though she was out for work the whole day, she had always made sure to have breakfast and evening tea with Ba. He spoke more to her than to Ma, even though it was usually to complain about his condition, about how nobody was telling him anything and how he couldn't remember the simplest things any more. She would patiently explain to him that Alzheimer's was that kind of disease and they were doing their best to manage it and that was why it was important for him to take his medicines on time without a fuss, even if it was only Ma who was around to give it to him most times. Sometimes, she would also try and tell him about whatever she had read about the latest research on the disease, although she wasn't ever sure he was really listening. It had been too long since she had last sat with him like this.

She was silent for a few moments and then answered him, 'Yes, Ba. I've come. Just had a really ... busy day.'

He didn't exactly say 'Humph!' but the angle at which he kept his chin stubbornly turned away from her indicated that he was still petulant and would be for a while.

'Have you had something to eat?' Trish asked gently. 'Tea?'

'That girl.' He turned his head away from the window to indicate Akanksha with a most accusatory and indignant expression. 'Every three minutes, she tries to give me something to eat! Every three minutes!'

'Uncle,' Akanksha protested. 'It was only twice, and I was trying to give you dinner.'

Ba ignored her, addressing Trish in a louder voice. 'I told you before that I don't need a nurse, I don't *want* a nurse.'

Akanksha was clearly hurt by this. 'Uncle, you've known me for years, I'm Akanksha.' Trish turned to her with a beseeching expression. Akanksha swallowed and then got up. 'Listen, honey,' she told Trish, 'I've got to go, Lisa has been calling nonstop since the afternoon. I really should get home.'

'Of course.' Trish smiled at her friend gratefully. Akanksha had been away from her small daughter the entire day to help out with Ba. 'Thanks, Akku.'

Akanksha gave the whole room a small wave and left, leaving behind a faint trace of the delicate, expensive perfume that she was wearing. Trish's mother followed her to the door. To exchange notes, no doubt, thought Trish, still irritated with her mother.

She was now alone with her father and he had turned his attention back to the waves. She sensed that he had thawed a little and was feeling better now that the other two ladies had left the room.

'Ba,' she said softly.

'Hmm?' Without looking at her.

'I ... saved a man today, I saved him from drowning.' Trish's words came rushing together. She edged closer to Ba's pillow to make sure he could hear her. 'It was on Marine Drive and I saw his arm, I thought it was a stick but then went to check and ... I went in and saved him, Ba.' She was surprised to find that her eyes felt like they had tears in them. That wasn't like her at all. She blinked the feeling away.

Her father was looking into her face now. Their eyes

met, after what felt like years, and he reached out slowly and patted her hand. She felt a little thrill to see that she was getting through to him. He was actually registering what she was saying. This could be some sort of a breakthrough!

'But you *couldn't* save him. Don't feel bad,' Ba said in a low voice, his manner comforting, still patting her hand.

'Huh?' Trish said blankly even as her heart went cold. His eyes had clouded over. She had lost him again. 'Ba. Listen to me.' She took hold of his thin, trembling hand in a bid to calm him down. 'I *did* save him. He's okay, at least they said he's okay, I couldn't see him, he wasn't around when I woke up at the hospital.'

'Yes, yes,' he said, his tone every bit as earnest as hers. 'Gone! What can you do about it? Nothing!'

Trish frowned at her father. She wondered what her mother had said to him before leaving for the hospital. She was about to ask him when Ma's voice floated in from behind her. 'He's getting upset, Trish.' It sounded like a warning.

'What's he talking about, Ma?' Trish demanded, turning her head to look at her mother. Ma stood in the doorway, tight-lipped and rigid. 'He's saying ...'

'I heard him,' Ma snapped. 'He's talking nonsense. You're upsetting him.'

Ba, who had been studying Trish's face, their hands still clasped together, stiffened at his wife's words. The trembling of his hands worsened and the frustration on his face forced Trish to ignore her mother. She quickly said to her father, 'Shhh, Ba, look, you'll miss the sunset.'

It was true. The golden sun was setting over the ocean, one brilliant beam of light stretching out over the water. Her father was distracted by this and, in a minute, he was staring out the window meditatively again.

Trish waited for her mother to leave the room, but Ma stood obstinately by the door. Finally, Trish released her father's hand – he didn't seem to notice – and she brushed past Ma, to escape that small room which was always far too crowded when the three of them were in it.

5

The Assignment

'Trish, try this laddoo. Is the sugar okay?'

Trish looked up from the classifieds section of the paper to see the moist, freshly prepared laddoo her mother was holding out to her on a plate about two inches from her face. Her nostrils had already been assailed by the achingly tempting smell wafting in from the kitchen. Who on earth made besan laddoos first thing in the morning anyway? Ma really knew how to make driving-Trish-up-the-wall an art form.

She said coldly, 'I'm having coffee right now, Ma. And *you're* the one always saying I should cut back on sweets.'

'Then why do you take two spoons of sugar in that coffee?'

Trish's hands tightened around the newspaper, crumpling the edges slightly, but she didn't say anything until her mother got tired of waiting and went back into the kitchen, clutching her laddoo and grumbling to herself.

Trish exhaled and tried to relax her shoulders. She felt so suffocated in here these days. The house hadn't felt quite this stifling when she had a job to escape to; but now, there were small clashes on a daily basis with her mother. They were constantly bumping into each other in this too-small flat with its tiny square rooms and narrow hallway. She tried to focus on the ads again. She was so desperate now she was ready to try anything. Her resumé was already up on all the major job portals, and she was sick of the emails they continued to send her: 'Exciting content writer jobs, 3-4 years, salary 3 lakhs per annum!' She scanned the classifieds listlessly.

'Didi.'

Munni, her fifty-something-year-old, small, efficient maid was standing before her. Trish looked up. 'Yes, Munni?' She realized the lady looked upset. Oh no. What had Ma done now?

'Didi. Please settle my balance today. I can't take it any more.'

'Munni, what happened?'

'*She* said ...' Munni's words came out in a hiss. Her prematurely wrinkled face was even more puckered up now. '*She* said I don't know how to make besan laddoos or anything apart from roti-sabzi-dal. I told her that I know how to make everything and she just taunted me saying that people like me were born liars. People like me! Means what? She has insulted me enough times. Two days ago also she got after me, did you wash the gobi properly? Ten times she asked me, did you wash the gobi properly? And when I told her that I bathed the gobi in Ganga-jal and did aarti of it also – I also get upset sometimes, didi – then she got angry and said I had better understand who was the madam of the house. I said I know who is madam of the house, it is Trish-didi, and then she says and I am Trish's mother so you need to show even more respect to me. And I said ...'

'Munni, Munni,' Trish pleaded. 'Look, we've talked about this before, she's an old lady, and old people are like this only.' Not that Ma was that much older than Munni, but still. 'And she's not going to change. You also shouldn't talk back, na, you weren't being polite either.' She tried not to smile when she thought about what Ma's face would have been like at the Ganga-jal remark. She went on quickly. 'This is why I increased your salary when they moved in, remember?'

'But how much will I have to bear, Trish-didi?' Munni wrung her hands. She was not the dramatic sort, so Trish knew she was really overwrought right now. 'I've managed this house for you for years without complaint.' She looked challengingly at Trish. '*Did* you have any complaint?'

46

'Er, no,' said Trish hastily. 'No complaint. And I want you to be around and happy and continue to manage the house.'

'Not possible now, didi,' Munni said obstinately. 'Please settle my dues today. I mean no disrespect to your mother. A mother is like bhagwan.' She raised her voice and Trish could see it was deliberate now because she also turned her head toward the kitchen as she bellowed, 'But I am NOT a LIAR and I CAN make besan laddoos and EVERYTHING else.'

'Is she cribbing about me again, that woman of yours?' Her mother's voice floated in from the kitchen. 'Rude, disrespectful, arrogant thing. Don't know why you've kept her around so long.'

Trish sighed and closed her eyes as they talked over each other for another few minutes. Finally, she looked up at Munni. 'Why don't you take the rest of the day off? Come tomorrow.' Munni hovered uncertainly. 'I'll talk to her, I promise.'

She must have looked really defeated. Munni's demeanor changed and she transformed back to her regular stoic self. She nodded once in grateful acknowledgement of her employer's support, adjusted the pallu on her loud, orange sari and left the room. A moment later, Trish heard the click of the front door. She was gone.

There was still lunch and dinner to be prepared. No matter, Trish would do it when she finished this morning's scan of job opportunities. She did have a lot of emails to write, she was still trying hard to get her resumé noticed. And a couple of people were coming to see her car later today, she remembered.

It would probably fetch at least two lakhs, or so she hoped. She had bought it for close to four lakhs a couple of years ago. It was hurtful, having to sell her car, but she had to be practical. She needed the money to tide her over for the next couple of months.

47

She wondered when Ma was going to offer to pay for something. Surely her parents had *some* savings piled up. There had been no discussion about it till now, of course, but Trish found it strange that even when she was clearly under monetary pressure, Ma hadn't figured out it was probably time to dip into their coffers so that they could make ends meet. But Trish herself wasn't going to bring it up, it was too uncomfortable a conversation, and there was no telling what kind of tangent Ma would go off on if Trish initiated it. Best to figure it out herself for now.

Every expense these days involved her doing a mental calculation about whether she could really afford it. She had never considered herself rich, but she had been fairly comfortable on her salary. The feeling of being so insecure about money was new to her. Why couldn't she make any breakthrough with the job market? She had been a good worker and had risen at a steady pace; she just didn't know how to sell herself. She resolved to figure something out about getting that damn MBA, maybe part-time when she was out of this jam and had the funds for it. She suddenly felt low. She glanced down at the dull, loose t-shirt and pyjamas that had become her daily wear these days. It made her feel even worse. Why would anyone hire someone like her, anyway? That bloody DNX Publications had let her go after so many years of service with barely any sort of notice and a minimal severance package. And of course, Trish had just accepted the decision and walked away quietly with her tail between her legs.

The fact was, she didn't think she *deserved* any better. She was a loser. And now she was going to be out on the streets within a matter of months, with two senile parents to somehow care for. She imagined holding out a begging bowl, her father lying prone on a tattered sheet behind her, while her mother nagged her continuously from next to him, 'Who will believe someone so fat doesn't get food regularly? I've told you so many times before to watch your weight. Even this begging business you've managed to mess up for us.'

48

Okay, this was going into the realm of the dramatic, which Trish liked to steer clear of. She shook herself out of it and went back to frowning at the wanted ads. Surely there would be *something*.

The doorbell rang. Trish grunted. Who could it be this early in the morning? The people for the car were supposed to come in the afternoon. She got up and walked over slowly to the front door. She definitely felt heavier these days. The little activity that she used to do while walking around in the office had ended, so she wasn't getting any form of exercise. And then Ma had taken to this irritating habit recently, of making besan laddoos and suji halwa and gulab jamuns and all sorts of other sweets. No matter how hard Trish tried, she would end up sampling them all. Ma claimed all this was for Ba, but the quantities she prepared were enough to feed a horse and there were always leftovers. Trish's midnight raids of the fridge were doing her in. She fumed as she reached out to open the door. It was all right for Ma, she had never had an extra inch of flab on her body. Trish had got her genes from her father, who had been a big, boisterous man in his prime. He had been tall too, so he had carried it off; but he was so shrunken and frail and thin now.

'Say hello to Trish-aunty.' It was Akanksha, with her small daughter Lisa.

Trish didn't like being called Trish-aunty, or for that matter, the baby-voice Akanksha always adopted around Lisa. The kid was seven years old, nowhere near being a baby, but Akanksha didn't seem to realize that.

'Hi there, Akku.' Trish pushed her unruly curls back from her face and peered through her glasses at Lisa. 'Hey, Lisa.'

'Arrey, say hello,' repeated Akanksha.

Lisa said sullenly, 'Hello, Trish-aunty.'

'Come in.' Trish moved aside to let them in.

Akanksha pushed Lisa forward and addressed Trish. 'Sweetie, I wanted to ask if you could just let her hang around at home with you today. I've got somewhere to be and didn't think she would enjoy being alone at home with just the maids. She'll read or something, I'm sure she won't be a bother at all. Is that okay?'

'Umm, sure.' Trish was a little taken aback. She had never had to babysit anyone before – Ba didn't count, he wasn't an actual kid. She did have a lot of work to get done. But still, this didn't sound too tough. 'What happened to school, though?'

'Summer holidays just began.' Akanksha rolled her eyes. 'Sixty days! Can you believe it? I don't know what I'm going to *do* with her. It's so great to have you around, though.'

'Well.' Trish began to say that it wasn't like she wasn't ever going to get a job. But then she recalled the day Akanksha had spent looking after Ba when she was in the hospital. She figured she would take the opportunity to return the favour. 'Sure. No prob—'

Akanksha cut in: 'Great, thanks so much.' She appeared to be in a hurry. 'I'll be back to pick her up around four, okay? You're a doll.' Trish did not think of herself as anything remotely like a doll and didn't like being called one, but Akanksha was already retreating towards the stairs, calling out, 'I'm sure you guys will have lots of fun bonding together.'

Trish looked down at Lisa's face. The kid was sulking; she looked positively hostile. Without a word, she stalked in past Trish on her long, skinny legs and disappeared around the bend in the hall. Trish thought about calling after her to tell her that shoes were supposed to be left at the door, but changed her mind. She shut the door wearily, already feeling spent.

Lots of fun bonding together. Sure, why not?

'I want to rewind and watch that ad!'

Trish looked over at Lisa, who was sprawled out on the most comfortable sofa in the house, the worn green three-seater in front of the television set. It had been over three hours and she had been glued to the TV the entire morning.

Trish cleared her throat. 'Lisa, we don't have a rewinding facility on our TV.'

'This is Tata Sky.' Lisa said accusingly. 'You can rewind and record on that. Don't you know?'

'You probably have Tata Sky *Plus* at home,' Trish said, trying to keep her tone friendly. 'That's different.'

'So why don't you get that?' Lisa demanded.

Trish said carefully, 'Never felt the need.'

Lisa looked like she was going to remark on the stupidity of this decision, but then she simply puffed out her cheeks and rolled her eyes and went back to staring moodily at the screen.

Trish wondered if she should just go and hide in her room again. But the WiFi was weaker in her room and she really did need to send out the application and follow-up emails that she had composed so carefully over the last couple of hours. She found herself getting distracted by the sound of the music videos that Lisa was watching.

'Babydoll main sone di, babydoll main sone di ...' Lisa began to hum along tunelessly.

Trish looked up again. 'Are you sure you don't want to just hop on over home and pick up a book? Your mom said that you would spend the day reading.'

'Mom doesn't know anything ... and she doesn't care either. And she said I should just stay here until she came.' Lisa didn't take her eyes off the screen, on which Sunny Leone was gyrating.

'I'm not sure this kind of music video is the best influence on you,' Trish began.

'What's influence?' Lisa asked distractedly, only mildly curious.

'Never mind.' Trish went back to her work. Who was she to try and educate anyone about this stuff? She didn't have any kids. Never would, given that she didn't plan on getting married. No nieces or nephews either – her mother had always been vague about her relatives and kept distant family at a distance. Must have fought with everyone, Trish thought uncharitably. Anyway, this Trish-aunty thing was new to her and, frankly, it didn't look like she was cut out for it. She hoped Akanksha wasn't planning to make a habit of this.

She spent the next few minutes focusing on sending out her resumé to various potential employers. Her phone rang just as she hit 'Send' for the last time. Ah. One of the people who were coming to see the car. The other guy had cancelled on her already. She answered. 'Hello? Haan ji. Yes, I'll be down in a minute. You can look at the car in the meantime. It's the Corsa next to the gate.'

She got up and called out to no one in particular, 'I'm heading out for a while.'

Lisa didn't acknowledge her words, she was still staring open-mouthed at the screen as if hypnotized. Trish's mother didn't bother to answer her either, though Trish was sure she had heard her from the other room. She stomped heavily out, wondering briefly why anyone bothered to have family and friends. Or kids, for that matter.

❦

By the time Trish came back upstairs, her mood was even worse. The fellow had been a short seedy small-office worker who had just moved from Agra and was shocked by the prices of Mumbai and was trying to negotiate his overall cost of living down on every front. He had complained about the state of the car and yet he seemed insistent on having it – at approximately half of Trish's asking price. Her polite response that she wasn't interested in negotiating was met with fiery gusto and he had kept talking at her for twenty minutes, trying to get her to change her mind. It was when she realized that his eyes kept dropping to her bosom – she had initially written his wandering gaze off as a nervous tic but then she finally noticed the pattern – that she cut the meeting short, saying, 'Thank you for your interest. Goodbye and good luck.' She walked away from him even as he still went on in that whiny seedy way of his. She was feeling disgusted and had the impression that his creepy eyes were now on her bottom. She quickened her pace and entered the building to walk up to the first floor.

She felt relieved to be back home. She turned the corner into the drawing room, glad that the music from the TV had stopped. Her jaw dropped when she saw what Lisa was doing.

That incorrigible kid was on *her* laptop. She was frowning at the keyboard, typing something slowly.

'Hey. Lisa.' Trish tried to keep it friendly. 'What the *hell* are you doing?'

She regretted using the cuss word but Lisa didn't seem to notice. 'YouTube. Why is this thing so slow?'

Trish went over and gently dragged the laptop away from the child's little paws, turning it around to face her on the other side of the table. 'This "thing" is mine,' she said through gritted teeth. 'And no one else is allowed to touch it.'

Lisa scowled. 'There's nothing to *do* here. And you weren't even using it.'

'Lisa.' Trish sighed. 'How about having your lunch now? It's getting cold. We all ate an hour ago and you said you would have it when you were hungry.'

Lisa made a face. 'It was some yucky sabzi.'

'It's alu-zeera. It's perfectly nice. You should try some.'

'Do you have any chicken?'

'No,' Trish said in a measured tone. 'We don't eat chicken at home.'

'What?' Lisa threw up her hands. 'What kind of house is this?'

What kind of kid are you, Trish thought, her blood beginning to boil again. There were just too many people who seemed to take her for granted. Her parents, her friend, her previous employer and now even this seven-year-old.

Her phone was ringing again. She frowned as she recognized the number. It looked like one of the office landlines. Strange. What the heck did they want? She picked up and snapped, 'Yeah?'

'Trish *darling*.'

It took Trish a moment to place the voice. She made a face at her phone. Nivedita. Smarmy woman from the print editorial team. What did she want? She had always behaved in a supercilious manner with Trish except when she wanted a favour. Everyone from the print side looked down on the folks who worked on the Internet business; they considered themselves 'real' editorial folk. But they'd had a lot of common content and Nivedita had been in the habit of picking up a lot of Trish's writing to fill print space – often without even giving her a byline.

'Hello,' Trish said guardedly. 'What's up?'

'Nothing, darling,' Nivedita gushed. 'We're missing you. So sorry that you were kicked out.'

'Wow,' Trish said. 'Thanks for the concern. I ...'

'So, look, darling,' Nivedita cut in, not bothering to listen. 'I have something interesting for you. I'm sure you'll love it.'

'Really?' Trish's tone was dry. She sincerely doubted it.

'Well, my stupid junior has gone and got some stupid chicken pox. The one who's currently writing the AMA column.'

AMA was the 'Ask Me Anything' column. 'The agony aunt thing?' Trish said, curious despite herself. 'That's still on?'

'On and off, actually. I know, I know, who reads that shit, right?' Nivedita's tinkling laugh grated on Trish's nerves. 'Still, there are lots of disturbed people in Mumbai – lucky for us, right?' She didn't wait for an answer. 'So anyway, since the idiot is out for a while, I need someone to do that column for me over the next three weeks. It won't pay much – you know the deal with how cheap this shithole is, right? – but I heard you still haven't found work and thought you'd jump at the offer.'

Trish had never thought of her as a subtle or pleasant person, but Nivedita had never actually managed to get her this angry before. She unclenched her jaw, noting the tightness in her wrists, and got ready to tell the presumptuous bitch exactly what she thought of her and her so-called offer.

55

But then she had a better idea.

'Okay.' She tried to keep her voice neutral. 'Fine. I'll do it.'

'Of course, darling. I *knew* you'd do it. I'm mailing you the questions right away. Answers by eight p.m., please. Don't be late. Tata.'

'Tata,' Trish mocked but realized that Nivedita had already hung up.

She looked up to see Lisa staring at her through narrowed eyes. 'You're still not using that *thing*,' she said in a whiny voice, pointing to the laptop. 'Can I watch YouTube *now*?'

6

The Letters

'All right! You want answers?' Trish growled, fingers poised over the keyboard. 'You'll *get* answers.'

She would teach that Nivedita not to reach out to her again so condescendingly. Stupid random assignment that paid peanuts, and she'd thought Trish would jump at it. Her offer was an insult for a writer of Trish's level. Well, erstwhile level. Now, she was apparently considered good for nothing other than composing responses to this drivel.

Dear AMA,
I am crushed. I found out by reading some messages on my husband's phone that he has been having an affair with his colleague at work. When I confronted him, he was honest and admitted to it, but says it's just that he finds his office women more powerful and attractive than me. I've never been a career woman and I know I haven't taken enough care of myself over the last eight years of bringing up our children,

but I never expected this. I wouldn't like to separate because
our sons would suffer. Please advise.
Crushed.

Trish's blood was boiling by the time she finished reading
the letter. Stuff and nonsense. What was wrong with people?
Her fingers flew fast and furious as she typed, barely thinking.

Dear Crushed,
Relax, darling, have yourself a nice cup of chamomile tea, or
three. Let me break this down for you (although you guys seem
to have broken things down pretty well yourselves so far). You
seem to have a rare talent for being able to find redeeming
qualities in that cretin you have the misfortune of calling your
husband. You say he was honest and admitted to an affair …
AFTER you'd already caught him at it. You sure he isn't a
direct descendent of Satyavadi Harishchandra? The man
has the balls to then confess that he really couldn't help it
because, after all, anything in a skirt in his office is naturally
superior to and more attractive than the devoted wife waiting
for him at home, caring for his children. Man, this guy sounds
like a keeper.
My sincere advice to you, dearie, would be to think about
what one of those powerful office ladies would do if they were
in your situation. Would they sit around like martyred cows,
forever subjugating their needs to those of all the men in
their lives (you mention you have sons, I hope they don't take
after Dad) or would they look to sue the arrogant bastard's
unworthy ass, taking his money AND the kids and resolving
to give them a better life than they could ever expect with a
man who takes his wife for granted like that?
Entirely your choice, of course. You could just choose to
play Mother Teresa in your own little world. Except that
from whatever I know about Mother Teresa, she had no time

57

for losers. More importantly, she had something called self-respect.

You may or may not end up getting yourself some of that. But oh, definitely get the chamomile tea.

Love,
Amy (I prefer that to AMA)

There. Trish felt immensely satisfied just getting those words out, even though she didn't quite know where they'd come from. It was as if she were releasing some of her own frustration by being overly caustic. She knew her letter would never reach the wretched woman, and she didn't want it to either; she just wanted Nivedita to get the point. Especially since, in her one-line email brief with the questions attached, she had informed Trish that the tone of the column had always been 'warm, friendly and understanding'.

Trish snorted to herself. She knew she'd be getting a plaintive call from Nivedita about this tomorrow. But it would be worth it.

She scrolled down to the next letter.

❀

'What the hell have you *done*?'

Trish cringed and held the phone away from her ear for a couple of seconds. She had been woken up by its ringing, so the call had caught her off guard. She was never fully prepared to face the world without a cup of coffee. Okay. So she had expected mild annoyance from Nivedita, but not this hysterical shrieking. And not this early in the morning. What was it, eight a.m.?

'Hey. Relax, Nivs.' She thought the use of 'Nivs', a nickname which Nivedita tried to force upon everyone and which Trish had never bothered with before, might calm her down. It didn't seem to be working at all, though, because Nivedita went on babbling incoherently, speaking so fast and in such a high-pitched tone that Trish couldn't understand what she was on about. She attempted to cut in. 'Listen, it was just a joke ...'

'Just a joke?' screeched Nivedita. 'A joke? My job is a *joke* to you? I'll be the laughingstock of the entire company. The chief editor has already texted me just now, calling me for a meeting as soon as I get in. I'm going to lose my job and be a worthless has-been like *you* by this afternoon.'

'Hey.' Trish sat up in bed. She hadn't meant to get Nivedita into trouble, but the worthless has-been stuff was getting a little out of hand. 'Watch it. And why all this drama anyway? You shouldn't have forwarded it on to the editor without reading it first. Anyway, it's barely three or four letters and it's not due till tonight.' She bit her lip and then sighed, closing her eyes. 'Okay, listen. You want me to redo it?'

'Redo it?' Nivedita's laughter had more than a tinge of hysteria. 'What's *wrong* with you? It's already out in *print*. That vile ... *bile* that you spewed was printed this morning.'

'What?' Trish froze. 'Today is Wednesday. The metro supplement is out only on Thursdays.'

'This column moved to the daily section weeks ago, you fathead!' Nivedita wailed so loudly that Trish almost dropped the phone. 'It was showing signs of picking up last month and we thought we'd try giving it a boost. Until today, of course, when you *sabotaged* the whole thing. And, more importantly, *me!*'

'Hang on.' Trish's heart was racing as she rolled out of bed and hurried down the hallway, past her parents' room, to the front door. There it was, the newspaper. She snatched it up and began turning the pages to scan them with her still-bleary eyes. The light was poor in the hallway, so she walked quickly to the drawing room, saying in a disbelieving tone into the phone, 'You mean ... you mean you didn't even *read* what I sent you before sending it out to *print*?'

'I HAD AN INTERN COPY-CHECK IT, OKAY?' Nivedita was so loud this time that Trish's mother, who was passing by to get to the kitchen, stopped and raised her eyebrows questioningly. Trish didn't notice, though: her eyes were glued to the paper. She couldn't believe it. Her sarcastic responses had actually been printed in the paper for everyone to see. She sank into her living room sofa as her heart sank into her stomach. Yes. All this was only too familiar.

60

Dear AMA,

I've got a major problem. My girlfriend still talks about her previous boyfriend and it drives me crazy. They were together for four years, and I was her best friend at the time. I kept telling her it would never work out. Her family saw it that way too. After they finally broke up, we got together, but I'm really not that sure she loves me the same way. I've told her a number of times that I don't want to hear about him any more, but she asks me why things have changed because we used to talk about him earlier. I always thought that we were meant to be together, but I'm not that sure any more. It's been almost three months since they broke up and she still goes on about it. How I can help her forget about him?

Frustrated and Jealous.

And there was her response, right below it. Trish groaned softly as she read:

Dear Frustrated and Jealous,

Of COURSE three months is more than enough time to get over a relationship of a mere four years. There's no way she should still be talking about him, or even thinking about him for that matter. With the several years of brainwashing that you've been painstakingly inflicting on your so-called best friend, and with the aid of her equally manipulative family, it's a wonder that she didn't abandon that loser earlier.

I say you're completely justified in feeling frustrated and jealous at this point. You waited so long, and swooped in before anyone could get a chance. Your timing was perfect and you've worked so hard. And for what? This girl obviously hasn't turned out to be completely amenable to your manipulations, and that's clearly a product defect. Did you get a warranty card with this doll? Either way, I say you send her right back to where she came from and find someone else.

Good luck with that, okay?

Much love,
Amy (I think AMA sounds too much like Amma, don't you?)

'Oh dear god,' said Trish.

'Yes. Dear GOD!' screeched Nivedita from the other end. 'Well done, *Amy*. I'm so going to screw that idiot Pervez. Brainless little twit. She messaged me saying that there were a few minor edits, but she had taken care of those.' Nivedita's voice dropped to a hiss. 'I trusted you, Trish. I figured it was *you* and that I could take it as a given that it would be all right. I had no idea you had so much bitterness inside you. I should have known. But now, you've got me up shit creek.' She raised her voice again. 'I'm going to get *fired* for this.'

'Now, listen,' Trish said quickly, the words running into each other as she tried desperately to make amends. 'I'm sorry this happened. It wasn't meant to be this way. I can talk to the editor – Zee? – if you like and I'll explain it was my fault.'

'What difference will *that* make now?' Nivedita's voice was harsh. 'You carry no credibility in the system. You never did, not even when you were heading the digital content department.' Her voice became colder. 'I was doing you a favour by sending some freelance work your way. There are a dozen people I could have asked to do this shit column for me. Instead, I reached out to you ... for *this*. I guess I should have stuck to never trying to do anyone else a favour. Well, I've learnt my lesson.' She paused for dramatic effect and ended her long speech with a final spiteful hiss. 'Thanks a lot.'

'Look, is there anything I can do? I feel terrible.'

'Well, maybe.' Nivedita's voice was now dripping with sarcasm. 'You should just have yourself a nice cup of, I don't know, *chamomile tea*?'

Even though she pronounced it 'shamomile', it still stung. With a muffled parting shot that sounded a lot like 'fat bitch', Nivedita hung up. Trish continued to clutch the phone numbly for a while, her head spinning and her eyes glued to the column with the words that had never been meant for public consumption printed right there in the newspaper with the highest circulation in Mumbai.

❀

'What's wrong with you?' Trish's mother asked curiously. 'Why aren't you eating? You didn't have breakfast either.'

The two of them had been sitting in silence at the lunch table. Ba had already been given his meal in his room earlier. Trish was just picking listlessly at the food on her plate.

'Not hungry,' Trish said.

Her mother swallowed another mouthful of dal-rice and said, 'Starving yourself won't help you lose weight, your body will just start to store more fat. Besides, you should cut down on dinner, not the earlier meals. And focus more on exercise. Your problem is clearly slow metabolism, so you must work on that if you've finally decided to do something about it.'

Trish's mind had been fully occupied with thoughts of what Nivedita would be going through at the office because of her prank; but now she was brought back to the present by her mother's words. She said sharply, 'What?'

'I've just been blessed with a different type of metabolism, Trish,' Ma went on. 'Never put on excess weight in my life. Except, of course, almost twenty kilos when I had you, but ...' She abruptly ended her sentence and looked up at Trish.

'Go on,' Trish said. 'Tell me that was also just my fault, because maybe I was too fat even when I was born?'

63

Her voice was getting louder and Ma looked fearfully in the direction of the bedroom. 'Shhh,' she urged. 'Ba will hear. Let him sleep right now, he needs his post-lunch nap.'

'What he *needs* is to get out of that *room*,' snapped Trish, not bothering to keep her voice down. 'Why is he always shut in there these days? He's losing it, and you're resisting the idea of taking him to a new neurologist. For all we know, he really needs physiotherapy or counselling or something. He's getting worse lying there, confined in that room all day.'

'You're going to upset him,' her mother said with a note of warning.

'You're *already* upsetting him.' Trish was quivering with anger. 'Why are you being such a control freak with him? At least think about what's best for *him* now that he's in this state.'

'What does *that* mean?' Her mother's voice was cold and furious.

Trish knew she was taking out her frustration on her mother, and had said more than she had meant to say. It was true that she had felt that Ma had always tried to dominate Ba and keep his attention on her, almost resenting the fact that Trish and Ba were close. Closer than Ba and her, or closer than Trish and her? Maybe both. But it didn't matter now. Ba was barely in his senses and they needed to be united in their effort to make him comfortable.

'Just please stop making jabs about my weight now,' she said in a low voice. 'Half the time you're trying to stuff me with your unhealthy laddoos, and the other half you're on about how I should work off the fat.' She added defiantly, 'I'm too old to care about the fact that I'm fat.'

Her mother didn't look like she was in any mood to stop the fight. 'If you watched your lifestyle, the occasional indulgence of a laddoo wouldn't be an issue. And it's not unhealthy, it's made of desi ghee.' She paused. 'And *why* don't you care about your weight? If you recognize you have a problem ...'

'It's not a problem, it's just the way it is,' Trish interrupted through gritted teeth, but Ma wasn't listening.

'... then you should do something about it.' Now Ma's voice was loud, and it was Trish's turn to worry that Ba might find it disturbing. 'You've lost your job, and you have no prospect of finding one. You're sitting around getting fatter and more lethargic by the day. You don't want us to talk about marriage, you don't want our help to arrange something. Well, I don't even know what we could arrange, with you in this state. You never want to hear what your own mother has to say about important issues. And if I do say something, you call me a ...' Her voice broke and, to Trish's annoyance, tears sprang into her eyes as she finished, '*control freak!*'

She turned away and dabbed at her eyes. Trish sighed and

threw up her hands. Control freak was an insult? Compared to lethargic fatty with no job or marriage prospects? Ma would win today – as usual. She always did this in moments of high emotion between them. She knew Trish never cried. But Ma herself had no qualms about turning on the tap, especially when it looked like it would play to her advantage. Such as now.

Trish sat there, silent and defeated. Her mother's shoulders were shaking as she sniffled in the martyred manner of the constantly wronged. She was still crying softly to comfort herself when Trish finally got up and walked down the hall to Ba's room and peeped in. She could only see the back of his white-haired head sticking out from under the sheet. He was still asleep. Good. She shut the door firmly to make sure Ma's crying wouldn't wake him up. She then walked back past the living room, ignoring the sobbing that was a few decibels louder now for her benefit.

She just headed towards the front door and let herself out of what felt like a madhouse – one where she was both inmate and warden.

1

Dear Amy

The seaside breeze was cool against Trish's hot cheeks as she stalked along on Bandstand. It had been a very trying morning, starting with Nivedita's call and her mother's haranguing. Apart from feeling sorry for what she had done to Nivedita, she realized only now that her impetuous decision had caused her to cut off a potential source of revenue. Small as it may have been, she actually badly needed some freelance work while the job search went on.

Akanksha was trying to reach her, but she ignored the calls. She couldn't take another request to bond with Lisa so soon. What was with Akanksha, anyway? What did she have to do that was so important these days? She didn't have a job. Trish had to admit to herself now that the one thing she'd always believed that she had that good-looking, rich, lucky Akanksha *didn't* have was a career – but that was now in the past. She glanced to see another message from Akanksha:

'Where are you? Call, please. Can you have Lisa over?' She pressed down hard on the delete button.

Akanksha really was fortunate to have Vinay – he wasn't just a rich, hardworking businessman. He was courteous, gentlemanly and kind too. Trish knew he was kind from the way his eyes crinkled up when he smiled. From the way Akanksha described it, almost complainingly, he tried to spend as much time as he could with Lisa when he was home. He travelled a great deal of the time and tried to compensate by being an involved father when he was around. Trish marvelled at the similarity between her situation and Lisa's – both had mothers who probably meant well at *some* level, but unconsciously competed with their own daughters. Hopefully, Lisa would grow up to be a lucky, competent woman who could take care of herself. Trish had always considered herself at least competent but was now beginning to believe that luck mattered much more. And looks, maybe.

67

She ignored the people walking past her at varying speeds on Bandstand. In Mumbai, people minded their own business, which was what she liked best about the city. Only occasionally would she come upon a gaggle of men who stared at her as she passed by and whispered to each other. She would pretend she didn't see them; they certainly made her wish *she* were invisible.

She walked around for a long time to let off steam and her feet were now tired. She approached a bench and sat down heavily, breathing hard.

Her mind was still racing as she looked straight ahead out at the rippling waves. Usually, watching the waves helped calm her down, but today her thoughts were coming in crashing waves themselves, one on top of the other:

No job, no job prospects. Fat bitch. Just screwed up possibility of regular freelance work. Couldn't even help you get an arranged marriage if we tried. Bile vile. Trishna, Trishna, where are you? Will have to rent a much cheaper place.

The buzzing of her phone interrupted her thoughts. She stiffened when she saw who it was. She contemplated not answering. Then, taking a deep breath, Trish picked up the phone and breathed, 'Hello?'

'Well hello there, Trish *darling*.'

What was she playing at now? Why did she sound so happy all of a sudden? Trish pulled the phone away from her ear and looked at the caller's name again, eyebrows drawn together.

'Hello? Trish darling?' Nivedita's voice floated from the phone. 'Are you there?'

'I'm here. I take it you didn't get fired for today's column, then?' Trish enquired dryly, trying to mask the relief she was feeling.

'Au contraire, ma cherie.' Trish made a face at the atrocious accent and pronunciation, and Nivedita went on. 'They loved it.'

'Who loved what?' demanded Trish, unable to believe her ears.

'Well, the Twitterati. They tweeted all day to the editorial handle about how fabulously refreshing today's AMA column was; it was clear, they said, that sometimes what was required was a slap in the face. The same worn, whiny issues being treated with a well deserved dose of sarcasm made for the most interesting reading of the day, and they're really looking forward to tomorrow's column now! Congratulations, darling. Your little gamble paid off. You have yourself a *column*!'

Trish closed her eyes, unable to fully register this. 'Are you serious? The editor liked it?'

'Listen darling, I just told you the who's who of Mumbai loves it, so do we. Now, listen, I'm sending you today's questions, you have to get back by tonight, and—'

'Whoa, whoa, hang on, Nivedita,' Trish protested into the phone, a scowl on her face. 'I didn't say I would do it. I only wrote that column as a joke, I can't answer people's actual letters like that.'

'What?' Nivedita shouted so loudly that Trish instinctively looked around to see if anyone was listening. No one was.

Trish tried to keep her tone neutral. 'I'm not going to do it. You were right, it was vile and sarcastic and I didn't enjoy reading it myself today. I didn't mean to make fun of anyone's problems. After all, how will those guys feel when they read the answers?'

69

'Who cares how *they* feel?' Nivedita was getting all agitated again. 'A much larger number of readers derived amusement from your answers. And besides, the big E thought that you made basic sense in all of them. If the people who wrote in have half a brain, they'll take your advice, and if they have less than half a brain – also a distinct possibility, of course – they won't get the sarcasm! And in the meantime, the intelligentsia like you and moi' – Trish gritted her teeth at the pretentious French again – 'will be happy to read both sappy question and snappy answer. See? It's a win-win!'

'I don't know about that, Nivedita,' Trish said.

'Hey, you tried to screw me over with this, remember?' Nivedita's voice rose a couple of decibels. 'And you said you'd do anything to help.'

'That was when I thought you were in trouble!' Trish retorted.

'Well, I'll be in trouble all over again now if you refuse to do this!' Nivedita screeched. 'What's wrong with you, Trish? This is the chance of a lifetime. You're going to get a regular *daily* column. That's a couple of thousand bucks a day.'

Trish froze. 'What?'

'Okay, okay,' Nivedita said quickly. 'Look, we figured you'd try to bargain, and so the Big E told me to tell you: you can start at three grand and we'll work it up further depending on the response going forward, okay?'

Trish did the math in her head. If it was really going to be a daily and it would hardly take up more than a few hours, it was actually pretty good money. It would certainly help tide over these difficult times and she could always continue to look for a regular job. She bit her lower lip and considered it.

'Well, well, WELL?' Nivedita said impatiently. 'What do you say, what do you say, we don't have all day. Of course,' she added craftily. 'If you don't want it, I could take a crack at it myself. I've got the sarcasm—'

'But not the sense,' Trish finished for her.

'What? What was that?'

'I said, because we're such good *friends.*' Trish emphasized the last word, putting her newfound sarcasm to practice. 'I guess I'll do it.'

'Fab, darling. Just fab. Sending you the mail. Hurry with the replies, and don't start drinking tonight to celebrate before you're done. Or maybe you should, your answers may come out even better then!' With her tinkling trademark laugh that always made Trish's toes curl, Nivedita hung up.

The sun was setting now and Trish watched the shimmering pink and orange rays splaying out over the ocean in silence. She couldn't quite believe it. Her impetuous act had actually paid off in a totally unexpected way. She knew that Ba would be watching the sunset from his window, and this made her feel a sense of oneness with him. Maybe – just maybe – things were going to be all right.

For what felt like the first time in weeks, Trish exhaled.

8

Babysitting

'Hey Trish! How goes?' Akanksha smiled at Trish through the open door as she simultaneously nudged Lisa forward. 'Go on! Say hello to Trish-*masi*!'

Trish-*masi*? She'd been promoted? Trish tried not to let the surprise register on her face. Akanksha had sounded so desperate on the phone that Trish hadn't been able to say no. She smiled down at Lisa. 'Hey. Got your books today?'

Lisa rolled her eyes and wordlessly held up a stack of four books. Her mother nudged her again. 'Stop pushing, Mom!' Lisa said and stomped into the flat past Trish, her thin shoulders drooping.

'Thanks *so* much for having her over again,' Akanksha said, backing away from the door.

Trish began, 'Okay, no problem, but ...'

Akanksha paused, shifting her weight from one foot to the

other, almost dancing with impatience. Trish frowned. What was the hurry? But she had to say her piece.

'Akku, it's just that … I've kind of got some work to focus on now. I've got a regular column and—'

'Hey! Congratulations! That's *great* news.' Akanksha trotted over and gave Trish an impetuous hug and then teetered away again on her high heels. 'And we *must* talk about it when I pick Lisa up later today, okay?'

'Okay, but …'

Akanksha gave her a wave just before she disappeared around the corner. Trish could hear the click-clacking of her heels as she trotted off down the stairs.

'Okay, okay,' Trish said. 'Whatever.' Then, in unconscious imitation of Lisa, she stalked into the house with drooping shoulders and a scowl.

73

❦

The kid wasn't being so bad today. She was engrossed in reading her Sweet Valley Twins books, her mouth slightly open. Trish thought about commenting that she had only read the Sweet Valley Twin series when she was twelve and maybe Lisa should be reading Enid Blyton, but she thought the better of it. Kids were different these days, they matured a lot faster – or so she'd heard. She'd better just stick to being friendly Trish-masi. Or even better, Trish-masi who just minded her own business.

She wasn't getting much work done. She spent most of the afternoon with Ba. He had announced loudly that he wasn't going to take his medicines any more, having developed a strange new conspiracy theory in his head. It took her a while to calm him down and convince him that her mother wasn't trying to actually poison him.

'But she is trying to finish me off, that woman!' He pointed an accusing finger at Ma, who bristled with indignation.

'Don't be silly, Ba, she's doing nothing of the sort.' Despite her worrying, Trish had to fight to keep the smile off her face. It was a preposterous accusation, so preposterous that she hoped it was just Ba's sense of humour making a comeback through the haze. 'Ba, let's play chess,' she suggested in desperation.

It was the one activity that her father still enjoyed. In a bid to keep him occupied, she had let him teach her the rules of the game, which she privately thought incredibly boring. He hmphed at first but then agreed. So they spent the next hour engrossed at the chessboard, with him half propped up against his pillows so he could see the board clearly. It was always surprising to her how his mental faculties appeared entirely intact when he was playing chess. He concentrated, strategized and beat her easily, complaining as usual that it was no fun playing with Trish because she was no challenge.

Still, he was evidently pleased with winning three games in a row. He quietly swallowed all his pills in quick succession and then lay down, turned over and drifted into his afternoon nap.

Trish tucked the light sheet around his shoulders and left the room, feeling relieved yet drained. Ma was sitting in the drawing room, reading the newspaper, opposite Lisa, whose nose was still buried in her book.

'He's asleep, Ma.'

Silence.

'He took his medicine.'

Continued silence. Trish realized that her mother was still

hurt about the whole poisoning-to-death accusation from her husband. Who wouldn't have been? Trish opened her mouth to say something sympathetic. But that wasn't what came out.

'I hope now you understand what I've been trying to tell you.' Trish was surprised at how much she sounded like Ma right now, but she couldn't help it. 'Ba needs to be reassessed – and quickly. His condition is clearly deteriorating and we can't just let this—'

Trish's mother folded the newspaper with such a violent rustle that even Lisa looked up for a millisecond from her book. Ma then got up from the chair and elbowed past Trish to go into the bedroom.

Trish stared after her. This was a first. Ma walking away from an argument before it even started? And what was with *her*, Trish herself, talking like that? The one thing she hated more than anything else about her mother was the smug I-told-you-so which she had heard countless times over the years. And here she was, doing the same thing at a time when she knew Ma least needed to hear it from her.

Feeling sorry but unable to actually do anything about it, Trish turned her attention to her pending work – answering the letters that Nivedita had sent for the day. She sat down at her laptop, noting with relief that Lisa had made no attempt to get near it at all.

She started to read the first letter. Hmmm. *Dear Amy.* Trish was amazed at how, within a mere two days, the newspaper had changed the name of the column from AMA to 'Dear Amy'.

Dear Amy,
My mother-in-law has been visiting us over the last month and I am sorry to say this, but she is driving me absolutely

crazy. She's constantly criticizing the way I do things, saying I don't spend enough time in the kitchen, referring to the dishes that I do make as 'flavourless' and generally comparing me – unfavourably – to her own daughter, who 'manages everything beautifully in London without any help, a job, a home, the kids, and always ensures a hot, healthful meal is on the table every evening'. My husband is a devoted son (are all Indian men like this?) and when I talk to him about it, he just tells me that I'm overreacting, that his mom is 'like this only' and that there's no point raking up issues with her when she's only here another two weeks. But I feel really suffocated holding back. What should I do?

Despairing Daughter-in-law

Trish bit her lip. Mother-in-law issues weren't things that she felt qualified to comment upon, but then, she felt that way about almost all the letters she received. Nivedita had been urging her to weave in a little more sarcasm, but she really didn't feel like it. Come on, she told herself, it's just a job. She thought for a couple of minutes and then decided to let her fingers do the thinking. She began to type.

Dear DD,
There comes a time in every woman's life when she has to decide to grow up. That is clearly a missed boat for your darling mom-in-law, but luckily, it doesn't sound as if it's too late for you. So here's what I think: It clearly bothers you a great deal that the mother-in-law appears to compare you unfavourably to the sister-in-law. I don't have any kids, but I imagine that those who do tend to generally think more highly of them than of other specimens of humanity. So isn't it natural that she sees the flesh of her flesh through rose-coloured lenses? (Also, doesn't that conjure up a slightly gross image?)

Anyway, stop and think: why do you care so much about this? Maybe this an opportunity to figure yourself out a little better. You know, reflect on your insecurities, dig deeper into your childhood, get some insight, write a journal, meditate and generally sort out your own shit. Seriously, it's an opportunity.

And also, talk to your husband about it. Talk his ears off. He doesn't want to hear criticism about his mommy? Well, he's not letting you talk to her, is he? Assume for the time being that he's right: Mom's not going to change, what's the point of upsetting her yada yada yada. He should still know how you feel. He signed up to be with you, right?

It strikes me as strange that Indian husbands don't seem to realize that their wives are going to be around a lot longer than their mothers (hopefully) and that they should start realigning their loyalties as soon as they can. But then, you have a lifetime to remind him of that fact, don't you? Either way, I say you keep the focus on yourself and on him. Attempting a heart-to-heart with Maa-ji is probably going to lead to some heartburn all around. And hey, maybe that's not such a bad idea: a little extra spice may change her opinion about your cooking being flavourless?

Much love,
Amy

Trish read it again and shook her head, frowning with disapproval. Had she managed to inject enough sarcasm into it? Maybe she would come back to this in the end and make a few spiteful remarks about the impossibility of having sex when your mother-in-law had her ear glued to the walls.

She read the next one and cheered up. This was going to be a piece of cake.

Dear Amy-ji,
There is a girl who I am in love since the last 2 year. I think she
also love me because we talk in the bus in a friendly manner
since the last 1 year. But I have not proposed her because she
is college student and I am 36 years. But more and more when
I think, I think I want to marry this girl only and am not liking
the girls that my parents are trying to arrange with. But how
can I ask her? Please advice me.

Hopeful in the Bus

Trish started typing almost before she finished reading
the letter:

Dear Hopeful in the Bus,
Ah, the good old bus romance. Thank goodness for public
transport! How else would so many people in our great
country find their partners on the bus journey called life? The
conductor rattles off the stops one by one, but who's counting
the many starts that are made on these wonderful moving,
matchmaking machines?

Now, to your question. I am afraid language proves to be a
bit of a barrier here. Are you asking me how you can possibly
ask a girl approximately half your age to marry you? Well,
since she's in college, she's at least an adult. Stranger matches
have been made, especially when the parties involved are a
young blonde and a geriatric millionaire. She's young but
probably not blonde; you're not quite geriatric and if I had to
place my bets on it, I'd say you're no millionaire either.

So go for it! What do you have to lose but your dignity?
Just in case she tells you she's always thought of you as a
friend – or an uncle – it's a small price to pay. As Nike says,
just do it. As long as she's not doing her BA in English, there's
a small modicum of a chance that she might actually say yes.

If your question was simply about <u>how</u> you should propose *to her, as in, whether you should wait till Valentine's day or pop a ring just before the bus reaches her stop, don't worry so much about it. You sound like a guy who's much more about content than style – or you had better be, anyway. Feel free to be creative! Ask her to meet you outside the bus if you're feeling really brave, maybe? If budget is an issue, McDonald's has a great twenty-rupee McAloo tikki burger you can hide the ring in. Ask for the no-pyaaz version.*

All the best, and I'd be highly tickled to hear how this pans out for you, okay?

Love,
Amy

p.s. Do me and all women a favour, including her. In the likely event that she says no to you, please do not stalk her. I'm sure you wouldn't dream of it because you sound lovely, but thought I'd just put in a word. Remember, there are always other fish in the bus.

There. That one wasn't so difficult. Some answers just came more easily to her than others. Of course, most of the time, she felt like a big fraud. The letters that came in were usually about relationship problems, and what did she really know about relationship problems? She had problems, of course, but not in the relationship domain. Largely because she didn't even have any relationships. She had lived almost three decades successfully managing to keep most people at a distance. She had never been in love, she didn't have any siblings or even cousins, only a kind of weird, twisted relationship with her parents. No close friends either to speak of, only …

As if on cue, the doorbell rang. Trish automatically looked over at Lisa, who continued to stare open-mouthed at her book and quietly turned another page.

Trish pushed against the arms of the chair to lift her heavy frame up and went over and opened the door. Akanksha stood there, smiling serenely, looking much more relaxed than she had a few hours earlier. In fact, she was glowing and radiant. Trish had resolved a long time back not to envy her friend her gorgeous looks, but this glowing business was getting on her nerves. 'Whoa, why are *you* so happy?' she grunted by way of greeting.

'Just.' Akanksha breezily wafted in past Trish. 'Isn't it a wonderful day?'

'Is it?' Trish peered outside the door, trying to get a glimpse of the weather. Looked like a regular sultry day in Mumbai to her. She shut the door and followed Akanksha inside to the living room.

'Hello, munchkin.' Akanksha sat down on the arm of the sofa on which Lisa was reading, and gently stroked her daughter's hair. Lisa ignored her completely, and when Akanksha bent down to kiss her cheek and nuzzle her, she just made a little annoyed sound and shrugged her off. Akanksha didn't seem to mind, she just sat there, gazing at her fondly, watching her read.

Trish cleared her throat. 'So listen. What I was telling you this morning?'

'Oh yes, darling.' Akanksha turned her big, pretty, kohl-lined eyes to Trish and beamed. 'Congratulations. I'm so glad you've found some work! It must be a big relief.'

'It is,' Trish admitted, and then added, 'But the thing is, I really do need time to be able to work at it.'

Akanksha nodded vigorously, big eyes staring innocently at Trish.

Trish tried again. 'Time to myself at home.'

Another nod. Complete agreement.

'Time *alone*,' Trish said, emphasizing the last word, hoping that now Akanksha would get it.

That asinine pretty-faced nod again. 'Of course.'

Trish gave up and rolled her eyes. The words came out in a rush. 'I won't be able to *babysit* all the time like this, Akku.'

'Oh.' Akanksha looked shocked and a little hurt. 'Did Lisa bother you today? I told her not to. Lisa?' Lisa didn't respond, burying her face deeper into her book, although Trish thought she was only pretending to read now.

'It's not that,' Trish said quickly. 'She was very good today, all she did was read. It's just … we'll need to plan things a little better. I need to balance a few things, including Ba's care, maybe start some therapy for him, and now there's the writing assignment and the job search.' She suddenly wished they weren't having this conversation in front of Lisa, who she was sure was listening. Yes, her ears were perked up. To make amends, she said, 'Lisa's welcome to come over, we'll just have to plan it in advance, unlike today.'

Akanksha sighed. 'Of course, darling. You're right. I shouldn't have just dumped her here like that without giving you proper notice.' Trish winced, wishing her friend wouldn't use the phrase 'dumped her' in front of Lisa. Oblivious, Akanksha went on. 'Well, the good thing is that my father is coming over to stay with us in a couple of weeks. So the last four weeks of summer holidays, he'll be home with Lisa and should be able to manage her while I'm out.'

'What are you so busy with these days, anyway?' Trish asked, but Akanksha was already jumping up off the arm of the sofa. She poked at Lisa's shoulder. 'Get up, Leez. We're leaving.'

'Sit, have a cup of tea,' Trish offered. 'I'm kind of taking a break right now from the writing, in any case.'

'Oh no,' Akanksha said, now dragging Lisa to her feet and then pushing her towards the door. 'We've imposed enough. I feel bad about that.'

'Hey, it's no biggie,' Trish said. 'I didn't mean to make you feel bad ...'

'It's okay, Trish.' Akanksha smiled at her. 'I'm glad you told me. Friends should be able to tell each other stuff, right?'

'Right.' Trish felt a little relieved as she followed them towards the door, but the feeling was still tinged with a sense of unease.

'Bye, Lisa,' she called after her as the small girl followed her mother, dragging her feet out of the door.

Lisa whipped around with a scowl on her face that was even darker than usual. 'You were not *babysitting*. I'm not a baby!' she hissed at Trish. And then, after one little stamp of her foot for effect, she ran off to catch up with her mother, leaving Trish open-mouthed with surprise.

82

9

The Contract

'Hold, please. Hold. HOLD.'

This felt familiar. Trish broke into a clumsy run to try and get to the lift before the doors closed. This time too, no one inside bothered to press the button to wait for her. She skidded to a stop right in front of the closing doors and cursed under her breath. Stupid assholes. She was glad she didn't work here any more.

She looked around and saw a tall, bespectacled young man watching her from a few feet away. He averted his eyes when she looked at his face. Another corporate snob, she supposed. Maybe even from her old office, for all she knew, although she didn't think she had ever seen him before. He was dressed semi-casually, in jeans and a dark green shirt. Good-looking in a lanky sort of way, she noted. They waited together, but when another lift door opened and she got in, he didn't follow her inside. Maybe he had been waiting to go down to the basement. Or maybe he just didn't want to share the lift with her. Whatever. She was glad to have the lift to herself. She rode up speedily to the tenth floor, adjusting her plain grey kurti over her faded blue jeans. She could have dressed more formally for the meeting, but she was irritated at having to come back here. Besides, she was just a freelancer now and didn't need any more corporate bullshit, especially after having been fired from this very company.

She didn't want to run into Akshay or any of the other Internet department folks, and was glad that Nivedita sat in the opposite wing, along with the rest of the print department. The reception guard smiled in recognition at her and she returned the smile but went past him quickly, not wanting to answer any questions about where she had been all this while.

Okay. This was the editorial section. It reeked of coffee and cigarette smoke. The décor was in blue and purple and had a distinctly bohemian feel. The office was totally deserted. She checked her watch. Eleven a.m. Wow. These people clearly had a different set of rules altogether. Well, fair enough, they probably were up late getting stuff to press.

Trish spotted a lone figure coming down from the far end of the office – yes, it was Nivedita. The latter saw her and waved in her typically overenthusiastic manner. She was dressed in a bright orange-and-white combination of flowing skirt and blouse with long dangling white earrings. She came up to meet Trish halfway and gave her a hug and even air-kissed her – not once but twice, on both cheeks. Unused to this form of greeting, Trish was totally embarrassed.

To cover it up, she said gruffly, 'So tell me again why we couldn't do this over the phone?'

'Oh *darling*, it'll avoid many iterations on the contract if we can have a discussion in person.' Nivedita smiled brightly at her. 'Anyway, you know Zee doesn't *do* phone conversations.' Trish didn't actually know anything about Zee at all, beyond the fact that she was the chief editor, but Nivedita went on. 'And besides, she *wanted* to meet you in person.' Her smile faded as she took in Trish's appearance, looking her up and down slowly. 'This is the best you could do?'

'What?' Trish said, her voice sharp.

'Never mind, darling. Follow me.' Nivedita breezily led the way to a room at the back of the office – the only one, Trish noted, that didn't have see-through doors. Well, it was made of glass but the view of the interiors was blocked by curtains of blue beads. The big E was clearly the big cheese here – her office was even bigger and fancier than Akshay's.

As soon as Nivedita opened the door, her attitude changed from breezy nonchalance to absolute deference. She poked her head through the door and said in a meek voice, 'Zee? Trish is here to see you.'

'Well, why don't you let her in then?' rang out a sonorous voice with a strange, unrecognizable accent.

Nivedita almost bowed in response and ushered Trish in. Trish walked slowly into the large office with its blue-beaded curtains and large, indecipherable pictures full of angles and colours which she assumed passed for modern art. Zee rose from her chair and walked slowly around her desk towards Trish. She was an imposing woman of about forty. She had a head of short tight curls and was clad in a flowing olive-green dress that looked rather like a gown. The manner with which she carried herself was distinctly regal. Trish smiled, but Zee's lips merely twitched fleetingly around the edges as she looked appraisingly at Trish.

'The column is doing well,' Zee announced. 'We've just concluded this month's research and it's already become one of top three in the paper. I always knew it had potential. I suppose it just needed the right tone.'

Her words didn't sound very much like praise, but Trish's automatic response was, 'Thank you.'

Nivedita was in the process of withdrawing, murmuring something about leaving them to it when Zee called to her. 'Nivedita. Will you tell the boy to get us two cups of green tea?'

'Of course, of course, Zee,' Nivedita grovelled and then escaped. Trish opened her mouth to protest that she would prefer coffee, but thought the better of it.

Zee sashayed over and seated herself in the large leather chair behind her desk. Trish lowered herself on to one of the smaller chairs in front of the desk and shifted around, trying to get comfortable. The seat was soft and squishy. She looked around surreptitiously, noting that Zee's office even had a separate lounge corner, with its own low table and sofa set. Impressive.

'You'll have to work at keeping the tone consistent, of course,' Zee remarked, eyeing Trish. 'I thought that last week's column was a little *soft*. And you gave away something about yourself in terms of not having any children. You do realize, of course, we need to avoid involving personal details of any sort in future columns.'

Trish didn't react. It wasn't that Zee wasn't making sense, it was just that she didn't like the tone.

Zee didn't seem bothered about her reaction anyway. Her attention had shifted. She was peering at something on her large, flat-screen desktop, grunting to herself, 'Incompetent fools, can't understand a simple thing.'

Trish waited for her to come back to their discussion, but a couple of more minutes passed and it looked as if Zee might have forgotten about her. She cleared her throat and said politely, 'You look like you've got an early start today. The office is empty.'

This succeeded in distracting Zee from the screen, and she looked over at Trish rather blankly, saying, 'Oh yes. Well, most people start their day here at noon and work late. But I wanted us to finish our meeting before anyone came in.'

'Oh. Why is that?'

Zee looked her up and down with what Trish instinctively recognized as disdain. Zee didn't bother to answer Trish's question. She suddenly changed tack. 'Well. Shall we look at the contract then?'

'I haven't actually received a copy of it from Nivedita.'

'Oh, that woman.' Zee rolled her large eyes. 'Indians can't get anything right the first time, can they?'

'Er. I'm Indian, too,' Trish offered.

'Oh, so am I, unfortunately. Part south Indian, part South African.' Zee's attention was back on the screen as she clicked repeatedly on the mouse. 'But I've had the advantage of spending most of my working life in more civilized places in Europe, mostly the UK. Just two years in *this* city, and it's been enough to drive me mad.'

Trish found herself bristling with anger, but figured that it was better to avoid saying anything. This candid little speech confirmed her initial opinion about Zee – she was just a self-obsessed egomaniac with a deep-rooted colonial hangover.

There was a knock on the door and Zee called out, 'Come!' in her deep voice. A scrawny young fellow entered and hurried over to the table with a tray with two cups of green tea in shiny white bone-china cups, gold-rimmed unlike Akshay's, Trish noted. She said a soft thank-you to the tea-boy, but he seemed too scared to respond. Zee ignored him completely, still staring at her computer. Trish watched curiously as the trembling boy proceeded to back out of the room.

'Here it is,' Zee announced and turned the screen all the way around to face Trish. 'I won't bother asking that buffoon Nivedita to take a printout. Just read it on the screen for now.' She helped herself to a cup of green tea and settled back in her chair. Trish tried to ignore the fact that Zee now seemed to be studying her expression. She kept her focus on the screen.

Hmm. Standard stuff. This contract between Ms Trish Saxena, hereinafter referred to as the party of the first part and DNX Publications, Mumbai, hereinafter blah-blah ... Okay, daily column, non-compete clause as far as this genre was concerned, contract validity for a year on renewable basis upon mutual agreement, termination from either side upon one month's notice, content to become the property of the publication, conferring the right to use it online, right to use material or reject it as per editorial's final judgment etc. etc. It looked all right, but the compensation structure didn't appear to be clearly mentioned anywhere so far, and Trish was about to remark upon this when she reached Clause 4D.

The party of the first part agrees that they will maintain complete and total secrecy about their identity in relation to the column in question, and will, in no circumstance, whether intentionally or through negligence, allow for it to become known that they write the same.

'What's *this*? In this privacy clause.' She looked up at Zee. 'I'm not supposed to tell even family and friends about the fact that I write the column, even *post* termination of the contract? Why?'

'*Have* you told anyone yet?' Zee had her eyebrows raised.

'Well, no, but ...'

'Good. Now. Trish.' Zee spoke with the air of one explaining something to a particularly slow individual. 'You probably have very little understanding of how these things work. But I'm trying to run a lifestyle supplement here. It's the most read supplement. In fact, our research tells us it's read even more than the main paper. This hasn't been easy for me to achieve, but I've done it. And it's because I keep in mind that there has to be a certain aura we must maintain and project for the key columns and columnists that we feature.' She waved one heavy arm around for effect. 'We have celebrities writing for us. Have you seen Deepika's column?' Trish shook her head, but Zee paid no attention. 'Well, *you* have the honour of being published alongside those columns now.'

'Yay,' Trish said dryly. 'But Zee, the thing is, no one knows that I'm Amy, and according to this contract, you don't want anyone to *ever* know either.'

'Yes, but that's for good reason,' Zee said sharply. She appeared to have caught the sarcastic tone in Trish's voice and seemed affronted by it. 'We would like Amy to be perceived as someone who's ... successful, glamorous, young, *hot*. The persona we'd like to create is of someone good-looking, well turned out, confident, in complete control of her life. And you ... well.' She paused and looked at Trish with an expression full of meaning, waiting for it to sink in.

'So.' Trish underwent an inward struggle to maintain her composure. 'In short, you want *Amy* to be all the things you think I'm not.'

'Exactly.' Zee sat back, with a pleased, condescending smile. Trish, who had been a little daunted when she walked in for the meeting, now felt like jumping up and challenging this woman to a wrestling match. She could take her, she would grab those tight curls and swing her around and then sit on her until she begged for mercy. She would ...

She took a deep breath to calm herself down. Her eyes fell on her neglected cup of green tea. She picked it up now to take a sip. It was lukewarm, bland and disgusting. She tried to contain her anger as she skimmed through the last couple of paragraphs on the screen facing her. She almost choked on her tea.

As compensation for the column and the agreed discretion, the party of the second part agrees to pay the party of the first part a sum of Rupees ...

They were *increasing* her payout? Trish's heartbeat quickened as she read on, hardly able to believe her eyes. And offering a six-month advance? It would take a great deal of pressure off her to know that she had guaranteed work at this rate. She had been prepared to negotiate, but the numbers in front of her were already well beyond what she had hoped for.

90

'So.' Zee spoke softly now, her tone almost ingratiating for the first time. She was still watching Trish's expression closely. When Trish looked up, the smile on Zee's face was already triumphant. 'I assume we have an understanding?'

Trish underwent another internal struggle that lasted several seconds and then nodded, saying in as neutral a tone as she could manage, 'I suppose so.' It was worth the stupid anonymity clause.

'And we can count on your complete and absolute discretion?'

Trish bit her lip. 'Okay, yeah.' She cleared her throat and said in a more decisive manner, 'Yes.'

'Wonderful,' Zee said dryly and then reached out and turned the computer screen towards her again. She now spoke with an air of dismissal, not looking at Trish. 'Nivedita will handle the paperwork with you. Only she and I know that you write the column. I intend to keep it that way.' She looked at her crystal-studded silver watch. 'So you should leave now. It's almost noon and people will start to come in soon. If anyone sees you, they'll wonder what on earth you were doing talking to me.'

It was rude and abrupt as a parting, but her short time with Zee was enough for Trish to know that she couldn't have expected any different. She pushed back her chair to stand up, making as much of a noise as she could by scraping the legs along the floor. She felt a slight twinge of satisfaction to see that this made Zee wrinkle her long nose.

She said, 'Bye, Zee,' when she reached the door, but Zee was staring at her screen again and didn't reply. Trish left the room, mentally slamming the glass door behind her, although the only sound she actually made was the tinkling of a few blue beads.

She didn't bother to speak to Nivedita before leaving and was still in a bad mood as she drove out of the parking lot. She was pissed off at Zee – what a complete bitch! But she was beginning to feel even more pissed off at herself. Had she just sold out? Why had she let herself be insulted like that?

The column must have really got the circulation and readership numbers of the paper to rise by a significant percentage. There was no other reason she would have been offered this kind of money. She couldn't help being mystified by the privacy aspect. Sure it was an anonymous column. But not to be able to tell her own *family*? If Zee had said they needed to maintain anonymity so that a future writer could also carry the column off, it would have been different. Instead, she had given her that condescending haughty look and implied – no, *said* in so many words – that Trish was too much of a loser to be identified with Amy. Trish should have thrown the contract in her face. Figuratively. No, literally. She should have tossed the damned computer screen at her.

She glanced moodily into the rearview mirror. Her attention suddenly shifted to one of the cars behind her. In it was the same tall, bespectacled man she had seen on the ground floor while waiting for the lift. He had quietly pulled out of the parking lot a few seconds after her in a nondescript grey Ford Fiesta. She now realized that he had taken the same few turns that she had so far and was currently maintaining a consistent distance of three cars behind her.

Trish was being followed.

10

Hello, Mister

'Okay, stay calm ... Stay calm!'

Trish tried to suppress her rising panic as she squinted at the rearview mirror. Unmistakable. Same fellow, and he was definitely after her for some reason. To test her theory, she flicked the indicator switch and took the first right turn that came up even though it took her away from her route home. Sure enough, after a few seconds, there he was again, four cars behind her now. Her heartbeat quickened.

She fiddled around on the dashboard to find her sunglasses. They were dusty from lack of use, but she quickly wiped them on her kurti and shoved them on to her nose. They made her feel less visible and she was now free to glance at the rearview mirror every three seconds. She took another couple of random turns in a bid to throw him off, finding it difficult to navigate the new, unfamiliar terrain.

What did he want? Was he some kind of psycho? A rapist?

A psycho-rapist? Why her? She was Trish, the girl to whom nothing ever happened, for god's sake. Just when she had become used to that, life was throwing this sort of thing at her.

Crime rates were growing at an alarming rate across all the large cities of India, and Mumbai was no exception. Her mother often exclaimed over newspaper reports, reading them out to Trish with a mixture of fascination and horror, usually over breakfast when she least wanted to hear it. The perpetrators were often innocuous-looking, well turned out men from decent families. That was just what this guy looked like, Trish thought grimly. There would be no point confronting him. What if he were armed? She took the next left turn. She decided it would be best for her to try and circle home. A few tense minutes passed and she couldn't see him any more. Maybe she had managed to lose him.

The grey Fiesta suddenly appeared behind her again and her foot automatically pressed down on the accelerator. She could call the cops, she realized. That would be the smart thing to do. Where was her purse? Oh god, she had tossed it in the backseat. She slowed down a little and tried to reach back for it, but it was just out of reach, and as she clawed desperately at the straps, she ended up pushing the purse farther away.

Could she stop and retrieve it? But she would lose a few precious seconds and he'd be right upon her. She accelerated again, zipping past the other cars, overtaking from the left and not paying any heed to traffic signals. Surely there was nothing he could do to her in broad daylight with other folks around. But she wasn't taking any chances. There was no way she was going to stop now.

Why wasn't she able to spot any cops? Usually, if she even broke the slightest rule, such as crossing the stop line at a red light, a policeman would magically appear, with his challan-book, ready to fine her. But now, even though she deliberately zipped through a red light, almost colliding with an auto-rickshaw approaching from the right, there was no cop in sight. The auto-guy held his palm out at her in the aggressive-but-curious gesture that was code for 'Ah, another stupid lady driver', but she just left him in a cloud of dust. She briefly wondered: would the Mumbai junta come to her help if she just stopped and said she was being followed? Somehow she felt it would be wisest not to try and find out.

Her heart was still racing as she got closer home. There had been several close shaves, but at least her crazy driving had served to throw the psycho off her trail. Anything could have happened, she realized. She took a deep breath and exhaled: 'Ommmmm.' Some sort of protective spirit had been at work, she thought. She felt a lot better as she reached the street leading up to her apartment and slowed down.

95

The protective spirit was apparently out to lunch now because she spotted the grey Ford Fiesta crawling along behind her, this time maintaining much more distance. She gritted her teeth and made a decision.

Cursing under her breath, she drove a few hundred metres past her own building. She wasn't going to show him where she actually lived and put her parents in danger. She whizzed past Shah Rukh's bungalow, with the fleeting thought that he certainly had a lot of security for his home Mannat; if she tried to barge in or something, it would attract a lot of attention and the psycho-rapist would be scared away. Abandoning the plan as both stupid and overly dramatic, she drove on until she spotted a parking spot on the right side of the road.

She pulled in, parked, took off her sunglasses to toss them on to the passenger seat and got out of the car. She opened the back door and pulled out her purse. Swinging it over her right shoulder, she walked with deliberate nonchalance towards the unfamiliar apartment building, trying to hide the fact that her left hand was desperately trembling as it attempted, without success, to locate the phone buried somewhere inside her purse.

❀

It was a bad, bad decision. At least her own building had one or two watchmen hanging around most of the time. This place appeared to have no security whatsoever, either at the gate or in the main hall, where she now stood. Where the heck was everyone? There was a ramshackle sort of lift and she thought of quickly getting in and making her way to a higher floor. But the thought of being shoved off a higher floor to her imminent death stopped her. She would probably hyperventilate in a lift right now anyway. She looked around desperately and then ran over to a narrow passageway just across from the lift lobby. It had long rows of mailboxes on the walls with the residents' names and house numbers. She crouched down in a corner there.

She rifled through her purse again, cursing herself for being so disorganized. Her ears were suddenly super sensitive and the sound of the click of a door made her freeze in her crouching position. Someone had come into the building.

He was obviously trying to be as quiet as possible as he walked around the lobby. She counted his steps and estimated that he was just a few metres away from her. Would he assume she had taken a lift up to her supposed flat? If he got into the lift, she could make a mad dash to the entrance. It was her only hope.

Then the sound of his steps became louder and Trish realized that he was heading straight towards her. This was it. She swallowed hard and clenched her fist. She wasn't going to go down without a fight.

The fellow turned the corner and his shadow fell on her. With desperate abandon, Trish sprang up and leapt at him with an enraged scream. He only had time to blink once in horror and say 'Wha—' before she made contact, grabbing him hard around the stomach region as she tackled him to the floor, his spectacles askew, hands flailing automatically towards his face to try and hold on to his glasses.

Trish not only had the advantage of surprise, she also had the advantage of several kilograms. She now sat on his chest, pinning his arms to the floor with her knees. Her face was red and hot, her curly hair wild and standing on end. She must have looked a frightening sight because all the guy could do was stare at her, his brown eyes opened wide in shock. He'd had the wind knocked out of him and was gasping for breath. Trish quickly clamped both hands around his throat in a vice-like grip.

She felt a lot more confident now that she was in control of the situation. 'Aha.' Her voice was shriller than she would have liked. She modulated it down to a growl. 'Picked on the wrong girl today, didn't you?'

'Excuse me, ma'am,' The fellow managed to choke out. 'But I think there's been some mistake.'

'Of course there's been a mistake, you creep.' Trish barked at him. 'You were following me and I suppose you thought you would ... would ...' She found that she couldn't say it. She finally finished with, 'Have your way with me, eh?' It sounded lame even to her own ears. To make up for it, she tightened her grip on his throat. This caused him to cough loudly, and she loosened her hold just a little, biting back the word 'Sorry'.

The thing was, this guy wasn't behaving much like a psycho-rapist. Not that she was sure what a psycho-rapist would do if caught like this, but he was making absolutely no attempt to fight back. In fact, he simply lay there quietly beneath her. She decided to loosen her grip around his throat a little further and his face became less purple after a moment.

'Perhaps,' he ventured tentatively when he could speak again, 'you might allow me to explain myself?'

'Explain, then,' she ordered. 'What do you want from me?'

'Well, you see.' He blinked up at her a couple of times, clearly uncomfortable without his spectacles, which now lay two inches away from his face on the floor. 'It's just that ... I've been ... disturbed.'

'I KNEW IT.' Trish tensed up, tightening her grip on his neck again, and transferred more weight on to her knees in order to press his arms down harder. He groaned in pain and was caught up in another coughing fit, while Trish yelled, 'Hello? Is anyone here? Guard? GUARD!'

'Ma'am. MA'AM!' the fellow managed to choke out. 'It's not *that*. As in, I've *been* disturbed, I'm not disturbed per se. And I'm definitely no criminal. I was just seeking your help. I mean, I've been trying to contact Amy, but they insisted that they couldn't let me meet her. I knew if I waited long enough, you would show up. And you did today! I wrote a letter, but I just really wanted to give it to you in person. That's all.'

His face was screwed up in discomfort, and those brown eyes looked up at her beseechingly. 'You expect me to buy that?' she hissed at him. 'What a cock-and-bull story. Who hangs around all day waiting for an anonymous columnist to land up?'

'I did. Five days, in fact,' he said, almost proud now. He had the temerity to even smile. 'And I found you.' She squeezed his throat again and he gasped. 'Look, look, you'll find the letter in my shirt, front pocket, right here.' He indicated with his chin towards his chest. 'Read it if you don't believe me.'

'Hah! Just trying to divert my attention,' Trish said, feeling increasingly unsure of herself.

'Please, Ms Amy,' the man begged. 'I can't breathe. It would be very nice if we could have this conversation standing up.'

'My name isn't *Amy*, you psycho,' Trish barked, but then she bit her lower lip, thinking hard. She didn't quite trust him, but she was confident she could pin him down again if it came to that. Of course, he might run away, but that would be no big deal, she had seen his face closely enough to identify him. With a grunt, she finally released her grip on his throat. She pushed her heavy body off his, teetered a bit and finally managed to rise to her feet in an uncertain and rather undignified manner.

She watched him warily as he sat up. He picked up his glasses and put them on, then fished around in his pocket. She tensed up. How stupid of her. She'd forgotten. What if he had a weapon? But he pulled out a small white envelope, slightly crumpled, and held it out to her.

'I don't need to see that,' Trish said curtly. 'Just get out of here and don't let me see your face again.'

'What?' he said incredulously. 'Hang on, you can't do that. You have to read my letter.'

'I don't *have* to do anything.' Trish stood up straight, towering over him menacingly. 'I'm giving you one chance to get your skinny ass out of here. Don't make me sit on you again.'

'Listen, hello. Excuse me,' the fellow said, blinking in indignation through his spectacles. 'You attacked me without

99

reason; and now when I'm making a simple polite request of you, you ...'

'Out! Out! OUT!'

'Okay, okay, OKAY.' The man scrambled to his feet. He hovered. Trish's face was hostile and she tensed up as if to attack him again. 'I guess I'll be off then,' he said politely, as if they had just concluded a cordial tea party.

'OUT!' Trish screamed at the top of her lungs.

With a start, the man dropped the envelope to the floor and beat a hasty retreat. He turned into the lift lobby. Trish scrambled after him to make sure he was really leaving. He didn't look back once, and she watched as he disappeared out of the main door of the building.

11

A Curious Letter

Trish's hands were still trembling as she fumbled with her key in the door. She usually avoided ringing the bell because there was no telling what time Ba would be taking his nap. Besides, this way she also got to avoid having to talk to Ma.

She swung the door open, feeling a wave of relief now that she was finally home. She stepped into the apartment and immediately found herself face to face with her mother. She was still feeling jumpy and just about managed to keep herself from visibly starting.

'Hello, Ma,' she said in as neutral a tone as she could. 'How's Ba?'

'Ba is fine,' Ma snapped at her. 'You could ask about *me* sometimes too, you know. I'm also old and weak.'

Privately, Trish thought that Ma was in the pink of health – still in her early fifties with no major complaints – and she was the one who went on about having a healthy metabolism.

But she decided she wouldn't give in and let Ma have a fight today. 'Okay,' she said calmly. 'How are *you*, Ma?'

'Too late now. You don't even sound like you mean it,' her mother said peevishly. 'You're just asking because I said you should.' Trish sighed and squeezed past her mother and went down the hall into the drawing room. Ma followed her. 'Have you had lunch?'

'No, Ma. I'll eat in a bit.'

Her mother continued to hover. 'Where were you today, anyway?' She sounded curious.

'The office,' Trish said automatically, as she dropped on to her weather-beaten, comfortable sofa.

'The office?' her mother cried. 'Why? Are they giving you your job back? I knew the good lord would answer my prayers!'

'Calm down, Ma,' Trish hissed, sitting up straighter. 'It's not that. They just ...' She stopped short. That ridiculous clause, it said she couldn't talk about writing the column. At all. Not even to her own mother. This was stupid. Why had she agreed?

'They just what?' Ma was looking at her through narrowed eyes.

'They just needed ... to finish some paperwork ... about my leaving.' Trish was not a skilled liar. She tried to avoid her mother's penetrating glare by examining a spot on the carpet.

Ma, usually so self-involved and cozy inside her own bubble, was suddenly acting like Sherlock Holmes. She crossed her arms across her chest and said, 'Why do I get the feeling that you aren't telling me everything? Why this secrecy? Why not just ...'

'Okay. OKAY!' Trish's nerves were still frayed and she lost her patience. Her voice rose involuntarily. 'How about *this*? How about the fact that I just got chased halfway across Mumbai by a guy who turned out to be a self-confessed lunatic? And that I led him into the wrong building and trapped him and sat on him until he finally gave up and agreed to stop stalking me and ran off? How's *that* for an exciting day in the life of your only daughter?'

Her mother was staring at her incredulously. Trish glowered back, breathing heavily. Finally, her mother broke the impasse by throwing up her hands and rolling her eyes as she said, 'Fine! I was only trying to understand what's going on with you. You don't have to make up wild stories like that! Being chased by a lunatic, it seems.' She turned away in disgust and stalked out of the room, adding, 'If only you could figure out a way to get paid for your sarcasm, we wouldn't be in financial trouble any more.'

Trish stared after her, wondering if she had heard right. Now how the hell did Ma know about *that*? No, of course she didn't know, it was just something random she had said. And naturally Ma wouldn't believe her about the chase. Her mother had this habit of downplaying anything that Trish said. When Trish was ten and had come home panting, telling her mother that she had been chased by a dog and had narrowly escaped being bitten, Ma had written it off as a gross exaggeration. Her logic included the fact that portly little Trish couldn't have actually outrun a dog. Trish cringed at the memory. This was precisely why she didn't ever want to tell her mother anything, even if it was important. Actually, *especially* when it was important. There just wasn't any point. She took a deep breath and exhaled slowly. Well, at least Ma had left her alone for now and Trish could indulge the curiosity that had been steadily growing inside her.

After a final glance at the doorway to make sure her mother

had really gone, Trish struggled to extract something from her jeans pocket. Ah, there it was. She looked appraisingly at the small crumpled white envelope and then proceeded to unfold the letter inside.

Dear Amy,

I hope you are doing well. I have been following your column with great interest over the last few days and I wanted to request a personal meeting with you.

I have called the DNX publication office several times, but I have got no response from them as to how I could give this letter to you in person. I did not want to send it to the column as I assume there is a screening process, and I would not like anyone but you to read this letter.

Allow me to assure you that I am a perfectly normal person, apart from certain issues, completely nonviolent in nature. However, in case you have concerns about your safety, I would be happy to meet you in a public place such as a café or any restaurant of your choice.

Since I have received no cooperation from the publication with regard to my request for your mobile number or personal email address, I am taking it upon myself to visit the office in the hope of being able to hand over this letter to you personally. If you are reading this, it means I have been successful in my search for you.

I beg of you to grant my request as my problem is unique and can only be adequately demonstrated in person, and would be too unbelievable if I tried to describe it in writing.

Please do call me on the number below.

Yours humbly,
Sahil Aggarwal

The neatly written letter ended with a mobile number. Trish read it again, her frown deepening as she realized that this particular letter raised more questions than it did answers. So much for satisfying her curiosity.

She folded it up, stuffed it back in its envelope. Whatever. She was hungry.

❋

'Are you really going to eat *that*?' Akanksha looked aghast at the large bowl of Maggi on the table with its slice of half melted cheese on top.

'Yep.' Trish tried to hide her annoyance. She had just prepared herself the Maggi from the double pack of Classic Masala and was settling down to eat when Akanksha had landed up, unannounced and with Lisa in tow. She had babbled brightly about how today was positively, definitely the last time she would be asking the usual favour of Trish since her father was arriving soon. And now, having barely entered the house, she was already remarking upon Trish's choice of food.

'Goes straight to your butt, you know,' Akanksha said knowledgeably. 'All maida.'

'I want some Maggi too!' Lisa announced and then looked up at Trish 'I mean, please can I have some too, Trish-masi?'

'Sure thing.' Trish was pleased that Lisa could remember to be polite. She had started to like this kid. She went into the kitchen to get another bowl.

She came back just in time to hear Akanksha tell her daughter, 'Well, your butt is skinny, so I guess you can have some. At least you're eating something.' Lisa ignored her mother as she sat down at the table, licking her lips. Trish decided to ignore Akanksha too. She transferred some of the noodles to Lisa's bowl and sat down next to her to eat. Akanksha took the chair opposite the two of them. 'So how's your new thing going? You said you have some new writing assignment?' Akanksha seemed to have realized that she'd been a tad insensitive with the Maggi thing.

Trish shrugged non-committally. She sensed that Akanksha was just asking out of guilt. Today was a change, though. Akanksha was hanging around. Usually, she just dropped Lisa off and hurried away somewhere. 'What are *you* up to?' She turned the question around on Akanksha. 'I've been asking you where you rush off to after leaving Lisa and you haven't really answered me. What's going on?'

'Oh. That!' Akanksha said breezily. 'Nothing, nothing. It's just … there are these new … classes I've been taking.'

'What classes?'

'What? Oh. Zumba.'

'Huh?' Trish frowned. 'What's that?'

'Zumba?' Akanksha threw her head back and laughed. 'You don't know what *Zumba* is? Come on, it's all the rage these days.'

'No,' Trish said calmly. 'I have no idea. What is it?'

Akanksha seemed not to know where to start and just kept giggling. Lisa, as if sensing that her mother was being dense, swallowed a mouthful of Maggi and said, 'Dance fitness. We had classes in school too.'

'Dance fitness,' Akanksha nodded. 'Exactly. And great fun, right, Leez?'

'I don't know, you never let me join those classes.' Lisa gave Akanksha a plaintive look.

'Where do you go for these?' Trish asked. 'It sounds interesting.'

106

'Really?' Akanksha laughed again. '*You're* saying some form of exercise sounds interesting? That's something. Maybe you should join me. I'll enquire about a friend discount.'

Trish worked hard to ignore her friend's jab. 'So where are they? Nearby?'

'Not too far.' Akanksha looked at her watch, appearing distracted. 'That Celeb Fitness Gym.'

'So what are the timings and charges?'

'Oh.' Akanksha picked up her bag and stood up. 'I'll do one thing, I'll message you the details, okay? I have a special plan with them because I'm a gym member, I don't know about the regular rates. Anyway, the afternoon batch wouldn't suit you, you usually seem to have your writing work to do at that time. In fact, don't you have your writing work to do now?'

'Well, yeah, but ...' Trish indicated her Maggi with her fork.

'I'll leave you to it then,' Akanksha said brightly. She waved at Lisa. 'Now you be a good girl, missy. Pick you up later.'

Missy continued to ignore her. She was good at ignoring her mother, Trish thought admiringly, she could learn a thing or two from Lisa. The kid took a huge mouthful of Maggi with so much delirious enthusiasm that Trish had to laugh, and Lisa spontaneously giggled through her mouthful too.

'All righty then, I'm off,' said Akanksha, waving at them, and then disappeared out the door.

Trish and Lisa were still giggling as Lisa struggled to get all the Maggi strands into her mouth. There was a little lull after which Lisa remarked, 'My mom is weird.'

Trish nodded along in solemn agreement and then their eyes met and they giggled again. They proceeded to enjoy the rest of their snack in perfectly companionable silence.

❀

'Trish-masi?'

'Yes, Lisa?' Trish looked up from her computer at Lisa. She was actually glad for the interruption. For some reason she was unable to concentrate on the letters today. She had just been staring listlessly at a medical blog, reading about Alzheimer's disease.

'I'm taking guitar classes in the summer holidays,' Lisa said. She was lounging on the sofa, her book dangling from her fingers. Apparently she couldn't concentrate on her reading today either.

'Oh? That sounds great.'

'My nanu is going to buy me a new guitar when he comes to stay with us.' Lisa spoke with warmth.

'Cool.' Trish smiled at the little girl. Lisa had seemed like a sullen little teenager the first few times she had come over, but had now transformed into a nice little seven-year-old. She couldn't know for sure, but she suspected that Lisa just needed someone to give her attention. Akanksha didn't seem to be giving her much time these days.

'You have pretty dimples,' Lisa remarked a little shyly.

Trish didn't quite know how to respond. She couldn't recall the last time someone had complimented her. 'Well, thank you,' she finally said, feeling self-conscious.

'Are you going to join the Zumba classes too?'

'I don't think so. It sounds like fun, but I don't think I'll be able to do it.' She looked down at herself and sighed. 'Maybe it's a little too late for me.'

'Why?' demanded Lisa. 'You're not older than my mom, are you?'

'Umm, about the same age.' Trish frowned. 'But your mom's so much fitter than I am.'

'So you need the Zumba classes more, that means,' Lisa

pronounced with an air of certainty that only a seven-year-old could carry off without being a know-it-all.

Trish had to laugh at that. 'Okay, okay,' she said good-naturedly. 'I suppose I could go for a trial class at least.'

'Yes.' This seemed to make Lisa happy. 'You go for Zumba class, I will go for guitar class.'

'Deal.'

Trish went back to reading her letters and Lisa to her book. Trish couldn't help but think that this kid made more sense to her than a lot of adults. Including those who had written some of the letters she had to read today. She tried to concentrate on formulating appropriate responses, but somehow the words just weren't flowing. She had to admit it. The one letter that was still playing on her mind was the one she was still carrying all crumpled up in her pocket.

Why hadn't she destroyed it yet? What was possessing her to even consider calling the fellow back and agreeing to his strange request to meet with her? She still had no evidence that he wasn't a psycho, although she had to admit she also had none that he *was* one. His language in the letter was quaintly formal and his manner had been polite and mild, even while she had been sitting on his chest and threatening to strangle him. Actually, the more she thought about him, the more she realized he had actually been kind of cute in a geeky sort of way. There was something about him, although she couldn't quite put her finger on it. His brown eyes had exactly matched the colour of his hair. She shook herself. Not that it mattered, of course.

Aha. *That* was it. She was just curious about how he had known that she was the one writing the column. Nivedita and Zee were the only ones at the office who knew, supposedly, and she was sure neither of them would have given it away to

109

him. So how had he figured it out? And what was that about having a problem so unique that he could only demonstrate it in person? All kinds of strange thoughts started making their way into her mind, but she pushed them out.

Maybe she would meet the guy, she thought. Just as some form of closure. It would be in a public place, a café like he had suggested. He couldn't do much harm. She would carry pepper spray. As per the terms of her contract, no one was supposed to know that she was actually Amy. She would have to find a way to ensure that he kept it a secret and it would have to start with hearing him out. She would call him in a day or two, she decided, and take it from there.

How odd her life had become. An anonymous column that was a strange hit with the general public; a strange man asking for a rendezvous with her; and a kid hanging around her home, urging her to try some strange new thing called Zumba.

Oh, well. She turned her attention to the day's letters again. She felt more sorted in her head now that she knew what she was going to do about that polite stalker. Time to dive into the mundane same-old-same-old.

Dear Amy,

I would like to try a threesome, but my husband is old-fashioned and refuses even though I have told him I wouldn't mind if we take on another woman ...

Trish sighed.

12

The Rendezvous

Trish tapped her foot continuously as she waited at her table at Costa Coffee. She looked out of the large glass window at the people passing by the café. She had chosen this place carefully. It was close enough to her home for her to get back quickly, but not so close that she might run into Akanksha.

Her choice of table was a considered one too. Table for two in a discreet corner towards the back. Right next to the window so that she could observe the folks on the sidewalk, but in the shadows so that she herself remained practically invisible. Exactly how she was most comfortable.

She noticed her own nervous foot-tapping and stopped herself. This was going to be fine. Only one other table in the café was occupied: three people having a languid discussion in between checking their phones, two guys and a girl, in their twenties, well dressed. What got to Trish was how comfortable they seemed to be about themselves. How confident and easy their movements were. She shifted around uncomfortably in her chair. What was she doing here anyway? She always tried not to compare herself with other people, but found herself feeling even more out of shape and out of place than usual.

She was here for a purpose, she reminded herself. She would meet Sahil and figure out what the deal was with him once and for all. And she was going to make sure that he understood he was supposed to keep her secret. She would just have to give him a patient hearing first. She could do that. Right? Right. It was fine. It was all going to be absolutely one hundred per cent fine. She reached out to her purse and felt around again for the pepper spray. Ah, good. Just in case.

She jumped as she realized that a figure was suddenly looming over her. 'Shall I take your order now, ma'am?'

Oh. It was just that overenthusiastic waiter with his wide, gap-toothed smile. He had already approached her to take her order three times so far. Once more, and he could forget about his tip, she resolved. She repeated slowly, this time through gritted teeth, 'I'm *waiting* for someone. I'll order when he comes.'

'Okay, ma'am.' The fellow inclined his head politely and withdrew again. Just like all three previous times, she got the impression that he didn't believe her. Why would a man show up to meet someone like her, eh? He had probably seen enough women being stood up like this. It made her want to wrench the menu from his hands and beat him over the head with it.

She glanced at her watch. She had arrived a little before their appointed time. Sahil should be here any minute now. She had decided to leave the house early. Ma was doing her evening puja, the ritual she had kept up for so many years even though Trish suspected her heart was not actually in it.

Still, today the ritual had served as a window for her to slip out of the house without being questioned. No matter how grownup you were, as long as you lived with your parents, you could expect to be interrogated regarding your whereabouts all the time. So much for that 'deal' she had struck with Ma. It annoyed her, but she didn't want to have yet another argument. For now.

The door of the cafe swung open. It was him. She found she wasn't prepared for his entry after all. She had been staring out the window, looking out for him, but had been lost in her own thoughts and had somehow missed seeing him walk up to the entrance. He was dressed in a white shirt and brown chinos, a simple yet rather tasteful combination. She felt herself stiffening, suddenly even more self-conscious. He paused and looked around the café, his spectacles glinting briefly in the light from the low chandelier, and then his eyes settled on where she was trying to hide. His face broke into a smile that looked both relieved and nervous. He made his way to her and hovered in front of her table, running his hand through his thick brown hair. She got the impression that he was keeping his hands in clear view as if to demonstrate that he did not intend to whip out a weapon.

'Hello ... Sahil,' she managed to get out.

'Hi.' He continued to hover. Trish gestured towards the seat across the table, inviting him to sit. After another moment of hesitation, he sat down. 'Thank you so much for agreeing to meet me. I really do appreciate it, Miss ... er ...'

'Trish.'

'Trish,' he repeated. 'So, um, what are you having?'

The overly friendly waiter arrived, as if on cue, beaming at the two of them. He looked genuinely pleased that Trish hadn't been stood up after all. That approving smile made her want to thwack him all the more. 'Double-chocolate doughnut,' she announced. She felt the need to fortify herself. A sugar rush always helped.

'Coffee to go with that?' Sahil asked. She shook her head, and he turned to the waiter. 'Doughnut for the lady, a cappuccino for me. Thank you.'

The waiter bowed and took off with the menus. Sahil turned back to Trish and smiled at her warmly. 'So. You do live around here, after all?'

Trish fidgeted a little and then nodded. She wasn't good with small talk in the best of circumstances. 'Sea View Apartments,' she said a little curtly and then mentally kicked herself for revealing that to him. 'Anyway,' she went on, the next words coming in a rush. 'Would you like to go ahead and tell me what you wanted to?'

'Oh. Sure. I guess ... you're in a bit of a hurry.'

'It's not that,' Trish mumbled. 'I'm just not ... you know ...' She gave up trying to explain. As a matter of principle, she never explained herself and she wasn't going to change that for a random stranger, even one with a rather appealing warm smile and clear brown eyes. Besides, she'd read before that most psychopaths possessed a certain innate charm. 'Could we just get to the point, please?'

'Sure. Sure.' Sahil opened his mouth and shut it again. He looked blank. 'I don't quite know where to start.'

'Well, start with why you wanted to meet me so desperately. Start there.'

'Ah. *That*,' Sahil said. Trish had to keep herself from rolling her eyes. Maybe she *was* dealing with a real loon after all. Sahil pursed his lips thoughtfully and appeared to come to a decision. 'All right. The thing is ...' He spoke in a low, urgent voice. 'I'm running out of options, Trish. I've tried the best psychologists and psychiatrists and counsellors in Mumbai and, in fact, all of India. You name a therapy, I've tried it. But it's no use. They can't help with my particular problem.' He hesitated again, looking anxiously at her face as if to gauge her reaction.

'Okayyy,' Trish said slowly. 'So then you decided you'd reach out to a random unqualified anonymous columnist for a lifestyle publication that's practically a tabloid?'

Sahil smiled. 'I always like the sarcasm in your column. I know you don't mean it. You're a good person.'

'How do you *know* I don't mean it?' Trish countered. 'Or that I'm a good person, for that matter? You don't know a thing about me.' She knew he was trying to be nice, but she didn't like any form of presumption. He didn't know her from Adam. Eve. Whatever. No one really knew her and she didn't want them to either. She went on, trying to sound less snappy. 'So what's the problem?'

He swallowed and then went on, his voice even softer now. 'For a long time now, I have had this little issue ... of being somewhat ...' He took a deep breath and then finished, almost whispering the next word. '*Psychic.*'

There was a long pause and finally Trish whispered back, in unconscious imitation, 'I see.'

'So actually, that's why I had to meet you.' He spoke quickly now. 'Because ... I ... *saw* myself meeting you. So I knew I would meet you. And that's why ... I had to meet you. That's all.'

He seemed to think that this bizarre statement passed for some sort of an explanation and sat back, gazing at her face appraisingly. His brown eyes flickered and she noticed that his expression now contained the slightest hint of a challenge. Trish's head was beginning to spin. On the one hand, this

115

seemed like a good time to say nice-to-have-met-you-bye-bye-now. But strangely, she found that curiosity was getting the better of her. What on earth was this fellow on about anyway? She became vaguely aware of a familiar scent tickling her nostrils. Double-chocolate doughnut. She looked up to see the waiter approaching them with a tray and his constant ingratiating smile. They suspended their conversation as the waiter placed their order on the table.

Sahil looked fidgety and agitated. As soon as the waiter retreated, he said, 'Look. I have no control over it, okay? It just happens, and I ... I ... *see*.'

'Dead people?' Trish suggested lightly, scanning the table for a fork. The doughnut looked good.

'You don't believe me,' he said flatly. Suddenly the light in his brown eyes went out. Trish had just taken a big bite of doughnut and, for some reason, his disappointed expression caused her favourite warm gooey chocolatey delicacy to turn to cardboard in her mouth.

She chewed and swallowed it with some difficulty and looked straight at him. 'Well ...' She bit her lip. 'It's just ... look, come on, you have to admit that something like that *is* a little hard to believe. You know what I mean?'

'Of course I know what you mean,' he said in the same flat tone. 'That's what I've been hearing for years. No one believes it. I don't know why I thought you might.'

'Okay, listen.' Trish put her fork down. 'Let me just suspend all judgement for the next few minutes. Go ahead. What's the deal?'

He shrugged. 'There's no deal. I mean, it just comes and goes. In flashes, really. I sometimes get these visions in my head. It started when I was a kid. Initially, I thought I was just daydreaming. Until I began to see that what I saw in my head actually happened a while later, sometimes a day later, sometimes a week or so. It was ...' His eyes clouded over. 'Disturbing.'

She found that she was holding her breath and exhaled. 'As in?'

'Okay, don't get me wrong. It's not as if I've ever seen gruesome things like murders taking place. I'm not *that* sort of psychic. That kind of stuff might actually be useful to someone.' He laughed nervously. 'It could be anything. Small things. Like knowing I'm going to run into someone a little before it happens or seeing my dad drop something to the floor and then watching him actually do it, mundane stuff. It's just ...' He seemed to be grasping for words. 'Very frustrating and makes me feel totally abnormal. I don't *want* it.'

She didn't know what to say. Sahil had his head in his hands now and was speaking so softly that she had to lean in slightly to hear him.

117

'It had stopped in between. For several years, I thought it was gone. I went to college, got a job. And then, two years ago, my parents insisted that I take over the family business. I really didn't want to do it, but they insisted I give it a shot. About that time, the stupid visions started again and I remembered how it used to be for me as a kid, not knowing when I might suddenly get a vision, wondering when I might actually see something really disturbing, you know, like maybe my own death.' He let out a short bark of a laugh which had no trace of humour in it.

There was a long silence. Trish still had no idea what to make of all this. She was a fundamentally practical person who had always scoffed at any form of mumbo-jumbo. Akanksha was a regular with this sort of whacked-out thing and had often tried to get her to go for things like past life regression sessions, tarot card readings and so on, and Trish had always laughed at her and flatly refused. And now, here she was, sitting across from a guy who claimed he had visions of the future in a chagrined but rather matter-of-fact way, as if he were confessing to disliking his mother-in-law or something. 'So what does your wife have to say about this?' Trish asked, feeling it was safer to ask more questions than pronounce her own opinion on this subject.

'My what? Oh. I'm not married.' Sahil smiled ruefully. 'Confirmed bachelor. Who would marry a loon like me?' Trish started a little at his choice of word because it had been running through her own mind a few seconds earlier. Could he actually be a psychic? She shook herself. Now *she* was beginning to act like a loon. He went on. 'Just haven't met the right person yet, I guess.' He looked thoughtfully into space. 'I know for sure right now I need to focus on getting this *thing* sorted out.'

'Hmm.' She nodded sympathetically. She decided to go ahead and just say it. 'Look. Sahil. I wish I could help you, but I really don't see how.' He opened his mouth to respond, but she held up her hand and said, 'I said I'd hear you out. I've heard you out. And let me tell you something. I'm not a trained psychiatrist or counsellor or anything. I just write a random anonymous column, trying to provide commonsensical advice to nonsensical problems.' He stiffened, and she quickly went on. 'I'm not talking about *yours* specifically. But you're really better off getting professional advice from someone who knows about this stuff. I have no clue whatsoever. Always lived a very straightforward, practical life. Don't believe in anything remotely other-worldly.' She searched in her head for what Akanksha might suggest in a situation like this. 'Maybe you should go to some sort of ... healer or reader or ...'

'I've tried all those, they're all crooks, Trish! I've even been to psychics and *seen* visions of how they were going to bluff about *their* visions!' He shifted his chair a little closer to hers. 'Look. It's okay if you don't think you can actually help me with this. I'm telling you, I just saw myself meeting you, so I knew I had to make this meeting happen. I've spent *years* trying to *fight* this thing. It's almost *killed* me.' She could sense the urgency and frustration in his tone. 'So now I thought I'd just follow the damn lead and see where it takes me.'

'How did you get Nivedita to tell you I write the column?' Trish asked suddenly, remembering that this was something she had meant to find out.

'Who's Nivedita?' he asked blankly.

'The one who ...' Trish swallowed. 'So how did you know *I* write as Amy?'

'I told you before. I read the column and felt that I was supposed to try and track down the writer. So I kept trying through the paper.' He sounded sullen now, as if sure he wouldn't be believed. 'And then when I saw you at the lift that day, I just knew. I saw it in my head that we'd be sitting together discussing this. Simple.'

'Simple?' Trish now found herself starting to get angry. What did this guy think he was trying to pull on her anyway? Why was she even wasting her time with him? But then, it wouldn't do to get angry with a nutcase. Besides, she had yet to ensure that he would keep her column a secret. Her nostrils flared as she fought to keep her emotions under control.

'You know what?' He seemed to suddenly be inspired by an idea. 'There is one other thing. Maybe it's how I can even prove it to you. *Maybe*. It often happens when I make physical contact with someone.' Trish unconsciously drew a little away from him, and he looked irritated. 'As in, when we shake hands and normal stuff like that. I see something about them, sometimes their future, but often their past too. I've seen a lot of stuff about people that way.' He shook his head ruefully. 'It's also why I usually try to avoid shaking hands with people.' He held out his hand towards Trish. 'Please?'

She glared at him. 'We already *had* physical contact that day.'

'Didn't count,' he countered. 'I wasn't concentrating. I had other things on my mind.' Without warning, his hand enveloped hers. To her surprise, her heartbeat quickened and she felt a warm buzzing sensation running up her arm. He went on, 'You know, such as whether you were actually going to strangle me.' He smiled at her and she squirmed a little. Sahil looked down at the floor and frowned. His eyes closed. Her heart was in her mouth. What *was* this feeling? Trish withdrew her hand more suddenly than she'd intended to. Sahil's eyes snapped open and he looked straight at her. He was still frowning, but this time in confusion.

'Well?' Trish demanded, trying to break the awkward silence.

He said slowly, 'This hasn't happened to me before.'

'What?' Trish said sharply.

'Umm.' He paused and then confessed, 'I couldn't actually *see* anything.' He saw the skepticism return to her face and continued quickly, 'But I definitely sensed something. Something strong. About ... something missing. Or someone. Missing for a long time?' He searched her face. 'Maybe a breakup from many years ago?'

Trish folded her arms across her chest. Clearly the fellow was reaching. Merely shooting in the dark. Good. This was good. She had almost lost it for a moment there. A part of her had actually almost believed his story. She spoke, more coldly

120

than before. 'Sahil. I have very few people in my life and those relationships are all intact, thank you very much. No breakups. I happen to be an extremely independent person. And I certainly haven't ever experienced the kind of thing you're talking about. So I guess your "powers" don't work. At least not with me.'

He winced a little at the way she had said the word 'powers'. When he spoke, it was with a tone of defeat. 'I usually get more than that from contact. I don't know why it isn't happening here. But I'm telling you, I do have a very strong sense about your ...'

Her jaw clenched and he stopped short. She tried to relax her face, she didn't quite know why she was getting so angry. But this guy who didn't know anything about her was making completely false statements about her life with such certainty, even though she had already told him they weren't true. How could there be someone missing from her life when no one had been there in the first place?

121

'So,' she said, as evenly as she could manage. 'Now I've heard you out. Will you please do me a favour in return?' He nodded mutely and she continued. 'I still don't know exactly how you found out that I'm Amy.' He opened his mouth, but she ignored him and went on. 'But it is vitally important to me that you do not tell anyone else about it. It's a part of my contract with the paper and I don't want anyone to think I told you. Even my mother doesn't know about it.' Not that Ma would have been the first person she'd have told, but he didn't have to know that. 'So please. It is my request to you that you keep this a secret.'

'Oh.' He looked surprised. 'Absolutely. I never meant to tell anyone anyway. You have my word.' He said it solemnly and looked completely sincere. Trish sighed. This was the best she could have done. She fidgeted a little and made as if to get up. 'You haven't finished your doughnut,' he remarked quietly. His voice was so despondent that she hesitated. 'I'm going to ask him to reheat my coffee,' he said. 'You sure you don't want one after all?' He smiled at her. It was a wan, slightly lopsided smile now. 'I promise we'll just talk about normal stuff like normal people. Okay?'

She paused, then shook her head. Somehow she'd lost her appetite. 'I've got to go. Maybe another time.'

His face fell again, but he nodded slowly. She opened her purse to fumble for her wallet, but he reached out and touched her hand, saying softly, 'Please, let me.' The strange electric sensation again. She averted her eyes as she said her thanks, pushed back her chair and rose to her feet.

122

She made her way towards the door without a backward glance, trying to ignore a strange and entirely unexpected twinge of regret as she stepped out into the light.

13

Getting a Move On

'Tish-tish, *darling.*'

'Hello ... um ... Niv-niv?' Trish made a face at her phone. Tish-tish, it seemed.

'Darling, *why* do you do these things to me?' Nivedita sounded peevish. 'The big E has her knickers all in a twist now. Why are you *refusing* to answer that question from the threesome-woman?'

Trish sighed. She had known this would come up again. 'I told you earlier, Nivedita. There are some questions I just think it's better to avoid. It was sex-related.'

'And you have no experience in that department,' Nivedita finished for her knowingly. 'Well, you don't even when it comes to marriage, kids, in-laws and all that other stuff, but you do just fine with that. So make something up! Go with the flow! Just ...'

'Hang on.' Trish felt her face getting hot. 'Just what do you mean I have no experience in that department?'

'Do you?' Now Nivedita sounded curious as well as a little disbelieving.

Trish swallowed her anger. Not for the first time, she reminded herself that it wasn't Nivedita's fault that she was a clueless dimwitted moron. She took a deep breath and said, 'Look. As per our contract, just as the paper chooses to reserve its right to pick and choose from my responses, I also have the right not to respond to certain questions.'

'It says that in the contract?' Nivedita demanded. 'Where?'

Trish felt like banging her phone against her head. 'That was the *only* change that I asked you to put in, remember? The final signed version has it. Go and look it up. Clause 16B or something. And show it to Zee, too.'

'Look, babes, Tish-tish,' Nivedita was pleading now. 'You don't have to deal with her on a daily basis, okay? She's a terror! And she just *cannot* take it when she doesn't get her way. So please, just answer that question today and we can all live happily ever after.'

'No.' Trish was adamant. 'I'm sorry, but I can't. It will only invite all sorts of other questions of the same nature. I want the column to remain family-friendly.'

'That's where the readers are, Trish!' Nivedita urged. 'We'll open up a whole new market. So what if that's the direction the column ends up taking? Be more of a visionary, like Zee. She can see that we'll build circulation if we include more of this! Sex sells, and you know it.' She lowered her voice and said, 'And come on now, the more popular the column becomes, the more valuable *you* become to the paper. Think about that.'

Trish said carefully, 'Give me some time to think about it.'

'Okay, sure, I'll call you later this evening.'

'I'm done thinking. The answer is no. I'm not going to turn this column into Fifty Shades of Shady!'

'Trish.' Nivedita's tone was still desperate but it contained a note of warning too.

'The big E won't like this.'

'Oh, she can go and shove it up her big A!' Trish was fed up now. 'Good luck, okay, Nivs? Now, if you want your responses on time for tomorrow's column, please give me the time to write them.'

She cut the call, and then just because it felt good, she pressed the red button on her phone a few more times. She missed the nineties when there were landlines and you could actually slam the phone down on people you hated.

Come, come now, she told herself. She didn't really hate Nivedita or even Zee. Or did she? Trish believed in restraint, she rarely allowed herself to feel strong emotions for anyone or anything. But she had to admit that these people really got her goat.

How dare Nivedita say that she hadn't had any experience with sex? Okay. So she hadn't, but that wasn't the point. Sex was something you had in a relationship – or so she liked to believe. And she had never been in a relationship, nor did she intend to be. But she got a glimpse of how the outside world saw her – big, fat almost-thirty-year-old virgin. Well, how dare anyone think about her sex life when it was so irrelevant to even her? And why the hell was it bothering her so much if she didn't care about it?

Oh, it wasn't that she couldn't write an answer to that threesome question. She just didn't want to take the column into that domain; she knew it would lead to the crowding out of other kinds of problems. The people who read it now might

125

not find the column readable any more. And she just didn't feel like doing it, damn it.

Still feeling grumpy, she went back to answering the day's letters on her computer.

Dear Amy,

I've been borderline obese since childhood. It's always made me feel low, but I learnt to adjust to the problem. However, last week when I went for my health checkup, my doctor gave me a warning about how it's reached dangerous levels after my two pregnancies. He said that I'm at high risk for a heart attack if I don't lose twenty-five kilos really quickly. But the issue is that I don't have the time for exercise. I've recently gone back to work and, when I get home, my kids need to be looked after. I just don't have the motivation to begin an exercise program either because I've never been able to stick to one before. Can you suggest a quick way to lose weight that doesn't take time?

Desperately,
Overweight

Great. Trish groaned, her head in her hands. First it was sex, now the column was becoming one about fitness. What was next, skin care and beauty queries? This was supposed to be a *relationship* column, at least in her head. Now she'd have to ignore one more letter and it would cause another issue with Nivedita and Zee. It almost wasn't worth the money.

Doing a quick mental calculation, she shook her head. Yeah. *Almost* wasn't worth the money. She began to type. As it often happened, the response composed itself as her fingers flew over the keyboard.

Dear Idiot,
Your letter pissed me off on several levels. First of all, you sign off as Overweight. Is that your only identity? Sure, popping out two kids and holding on a fulltime job is given only a passing mention because it's so easy, right? Let's define ourselves by our body weight. It's just so damn measurable.

I wasn't going to reply to your letter because this column addresses relationship issues. But I see a major issue here in the relationship that you have with yourself. You say you've been obese since childhood, and yet you haven't felt the need to do anything about it? Even though it made you feel low emotionally? For years? With regard to your health, it's only upon a warning from your doctor now that you feel the danger of being in such a state? Do you read at all? And now, you want a quick fix that doesn't involve any investment of time on your part?

For the love of god, don't be so ridiculous, will you? You may not have been able to stick with an exercise programme before, but your doctor is trying to tell you something and I think it would be wise to listen. So here's my advice (and the usual caveats about this column not being intended as a substitute for medical yada-yada apply): Get a personal trainer. Get on a diet and exercise plan that's suitable for you, and expect results according to the time and energy that you put into this. Get professional help with regard to your self-esteem issues. In short, get off your butt and do something about your problem. Even shorter, get yourself a damn life.

Love,
Amy

p.s. And I hope you make that life a long one.
p.p.s. I hear there's a little new something called Zumba that's all the rage.

Trish glowered at the laptop screen. She had started by feeling irritated at the letter writer, but her ire was now almost wholly directed at herself. What a fake she was. *She* had a weight problem, she'd had one all her life. Okay, so while she wasn't exactly obese, she knew that she had always been carrying around at least eight to ten kilos of excess fat, as if it were some sort of protective layer. As if she were making some sort of damned point about not caring for her health and appearance. As if it helped her somehow be more thick-skinned. She'd been defiant about it, almost proud. When had *she* ever made any form of concerted effort to watch her own diet? And as far as exercise was concerned ... Hah. She had just been plain lazy. So where did she get off advising anyone else to go out there and get fit when she hadn't lifted a finger in that direction herself ever?

Well, why not? She shut her laptop down and got up. She'd go over to the nearby gym that Akanksha had mentioned. Maybe she'd even find her there right now.

She had to do something. She had to get off her butt. Time to practise what she was preaching.

128

❦

She was the fattest person in the room.

This was painfully clear to her as she faced the mirror, feeling exposed and uncomfortable. Twelve ladies, all of whom seemed to know each other, were standing about laughing and chatting easily, from what were clearly their regular spots. They were all waiting for the instructor Raj to start the music.

She had wanted to back out as soon as she had entered

this large room with its wooden flooring and bright lights and unflattering large mirrors; but the nice man at the reception in charge of new members had insisted that she try a free class when she had enquired about Zumba. Akanksha wasn't here. In fact, when she mentioned her name, he had frowned and said he was unable to place her. But then, he'd added, they had so many people coming and going, it was tough for him to keep track of everyone by name. Trish doubted that with Akanksha's striking looks, a member of the male species would have forgotten her. Maybe she just had the wrong gym. Trish had been about to refuse the offer of a free class when the well built Zumba trainer had landed up in his neon shorts and coloured mohawk, greeting her loudly: 'Hello! I'm Raj! New student? What's your name? Trish, eh? Nice!' Then, overriding her weak protests, he had shepherded her into the class before she knew what was happening.

129

So there she was, in dark blue track pants and an oversized grey t-shirt, which she had assumed would pass for workout clothing. The other women wore slick shorts or workout capris and figure-hugging sleeveless tops. They were mostly young, in their twenties and thirties, and had straightened, silky hair held back stylishly in colourful headbands. Trish stood out like a sore thumb and felt about as attractive as one. Raj didn't seem to care, though. He just pulled her to the front of the class and stationed her right beside himself so that she could follow his moves easily. Great. She was now standing where every single person in the class could watch her make a fool of herself.

Trish couldn't remember the last time she had danced and felt nervous. This was all one big mistake. Some thumping fast-paced Latino-sounding music started up and Raj yelled at her, 'Just go with the flow and have fun.'

Yeah, right. Fun. What the hell was she even *doing* here? Trish stood frozen as everyone began to follow Raj's steps. Could she make a bolt for the door now? Raj caught her eye, giving her a huge, friendly grin and an encouraging nod. Trish stared into the mirror, thought, 'What the hell', and started to follow his moves.

Hmmm. This wasn't so bad. The moves weren't tough. Okay, it took a lot of energy and she found herself getting breathless almost immediately. But she tried to keep it up. The music was loud and peppy, and Raj had some incredibly infectious energy. Trish, who had never paid much attention to music, discovered that her body had a certain natural rhythm and, to her surprise, she was actually able to keep up with the class.

She was expecting a break after the song, but even as it faded out, the second one started up. She swallowed and kept going. Again, without a break, the third song. She was actually enjoying herself now. This was fun. Only after the first five songs were up did Raj allow the class to take a break. Trish was panting as she headed over to get a glass of water from the cooler. Raj came up to her and smacked her on the back saying, 'So! You've done Zumba before?'

'Nope.' Trish ignored the over-familiar smack on the back which she wouldn't usually have allowed anyone. She gulped down a glass of water in one swallow and looked up at him.

He was gazing at her with an incredulous smile. 'But you kept up with every song! These other girls have been part of this batch for three months and you're getting most of the steps right on the first day! That's awesome.'

'Yeah?' Trish couldn't help but smile too. 'So you think I'll be able to do this?'

'You're already doing it! You've got the moves, girl!' He

grinned at her and then added sincerely, 'Zumba's great. You'll have lots of fun.'

'And it really does get you fit?' She couldn't help but run an envious eye over his toned body.

'Totally, man. I was a gym instructor, but I love dancing and this is a fabulous total body workout. Plus, there are specific exercises we build in for specific body parts. You can burn up to a thousand calories a session!'

'Wow. Er, how many calories in one besan laddoo?'

Raj threw his head back and laughed loudly, even though Trish had meant her question quite seriously. The other women, already back in their positions, looked over to see what was so funny, and Raj gave Trish another over-familiar thwack on the back before trotting off to his place in the front and calling back over his shoulder, 'Welcome to class, Trish!'

Trish was in an unusually good mood by the time she got home. That one hour of practically nonstop dancing had totally taken the wind out of her, but paradoxically, she felt full of energy. A certain lightness was in her step and she even heard herself humming as she turned the key in the door and let herself in.

Ma's sour face peered out of the kitchen to look at her as she walked down the hallway. 'Hello, Ma,' Trish said cheerfully, 'How's B—I mean you?'

'What's that?' said Ma sharply, cocking her head to the side.

'How's you?' Trish said breezily. 'It's the new lingo. Everyone says "how's you" nowadays.'

'Why are *you* in such a good mood?' Ma grumbled, coming out of the kitchen. 'Where have you been, anyway?'

Something stopped Trish from answering. There had

been too many instances of a cutting remark from her mother taking the wind out of her sails. Today had been fun, and she felt that it could be the beginning of something new. She didn't want to risk spoiling it, so she just breezed past her mother, saying 'Just out and about. You know.'

'I do not know,' her mother said, her hands on her hips. 'You don't tell me anything these days. You keep working on something on your computer and you say you've got some new assignment for the paper, but I don't see your name on any articles and you haven't even told me which supplement you're writing for.'

Trish started humming again as she headed for her room. She was thankful she had carried a set of clothes and showered at the gym. She was determined not to rise to Ma's bait at all today.

And then Ma gasped with a shock of sudden realization. 'You're doing drugs!'

Trish whirled around. 'Huh?'

'It *must* be drugs. You've been cagey about everything for so many days. And now you come home all happy.' She stepped close to Trish and sniffed suspiciously, making Trish glad once more for the shower. 'I can't smell any alcohol, so it must be drugs.'

'Wow. Great deduction, Ma.' Trish resorted to her usual defence mechanism of sarcasm. 'Can you tell how many ounces of coke I've snorted?'

'I'm not talking about Coke or Pepsi. I'm talking about *drugs*.'

Trish threw up her hands in defeat. The doorbell rang. Mother and daughter continued to stare at each other malevolently. Trish broke her gaze and went over to the door, sputtering with incredulity. 'Drugs! Never heard anything so crazy.'

She opened the door. It was Akanksha standing there, with Lisa and an elderly gentleman behind her. 'Trish! Meet my father. Dad, this is the wonderful girl I was telling you about. One of my best friends.'

'Pleased to meet you, Trish,' said the tall white-haired gentleman with a gentle smile.

'Oh. Hello, Uncle.' Trish made an effort to soften her face. Akanksha's father looked like a very nice man.

She realized it would probably be appropriate to touch his feet and she began to bend over to do so, but he laughed and quickly pulled her up by the shoulders and put a friendly arm around her, saying, 'Arrey, none of that feet-touching business, dear. In our family, women are treated like goddesses, they don't touch anyone's feet.'

Trish straightened up and grinned at him a little shyly, liking him already. He was dressed in an elegant grey kurta and somehow reminded her a lot of her own father when he was just a little younger and a lot healthier. But Ba had rarely put an arm around her like that, even when she was a kid. Trish's had never been a physically affectionate family, and it was only now that he was so ill that he seemed to need and accept comforting little gestures from Trish such as a touch on the hand to calm him down. It was too little too late. Trish was surprised now to feel a little pang as she saw the ease and comfort with which Lisa clutched at her grandfather's arm, all but swinging from it now, full of glee.

'Trish-masi, my nanu's going to buy me a guitar today!' Lisa was dancing about, shifting from one foot to the other, barely able to contain her excitement.

Trish laughed and chucked Lisa lightly under the chin, saying, 'That's great, Lisa.'

'Yes, but calm down, will you, Leez?' Akanksha patted her

133

daughter on the head. She added to Trish, 'Sweetie, we were just on our way out for that guitar, but I thought we'd take a chance here for a second. I really wanted you to meet Dad.'

'Won't you come in for a cup of tea, Uncle?' Trish said politely.

'Would you please stop calling me Uncle?' He laughed. 'Goodness. You make me feel so old.'

'Yeah, Nanu said I don't have to call him Nanu and that I can call him by his name.' Lisa was dancing about in excitement again.

'Which you're not going to, young lady.' Akanksha rolled her eyes and turned to Trish. 'As you can see, Lisa's only a little overexcited about that guitar, so we'll stop by another time. Dad's here for the next few weeks anyway.'

'Okay.' Trish smiled. 'Hey, Akku, I went to the Celebrity Fitness Gym today for the Zumba class, and they didn't seem to have your name listed. When did—'

'Oh you went?' Akanksha cried. 'We must catch up on that, okay? Right now, got to go. Lisa needs that guitar.'

But Lisa was looking up at Trish wide-eyed. 'You went for Zumba, Trish-masi? And on the same *day* that I'm getting my guitar?'

Trish nodded and grinned at the little girl. 'Yes, and it was fun!'

'Let's go, let's go!' Akanksha took hold of Lisa by the shoulder and her father by the arm and steered them both away. 'Bye now, darling, we'll see you again soon!'

She bustled her family off quickly, leaving Trish wondering, not for the first time, why her only actual friend was such a weirdo.

14

A Walk

'A blog?' Trish repeated.

'Yes, darling!' Nivedita's voice floated over the phone gleefully. 'Amy's going to go online! Yayyy!'

Trish rolled her eyes. She'd always known it would only be a matter of time. DNX Publications didn't have that stupid Internet division for nothing. 'Digital is the Future' had been their rather unoriginal mantra for the last three years. 'And you'll put up the same material that appears in print, right?'

'Absotively positutely, hon.' Nivedita sang. 'But also, so much *more*! We're thinking we'll be able to accommodate many more letters, real time responses, comments. We'll cross-post to our Facebook page, set up live chats and even give you a Twitter handle!'

'Hang on,' Trish protested. '*I'm* not going to be able to put in that much time. I have to figure out something else to do with my life apart from being Anonymous Amy.'

'Oh, but you're becoming a huge celebrity, Tish-tish. Do you know the monthly survey results have come and yours is now *the* most read column, even more than Deepika's style column!'

'Wow,' Trish said, adding caustically, 'So I write better than a Bollywood celebrity, huh?'

'Oh, it's not *that*,' Nivedita said, oblivious as usual to the sarcasm. 'I think the whole aura, the whole mystery that we've built up about the Amy persona has worked. *Everyone* wants to know who it is.' She sounded gleeful. 'We're even getting enquiries from other publications, snoops claiming to want to interview you as part of a story on anonymous columns, but we know what they're up to, just trying to blow it for us by revealing you and destroying the secret. Well, hah! We're not letting that happen.'

'So what are you telling them?' Trish was interested in spite of herself. 'The reporters, I mean.'

'Generally, false trails.'

Something about Nivedita's vague answer made Trish narrow her eyes in suspicion at her phone. 'False trails such as?'

With some hesitation, Nivedita continued, 'Well, we've let it slip that *perhaps* the chief editor herself ghostwrites the column; but then, we've also thrown in that maybe it's actually a gay Bollywood celebrity.'

'Ah,' Trish said quietly. So Zee, the pompous big E, was quietly basking in the glory of the column. No wonder there had been fewer complaints from that quarter over the last few days. Well, she could continue to take all the credit she wanted. It meant nothing to Trish. She hated attention anyway. This was all stupid. Which was why she had to focus on getting herself a real job, and that brought her back to the point. 'So anyway.' She cleared her throat. 'Good luck getting a team to manage the digital engagement part of it.'

'Hey, hang on,' Nivedita protested. 'You know it's going to be a piece of cake for you. You handled the whole content business earlier, and you know how the whole blogging and social media thing works.'

'Nivedita.' Trish sighed. 'I never said I *can't* do it. It's just that I *won't* do it.'

'Why not?'

'It's my decision,' Trish snapped. 'It's not part of the contract; I never signed on to let this take over my whole life. I'm trying to figure out what I'm going to do next, and this is just a stop-gap arrangement for me. And you're right, I do know what the digital content part of it involves, and it *is* a lot of work.'

137

'We're offering *double* for the digital part,' Nivedita said in the quiet, smug tone of someone laying down their trump card.

'Stop throwing money at me each time I say I don't want to do something,' Trish snarled.

'Oh, but darling! I'm not throwing money at you!' Nivedita managed to sound genuinely hurt. 'I'm just giving you the facts. I mean, come on, Tish-tish, haven't you ever heard of making hay while the sun shines? You of all people should be milking this for all it's worth! Anyway, Zee said in case you have doubts about taking this on, she would be happy to meet with you to discuss it.'

'Wow. As tempting as that sounds,' Trish's voice dripped with sarcasm. 'I think you can tell Zee that I'll make my *own* decision on this and get back to you guys in a few days. Okay?'

'Okay, sure. Take your time. Will you let me know tomorrow?'

'I said a *few days*, why don't you ever listen? I've got to go now.' The doorbell was ringing and Trish was totally fed up of the conversation.

'But Zee said ...'

'Bye.' Trish hung up on her. This was the way most of their conversations seemed to end. Sometimes she felt sorry for Nivedita. She was clearly just the messenger and got shot a lot of times. But then, she always seemed to bounce back easily and the next time it was all 'Guess what, darling?' all over again. Trish decided she might as well save her sympathy for someone who deserved it.

She went over to the door, but her mother had beaten her to it. Ma turned around and looked at Trish wonderingly. 'Trish. There's a boy, I mean, a *gentleman* named Sahil who's come to see you.' She stepped aside to reveal a tall bespectacled man who stood outside the door, smiling politely, looking boyish in the blue jeans and brown t-shirt just a shade darker than his hair and eyes.

138

'Oh.' Trish's heart skipped a beat and she told herself it was just the shock. She didn't know how to react. Of course Sahil knew where she lived. She had let her apartment name slip that time they had met at Costa. It wouldn't have been difficult for him to get her flat number from the stupid, easily-charmed-or-bribed guards downstairs. But still, to land up unannounced like this? What was that in his hands? A bunch of *flowers*? She hated flowers. And, oh god, she was dressed in her Winnie-the-Pooh pyjamas and an old pink t-shirt with yellow flowers on the front. Okay, she hated *real* flowers, not flower designs. She hadn't been expecting to see anyone from the outside world today, and here *he* was, looking so good, in his impeccably pressed clothes. Who pressed their *jeans*, for god's sake? This guy always managed to make her feel stupid. Why the hell was he here?

Ma was looking back and forth at the two of them, a curious smile on her thin face. Uncomfortable under her mother's scrutiny, Trish finally said, 'Well, come on in, Sahil.'

Sahil smiled, not without a hint of relief, and walked into the flat, past her mother, who looked on with unabashed wonder and joy. *Easy, old lady*, Trish thought to herself and once Sahil passed her to go into the drawing room, she whipped around to give her mother a warning glare. Ma tried to look innocent. Trish frowned at her and then followed Sahil inside.

'So, er, how come you're ... here?' She knew it wasn't the most hospitable thing to say, but she was embarrassed by his presence and couldn't help herself.

In contrast, Sahil seemed totally at ease now. He was standing with his back to her, staring out of her window. He let out a low whistle. 'Wow. I don't *believe* it. What a fantastic view you've got!' He turned around and looked at Trish and smiled. 'I actually ... just felt like seeing you, that's all. I hope this is okay. You kind of mentioned catching up another time the last time we met, so ...' For the first time, he seemed to notice her attire. 'I'm sorry. I didn't mean to intrude. I guess it was rude to drop in without calling.'

'And *why* didn't you call first?' Trish had her arms crossed over her chest, hoping this way she was blocking his view of the yellow flowers.

'I guess I knew you'd say no, huh?' Sahil grinned at her winningly.

'Wow. You must be psychic or something.' Trish was sorry as soon as the words came out. She hadn't meant to make that wide grin of his flicker.

He seemed a little subdued now, but he took a step towards her and held out the flowers. 'For you.'

139

'Thank you,' Trish said, feeling ashamed and, therefore, accepting the flowers. She was beginning to blush. To hide it, she turned away and began to look for a vase to put them in. They were lilies, pink and white, and she had to admit they were kind of pretty and had a nice scent.

'So you're Shah Rukh's neighbours, no, aunty?' Trish snapped her head around to look at him. Oh, good. He wasn't talking to her. He was addressing Ma, who was hovering at the doorway.

Maybe Sahil *was* actually psychic, Trish thought dryly to herself. He certainly seemed to have an intuition about the right buttons to push. Ma lit up at this observation and said, 'Well, yes, we are! I've so often hoped that one day he'll just step out of Mannat to buy eggs or something from the kirana shop across the road, and maybe I'll be able to ask him for his autograph or tell him that he was just so good in *Veer-Zaara*, it's my favourite movie of his. But we've never seen him,' she finished, slightly deflated.

'Yet,' Sahil reminded her gently, and Ma brightened up at this.

'Shall I make pakoras?' she said with more enthusiasm than Trish had seen from her in a long time. 'It'll be very nice with the chai. Such nice weather outside.'

'Yes, Ma, actually,' Trish cut in quickly. 'The weather is so nice that we were just about to go for a walk.' She didn't know where the words came from because a walk with Sahil was the last thing she had planned, but it was sure to be a hell of a lot less awkward than sitting inside this small house, with a simpering Ma hovering around, constantly offering to ply them with chai and pakoras. She turned to Sahil and said firmly, 'Right, Sahil? Walk by the sea?'

Sahil looked mildly surprised but quickly recovered and nodded. 'Exactly. A walk by the sea. Lovely weather.'

Ma looked a little disappointed at being deprived of Sahil's company so quickly. Sahil smiled at her so charmingly that Trish was afraid that he was going to invite Ma along on the walk. But he didn't, and Ma simply smiled back. Trish could almost see the wheels turning in Ma's head. Ma was thinking that it would be nice to let the two of them spend some time alone. Wonderful.

Trish muttered something about changing into her walking shoes and hurried out of the living room, pushing past Ma. She would also have to find something without that damned Winnie the Pooh on it. She wasn't done with her work for today and Sahil was throwing her off her schedule. She would have to get rid of him quickly.

She rifled through her cupboard, trying to ignore the question of why she was feeling so damned pleased.

141

❀

It *was* a beautiful evening. June in Mumbai was usually hot and sticky, but there was a cool breeze and it blew the occasional light spray from the water on to them. Maybe the rains would come early this year, Trish wondered idly. It was nice to be out although she was still feeling very conscious having Sahil by her side. Usually only couples walked in pairs like this on romantic Bandstand, often holding hands as a firm show of their everlasting commitment to each other. He had better not try anything of that sort with her, she thought, even though her fingers already seemed to be tingling at the very prospect.

She felt a lot better now that she was wearing reasonably presentable clothes: a light mauve top and a pair of practically unworn old jeans she had recently discovered she could fit into again, although it was still a bit of a squeeze. Her Zumba classes, three times a week, over the last month were already paying off. She was glad she was sticking with them, even though the first week had been tough, with aches and pains in places she hadn't even known existed. After her body adjusted to the routine, she felt she had a new sort of energy. In fact, on evenings when she didn't go to Zumba, she tended to feel a little listless, and so brisk walks on Bandstand served to fill that space. Right now, she was content to stroll along slowly with this strange tall fellow she barely knew.

Sahil broke the silence only after they'd already walked about a hundred metres away from the direction of her house. He turned towards her and said warmly, 'So how've you been?'

142

'Me? Oh. Fine.' Trish realized with a start that she was rarely ever asked that question. It was strange, now that she thought about it. The most inane, polite form of greeting, the blandest of social niceties was hardly ever posed to her. And Sahil even sounded like he genuinely wanted to know.

He was gazing at her appraisingly. 'You're looking different from the last time I saw you.'

'Different? No. Much the same,' she said, deliberately breezy, trying to hide how self-conscious she felt about being observed so closely by him. The intensity with which he looked at her, as if she were the only other person around for miles, was definitely not something she was used to. 'You're probably just confusing me with someone else, that's all.'

'No, I'm not.' He pressed on, 'Why don't you just tell me what's different?'

She knew she had actually lost weight. Getting regular exercise had quickly burned away some of the excess fat. Even Ma had remarked on it a tad begrudgingly two days ago and that meant it really did show. But Trish didn't want to tell him that. It seemed very trivial and silly. Why should she tell him anything anyway? She shrugged and looked straight ahead, the invisible walls going up around her again.

They walked on in silence for a little while longer, and then Sahil said, 'I guess you're still wondering why I came to see you today, huh?' She nodded wordlessly, still staring straight ahead. 'Would you believe me if I repeated that I genuinely just felt like it?'

'Not really,' she admitted.

'You think I have some agenda.'

'Yep.'

'I don't have an agenda, Trish,' Sahil said earnestly. 'I'm just going with the flow here. I feel some sort of pull ...'

'Oh, please.' Trish rolled her eyes.

'What oh-please?' Sahil demanded. 'Why are you always so ... closed? What do you get by being so skeptical?'

Well, for one, I get to not be disappointed ever. But she didn't bother to answer him out loud.

He sighed with exasperation and then went on. 'Okay, look. I just felt we could get to know each other better, okay? Just be friends. No harm in that, right?'

'I don't know,' Trish said carefully.

'Come on, Trish! Don't you believe it's possible for two people to make an instant connection?'

'We did,' she pointed out. 'I attacked you.'

He laughed, shaking his head. 'Yes. I remember that distinctly. I couldn't forget that one even if I tried. But you know that's not what I'm talking about.'

'What are you talking about then?' Trish was getting exasperated with all this. This dude was too instant-karma-ish for her liking. He was much cuter with his mouth shut.

'I just want to get to know you better,' Sahil said firmly.

'I'm *not* going to help you with that psycho stuff. I can't.'

'Psychic,' he corrected automatically and went on. 'You *said* that already, and it's fine. What if I say it's just that ... there's something about you that I really like?'

'Then you're even crazier than I thought,' Trish quipped.

'And why exactly are you so down on yourself all the time?'

'Please,' Trish sighed. 'Don't you try to counsel *me*. I'm fine.'

'Of course you're fine,' Sahil said firmly. 'That's exactly what *I'm* saying. See, we're just agreeing!'

She couldn't help smiling at that, but wasn't comfortable with this line of conversation any more. They were nearing her favourite bench. Without a word, she steered away from him and sat down. He followed and sat down next to her. After a few seconds, he said, 'Do you know you're pretty stubborn?'

'Yes.'

'Do you know you're pretty?' Without missing a beat.

'Do you know you're beginning to piss me off?' Trish's eyes were flashing as she turned towards him. What did he mean, making fun of her like this? Pretending to flirt with her, as if she couldn't see through it.

He laughed incredulously and said, 'I have a strong feeling that *anything* I say would piss you off. But hopefully that will change over time.' She didn't bother to respond. She was still fuming. 'So,' he said cheerfully. 'Would you like to know more about me or not?' Sahil seemed to take her silence as an invitation to continue. 'Since you're clearly dying to know more about me, I must first tell you about my origins.' He took a deep breath. 'I come from the Aggarwal Sweets family.' He said it with the air of someone confessing to a big crime. 'Heard of them?'

She couldn't keep the surprise off her face. Aggarwal Sweets was a huge enterprise, but somehow it seemed not to fit with Sahil.

'Yes, yes.' He sighed, noting the change in her expression. 'I'm the youngest son, and so far I've escaped the destiny of my two older brothers. They've both been roped into the family business. But I can't stand the thought of it. And so, since I'm the rebellious one, my father keeps threatening to throw me out of the family.'

'Well, that's a little drastic, isn't it?' Trish was intrigued, in spite of herself. 'Why should you be forced into doing something you don't want to do?'

'Yes. Try telling Babuji, though. He's one of the "Phamily business is the phamily's business" types.' Sahil gave a short bark of a laugh and then ran his hands through his brown hair. She noticed a pattern: he seemed to do this when he was thoughtful or nervous. A ray of light from the setting sun sparkled off his glasses. 'I just can't imagine myself handling that stuff.' He wrinkled his nose. 'Mithai, namkeen.'

'Hey, you guys make a mean bhujia sev though.' Trish felt duty-bound to express her loyalty to her favourite brand of namkeen.

His laugh this time was more genuine. 'That's true.'

'So maybe you could just tell them that you don't have an interest in baking or cooking or whatever it is,' Trish suggested quickly, uncomfortable under his direct gaze again.

He laughed even more loudly this time. When he stopped, he said, 'Trish, we don't actually sit and make the stuff ourselves, you know, we run it as an enterprise. Sales,

145

distribution, merchandising, advertising, finance. I still don't see myself being excited by it, though.' He grinned at her again. 'You're funny, you know that?'

She hadn't meant to be funny, so she felt her face getting hot. Why had she gone and said something so stupid to him? Of course. Just because they ran the business didn't mean that they were actually halwais themselves. She felt like an idiot.

'So,' he said, his voice getting serious again. 'With the combination of all that stress with the family, and then the flashes returning again a few months ago, I kind of did something really stupid a while ago.' He turned towards her. 'I sort of tried to … *end* it all.'

She wasn't sure she had heard him right. 'You did *what*?'

'Well, it was also kind of an experiment,' he said quickly, sounding defensive. 'I was getting really stressed out and couldn't accept that what I had successfully suppressed for so many years was coming back to haunt me again. And then Dad gave me this ultimatum. It was all kind of closing in on me. So I figured that I might as well put my "powers" to the test. I mean, I always wondered if I'd see a vision of my own death, so I thought I'd check what would actually happen if I planned it.'

'Oh yeah, that makes a lot of sense,' Trish said sarcastically.

'I know it sounds nuts. It *was* nuts. But it didn't work anyway.'

'You don't say.'

'Oh, stop with the sarcasm for a minute, will you?' he snapped at her, looking actually angry. His eyes had darkened, turning to molten chocolate. 'I'm telling you stuff I've never told anyone else.'

'Well, I didn't ask to hear all of this, Sahil.' She was stung by his tone. It was the first time he had spoken to her like that.

'So you *don't* want to know?' he asked challengingly.

Trish tore her eyes away from his and looked at the ground. 'Go on.' She paused, then added softly, 'Sorry.' She stole a glance up at his face again. He was smiling at her, the light back in his eyes. Her heart skipped another beat, which annoyed her a little.

He resumed, 'So as part of my great big jackass plan, about three months ago, I went out to Marine Drive. I know it'll sound dumb to you, but I can't swim. Never tried. I guess I'm kind of afraid of the water. It was really rough that day. I parked my car and waded into the sea, fully clothed and all. I guess I had this idea of being swallowed up and all my troubles coming to an end.' He exhaled heavily. Trish was holding her breath. She was getting a weird feeling about this. 'But I couldn't even get my suicide act right. It was a really secluded spot, but somehow I still got spotted and pulled out. Someone told me it was a woman that had stopped to buy a bhutta who raised the alarm. They said she jumped in to try and save me; I couldn't find out anything about her though. My father had me taken out of the hospital as soon as I regained consciousness. I think he paid the cops to let me off from the attempted suicide charges or something.' He laughed lightly and then became quiet. 'I've often wondered who she was.' He turned towards Trish now. 'You know what I mean? Who would do a thing like that for a random stranger?'

Trish, whose jaw had been dropping further and further as she listened, quickly snapped her mouth shut and tried to look as neutral as she could. Her heart and mind were racing. It couldn't be. Too much of a coincidence. She just couldn't believe it.

It was *him* that she had saved? This was stuff right out of the movies. She couldn't let him know about this. He

147

was already into this whole kooky scene of other-worldly happenings and following his gut and instant connections. Next he'd be telling her about the law of attraction and giving her a copy of *The Secret*. He already kept popping up like this when least expected; if he found out she had saved him from drowning, he would probably decide he was meant to be her shadow for life. It was all just a strange coincidence. No need to panic. She would have to end this conversation now or she would end up giving something away.

'It's getting late,' she said, trying to maintain an even tone. 'I'm sorry, but I've got to get home now.' She got up quickly from the bench. A little too quickly because the sudden movement caused a wave of dizziness to overcome her and she teetered a little.

'Whoa. Are you okay?' He was on his feet in a second and caught her by the arms to steady her.

148

She managed to regain her balance and immediately tried to shake herself free, though she was still feeling disoriented. She stammered a quick thanks.

The physical contact was strangely magnetic, like the previous time. It was as if there was some sort of electricity between them; her arms were tingling where he touched her. He seemed to feel something too, because his hands stiffened and tightened their grasp before he finally let go of her.

She glanced up at his shocked face and saw something strange in his eyes. It was an intense flash of understanding. No, it was more than that. Recognition. For the first time, Trish realized a part of her had always believed him.

She turned away from him and began to walk quickly. Fully aware of his gaze boring into her back, she broke into a trot, and soon, she was practically running the rest of the distance home.

15

A Working Day

'What are you *doing*?' Ba snorted. 'Why are you making foolish moves?'

His gruff complaint startled Trish back into the moment. She looked down at the chessboard, trying to see what he was talking about. Checkmate. Already? 'The king is dead,' she announced in a deadpan manner, trying to lighten his mood. 'Long live the king.'

Ba swept the pieces off the board with childish petulance. Trish noticed the trembling of his hands seemed to be getting worse. 'There's no point in playing with you, Trishna,' he barked. 'You aren't even *trying*.'

'Hey, Ba,' Trish said gently. 'Come on, you know I haven't played chess as long as you have.'

'Hah. It's not that,' Ba said with a shrewd expression that rarely appeared on his face these days. 'Your mind is elsewhere.'

Chess made Ba far more lucid than anything else, which

was why she tried to get in a game with him as often as she could. Ma still refused to learn the rules. She claimed it was because she was 'too old to learn new things', but Trish privately thought it was probably because she couldn't stand to lose at anything.

She sighed and glanced at the clock. The day was getting on and she had yet to start working. Ba was right, her mind *was* all over the place and she found herself unable to concentrate. She looked out of the window. The waves were calm and slow, approaching the shore with majestic ease, breaking over the black rocks gracefully before retreating and then advancing again in a rhythmic manner. Much like those thoughts of hers, insistent and repetitive. Once again, she tried to push them away.

'Are you thinking about a boy?' Ba asked, frowning at her curiously, his bushy white eyebrows knitted together. His perspicacity amazed her. But Trish and Ba had never had a serious conversation about anything of this sort before, and she certainly wasn't going to start.

She forced a laugh and repeated, 'A boy? Ba, do you think I'm a teenager or something?' She sighed again. 'No, it's not that. It's nothing.'

'Well, I want you to know,' Ba spoke fiercely now, 'only a *really special man* could ever be good enough for my Trishna. And it's all right to wait, beta.' He reached out, patted her hand briefly and then leaned back against his pillows. 'And he had better ask me first.'

This was so unexpected from Ba, and it sounded so ludicrous, that Trish's laugh was genuine this time. 'I'm not waiting for anything, Ba.' She couldn't help feeling touched by his fiery speech. She continued lightly, 'Some people are better off not getting married.'

Ma's voice floated in from the other room. 'Are you two talking about me again?'

'Yes!' shouted back Ba immediately, looking irritated. 'We were just talking about you only.' He lowered his voice and winked at Trish. 'We were, you know. Some people are better off ...'

'Ba!' Trish scolded, a little shocked but barely able to control her giggling at the same time. 'You wouldn't have had *me* if you guys hadn't married!'

'That's true.' Ba suddenly looked very tired and Trish saw that his eyes were far away again. He patted her hand again, but now it was just a mechanical gesture, almost dismissive.

'You want to sleep?' she asked gently.

He nodded, no longer looking at her. His gaze was fixed out of the window again. For about the hundredth time, Trish felt a familiar sense of disappointment. The feeling of having lost her father – again.

151

🌰

'So what's all this I hear about a handsome man coming to see you at home?' Akanksha's voice demanded over the phone. Trish rolled her eyes towards the ceiling. Couldn't people just shut up about this nonsense?

She shot a malevolent glance towards the kitchen where Ma was currently in the process of harassing Munni. She growled in a low voice into the phone. 'Akku, you know I hate it when Ma and you talk about me.'

'Oh come on, Aunty's just concerned! And you guys can't have a conversation without fighting, so she ends up telling me stuff.'

'Well, *I'll* start fighting with you if you don't cut out this *gossiping* with Ma. You know she's got a twisted view on everything to do with me. If you want to know what's going on with me, you're better off talking to me directly, okay?'

'Okay.' Akanskha's voice was gleeful and curious. 'So come on, come on, who's this mystery man of yours?'

'No one. I mean, he's just ... a guy I, uh, ran into.' Trish bit her lip and then repeated, 'No one, really.'

Akanksha let out a sigh of defeat. 'See? *This* is why it's more fun to talk to your mom than to you. She at least tells me whatever she knows, I don't have to coax things out of her!' She changed gears. 'So listen, how're you placed today? You think you'll be able to ...'

'Bring Lisa over,' Trish said gruffly. 'It's been a while since she's been here, it'll be nice to have her around.'

'Well, I must warn you, she's gone back into this brooding phase again. I don't know. She's always fine around Vinay and Dad, but sulks with me. I'm telling you, it's tough to raise a girl these days.'

Trish didn't see Akanksha doing too much active raising, but decided it wouldn't do to be judgemental. 'She'll be fine here, she'll just read or something. What's Uncle doing, would he like to come and have a cup of tea later?'

'Oh, thanks. But Dad's going for a checkup today, so he'll be out for most of the day. That's kind of why I need you to watch Lisa.'

'Is he okay?' Trish asked, recalling the tall elderly gentleman. He'd looked so fit.

'Pink of health, honey,' Akanksha sang out gaily. 'Just his annual medical checkup. He's very careful about looking after himself, especially after Mum passed on. So anyway, thanks so much for keeping an eye on Lisa! It'll just be for two hours in the afternoon.'

Trish no longer asked Akanksha where she was off to because she never got a straight answer anyway. She just said dryly, 'You sure you'll be done in two hours?'

'Oh. Yes. Just a parlour visit, you know.'

'Right.' Trish muttered. 'See you later.'

She hung up and finally began to try and answer those damned letters piling up in her inbox.

＊

This was all getting to be too much. Trish's eyes glazed over as she scanned through the word document to see how many letters she still had left to answer. Oh, lord. But then she had done this to herself. She had signed up for the online portion of the work and, as per the addendum to their agreement, at least a dozen additional questions had to be answered for the blog alone every day.

It was increasingly obvious from the tone of the letters that people really seemed to think she was a qualified professional of some sort. The respect that came through was unmistakable, as was their desperation. This thing, a stupid little column, which no one used to take seriously, had suddenly become people's saviour, despite its nasty tone. Or because of it? No matter how hard she tried to shake it off, Trish felt a nagging sense of being a big fraud. People were pouring their heart out to her, and it made her feel a sense of responsibility that was burdensome. After all, there was no real substance in anything that she was able to offer. Most of her advice was just pure common sense. Why the hell did people seem to be taking her words so seriously?

Nowhere had this become clearer than in the online section, which was naturally far more interactive and

153

responsive than the paper. Just an hour after she had sent her first set of answers for the blog, Nivedita had published them. Trish watched as the comments flew in fast and furious, as if people had been waiting for this all day.

Some comments were so pseudo-intellectual that she couldn't help cringing:

Love, love, love your style, Amy. My sympathies for your having to deal with these losers.

This week's answers were my favourite, Amy. You really know how to give it to them.

Wow! It frightens me that these are my fellow Mumbaikars. Keep it up, guys. You provide a lot of amusement for the rest of us.

Trish herself, on the other hand, had started to feel a genuine sense of sympathy for most of the people who wrote in. Some, she sensed were doing it just to be sensational and get attention, and she mostly ignored them. But many others were writing in with genuine hope about resolving something that was bothering them. It felt wrong to make fun of them while writing answers 'in keeping with the tone' of the column. And now it also felt very wrong that the exchanges were publicly available for other people to view and laugh at. She tried to shake herself out of it again. After all, this was no time to start having moral issues or to get emotional about the whole thing. This was just a job. Not even a job. A temporary assignment. Which just seemed to somehow be taking over more and more of her life.

She had decided to take over the online portfolio because of the extra money, but she had to admit it was partly also an ego issue. She just didn't want someone else to be handling answers under Amy's name on another platform. She *was* Amy, even if nobody knew it. Besides, it was not like she had very much else to do. And given that she was trying hard not to let thoughts of a certain person come into her head, it made sense to try and bury herself under more work.

The problem was that she was having trouble focusing; and she certainly no longer had the confidence that she was doing justice to each letter. Earlier, while doubts about her own limited life experience would occasionally gnaw at her, she had at least been able to spend time mulling over a difficult letter and edit her response appropriately before sending it out to Nivedita. But now, the load had become so much that she barely had time to read what she had written.

The bell rang and she got up, glad for the distraction. Her back was hurting and she groaned a little as she headed for the door. Maybe she'd have to give up the Zumba after all. But it was the one thing that brought her some sort of joy. Besides, the backache was probably more from just sitting stiffly and staring hard at the screen for hours. Or maybe from hunching over the chessboard on Ba's bed. That was it. Chess. Stress. Whatever.

155

She opened the door and saw Lisa standing there. Over her thin shoulders were the straps of what looked like a large guitar case, and this made her look even smaller than usual. She also carried a couple of books under her arm. Trish smiled at her warmly. 'Hey, Leez, come in.' Lisa gave her a shy smile and went into the house.

Akanksha's voice rang from the stairway: 'Dad will come and pick her up for her class at five, sweetie. Thanks so much!'

Trish poked her head out and only caught a glimpse of the back of Akanksha's red-and-purple peasant skirt as her friend disappeared down the stairs with her heels click-clacking and leaving behind the scent of a delicate and presumably expensive perfume. Trish shook her head disapprovingly once before slamming the door with all her might.

Not that she had much hope, but maybe, just maybe, for once Akanksha would hear the door slam and understand *something* about how someone *else* felt.

⁂

Dear Amy,

I've just moved into Mumbai with my dad. My mom's still in the US. They've been divorced two years now. I've been finding it tough to adjust to living in India again. I lived here only till I was five, I've been in New York since then. I finally made some new friends at school, but when they asked about my mom, I lied and said she's just wrapping up her work back in the US and that she's going to be joining us over here in a few months. I know I shouldn't have lied about this. Now I feel stupid. But I think if I do tell my friends ... well, they won't be my friends any more. And things are hard enough for me here without having to deal with that. What do you think I should do?

Feeling Fake

Trish stared at this letter for a really long time. Now a school kid was writing to her? And this was yet another example of a perfectly genuine problem, painful and confusing for the person undergoing it. How on earth was she supposed to maintain the sarcasm when this kid sounded like he – or she – needed a big hug first?

Trish turned and her eyes strayed to the kid in the room, sitting in her usual corner. Little Lisa was staring at her book, mouth slightly open, eyes unblinking as usual. Trish observed her for a couple of minutes.

'Hey, Lisa.'

Lisa looked up, her expression blank, her eyes so far away that she reminded Trish of Ba.

'What're you reading?'

Lisa held up her Sweet Valley Twins book: *Twin Against Twin*.

Trish nodded in mock earnestness and then asked, 'So why aren't you actually reading it?'

'What do you mean?' Lisa said sullenly. 'I *am* reading it.'

'So why have you been on that same page for the last five minutes?' Trish asked, not unkindly.

Lisa slammed her book down and pursed her lips. 'It's boring.' She looked at Trish squarely and said, 'Why have *you* been on that same page for the last ten minutes?'

She pointed to Trish's laptop, and Trish had to laugh. Lisa was right. She had been staring at her laptop for long stretches of time without typing. The room, usually filled with the quick clattering from her keyboard, had been completely silent.

Lisa gave her a wan smile. Trish said, 'Hey. Why don't you show me what you're learning on the guitar?'

'Guitar?' Lisa looked over at her instrument in the corner, as if seeing it for the first time. She then looked back at Trish and shook her head. 'Not learnt much.'

'Okay, so whatever you've learnt?'

'I don't feel like playing,' Lisa snapped. 'I hate the guitar. I hate Mom for making me go.'

'Whoa.' Trish was really surprised by her vehemence. 'Just the other day you were so excited about it. What happened?'

'Nothing!' Lisa was clearly getting angry. 'I didn't *know* before that I wouldn't like it! It's too *difficult*. I've told Mom so many times now that I don't want to do it. Even Nanu told her. But she just doesn't listen, she *still* makes me go. She just doesn't want me around!'

Her face was red now. She snatched up her book again and stared at it unseeingly.

Trish, feeling upset, but trying not to show it, turned her attention back to her computer. Akanksha was so disconnected from her own kid. If Lisa hated guitar lessons, why was she forced to go? Why couldn't Akanksha at least talk to Lisa and understand what her issue was and work things out with her? The kid was clearly feeling unwanted, for heaven's sake. Trish would talk to her about it later. Or maybe not. Ignoring things as far as Akanksha was concerned was usually a more trouble-free policy.

She scanned through the other letters, trying to find something that looked as if it would be easier for her to answer than one from an America-returned schoolkid with a broken home and heart.

That was when she spotted the letter that would hold her attention for the rest of the day. At first, she couldn't make head or tail of it. And then she read on with gradual understanding.

Dear Amy,

I have this major problem.

There's this woman I met recently with whom I feel a certain strange kind of connection. Unfortunately, she's the skeptical type who doesn't seem to feel the need for new relationships, and she certainly doesn't believe in connections and fate and so on. In the short time that I've known her, I've ended up telling her more about myself than I have ever told anyone else. She knows my biggest secrets already, but the minute I discovered just one of hers, she panicked, even though there wasn't any real reason to, and ran away from me. Literally. She ran, Amy! You should have seen her go. It was like Cinderella when the clock struck midnight, only in sneakers instead of glass slippers.

For the last couple of weeks now, she hasn't been taking my calls. So I've stopped calling and emailing her altogether. I just thought in case she gets to read this letter somehow through your column, she might realize that relationships aren't things you have to run away from all the time. She seems to think getting close to someone will make her weaker instead of stronger and more fulfilled. Isn't that wrong? I can't quite figure her out, but it would be enough for me if she at least believed me when I tell her that I just really like her for who she is, damn it.

Could you please let her know that she has two choices? She can reach out to me and we can see where it takes us. Or she can continue to ignore me, pretend I never existed and go back to her own life. Either way, I would like her to know I wish her well and I'm immensely grateful for all she's done to help me. In some ways, I feel I owe her my life.

Warm regards,
Drowning in Sorrow

p.s. My sincere apologies for treating your wonderful column as if it were Miss Lonely Hearts. I look forward to having my head bitten off. But I still carry the hope that she sees this.

p.p.s. And if you ARE reading this, T, please know: there's something about you that fascinates me, and I'd love the opportunity to figure out what it is.

Trish's cheeks were burning hot by the time she reached the end of the letter. She scrolled back up and read it again, and then a third time.

Even though this particular letter would never make it to actual publication, she knew it would be running through her head for a long time. Oh, he was a big one for letters, that Sahil. A royal pain, that's what he was.

159

She had successfully managed to avoid him for so many days, until she was sure he had given up, and now he turned up *here*, of all places. Did Nivedita do any actual screening at all? No, Trish guessed that she didn't, especially now that the online forum had opened up. She probably sent her the entire deluge of letters. Anyway, Sahil's letter was oblique enough so only *she* could have figured it out. She would have to kick him for this when they met next, she decided as she tried to focus her attention again on trying to find another, answerable letter.

Yes, they would have to meet again. He had unwittingly struck a real chord with her through his invitation for her to just ignore him and go back to her regular life.

Because Trish had a strong feeling she'd had enough of that life.

160

16

The Meeting

The lift door opened on the ground floor, revealing a crowd of about seven people inside. 'Coming?' the young man up front enquired politely of Trish.

Trish was about to get in, but then the familiar sense of panic set in. She managed a smile. 'Uh, no. Thanks. Carry on.'

The man smiled genially and pressed a button. The doors closed. Trish bit her lip. Why not? For a change, she would try taking the stairs.

Ten floors. Trish couldn't remember the last time she had climbed more than four floors in a row. She was in no hurry. Meeting Zee was hardly a prospect that filled her with delight. But since the snotty chief editor wrote the cheques, Trish could only put off her requests for meetings so many times. Trish wondered what she had to say to her now. Judging from past experience, it couldn't possibly be anything very good.

She reached the stairwell and started to climb. The first couple of floors weren't much of a problem, she managed to keep her breathing even. She knew her exercise regimen was helping, and she had made a genuine effort to keep her diet healthy over the last few weeks, reducing sugar and fat, and actually managing to resist Ma's constant flow of sweets. Akanksha had been effusive in her remarks about her weight loss, although Trish didn't take anything Akanksha said too seriously. Lisa's quiet nods accompanying her mother's statements meant more to her. She had a strong feeling that the kid wouldn't lie.

The next few floors were tougher, but Trish kept climbing valiantly even though it was getting harder to breathe. To her surprise, she made it to the seventh floor without a break. Not bad. She was doing it! Raj had, just the previous week, declared her his best student, claiming she kept up with his moves better than anyone else. In fact, he had exclaimed while slapping her on the back, a habit of his that she had just got used to, that sometimes when he forgot the steps, he only had to look at Trish in the mirror and follow her. She had turned pink with embarrassment as the rest of the class laughed and clapped. It was true, though. She had a sharp memory and a good sense of rhythm, and she'd figured out the general pattern of the moves, so much so that she could sometimes actually predict the next steps, even for a new song that Raj had just choreographed.

Smiling at the memory of his compliment, she walked up the remaining three floors with a jaunty bounce in her step that she was glad no one could see. The bounce faded as she reached the top floor and turned in towards the familiar landing where her erstwhile office was situated. She didn't feel the need as much as before to sneak in and try

162

to be completely invisible, but still, this would always be the office from where she had been fired, of which she had no good memories.

'Trish?' A voice rang out in surprise from just behind her near the reception. She froze and then turned reluctantly to face him.

Just great. Akshay. Her ex-boss *had* to be taking some sort of a loo break or something at the exact moment that she reached the reception. What luck. She adjusted her bag over her shoulder and said casually, 'Hello, Akshay. How are you?'

'I'm fine, Trish.' She noted that he was gazing at her in what appeared to be an appreciative manner. 'How are *you*?' Without waiting for an answer, he looked her up and down and said, 'You look like you're doing well. You're so ... *different*. I almost didn't recognize you.'

Trish shuffled her feet a little. She was fitting into her older clothes now and had picked out a flowing black skirt with a practically unworn blue blouse that she had bought on a whim years ago. The blouse fit her curves well, but suddenly it felt too tight and low under Akshay's ogling. Irritated by his eyes lingering on her cleavage, she practically snapped at him, 'Got to go. I have a meeting.'

'With Zee,' he said knowingly, and she couldn't hide her surprise. He went on, 'She mentioned that you were applying for a position in editorial and asked me for a reference.' He gave her a smile that, with shock, she recognized as the flirtatious one she had seen him use on the young, attractive new girls in the office while she had worked with him. 'I told her you were a solid, reliable worker.' Trish felt a spark of anger as she recalled the way he had spoken to her while asking her to leave, and instantly knew that he was lying.

'Oh, you did?' She batted her eyelids at him with a smile.

163

She was being totally sarcastic, but like most thick, self-involved people, he couldn't pick up on it, and his smile widened as he leaned in and said, 'Tell you what. Come and see me after your meeting with Zee. We're expanding. There are some exciting new positions we're putting in place now. You've been part of this system, so we know your calibre.' Another downward glance. 'We may just be able to work out something even more interesting than what Zee's got for you. You know, start afresh?'

He had the audacity to wink at her. Trish held her ground. She said carefully, 'Okay. Sounds interesting. I'll see you in your office then.'

'Great,' he said breezily. 'I'll be waiting.' And then, with a smarmy little wave, he turned and walked into the office. She made a face at his back and spun around to walk towards the opposite wing. Only then did she note the amused expression on the face of the old security guard at the reception who had apparently been watching the entire exchange. He gave her that happy toothless grin of his that had always cheered her up in the old days, and she couldn't help laughing. Throwing him a broad conspiratorial wink, she headed to her meeting with Queen Zee.

❀

She looked more like a queen bee than ever, sitting on her high-backed chair, nose tipped in the air, her army of editorial assistants, designers and other sundry yes-men swarming over her as they all examined something on her large flat-screen desktop computer. Trish cleared her throat once and then again, louder, as she stood with her head poking through the half open door. It was now fifteen minutes past the scheduled time of their meeting, and she had decided to ignore Nivedita's simpering plea that *no one* interrupted Zee in the middle of a meeting.

Someone at the outer fringes of the mob heard her cough and turned towards her. Soon, everyone in the room, including Zee, was staring at Trish. The others looked aghast. Zee merely looked pissed off.

'Sorry to interrupt,' Trish said brightly to Zee. 'But we did have a meeting scheduled at twelve today, right?'

Zee opened her mouth as if to retort with something biting, but appeared to change her mind midway. She glanced up at her team members and said crisply, 'You people come back at one.' As they began to file out, she added in a dangerous tone, 'And don't be late. We'll work through lunch if we have to.'

Trish stepped aside, and soon the room was empty but for her and Zee. Zee continued to sit with her head tipped back, looking down her long nose at Trish. She raised her arm towards a chair across the table from her to indicate that Trish should sit. Just to be contrarian, Trish walked over to the lounge area and took a seat on the sofa.

Zee's black eyes flashed for a second. She smiled coldly. 'I suppose you're wondering why you were called here today?'

'How are you, Zee?' Trish said, by way of polite greeting.

'Fine,' Zee snapped, and Trish was pleased that this seemed to throw her for a second.

Trish kept her tone pleasant. 'Yes, I'm wondering what was so important that it couldn't be discussed on the phone. I'm also wondering why you called me today in front of the entire office instead of like last time when you wanted me to sneak in and out.'

Zee replied dismissively, 'That was when we had to be very

careful about Amy's identity. Now, no one would believe it's you, anyway.'

She was as rude as before, but Trish just smiled and said, 'It might also have something to do with the fact that there are rumours about the column being ghostwritten by you. Which, I'm told, are heartily encouraged.'

Zee crossed her arms over her chest and said in a warning tone, 'Look, Missy.'

'It's Trish.'

'*If* I wanted to, I could write this column with my left hand,' Zee spat out, ignoring Trish's interruption. 'It's just that I have more important things to do. I have a whole paper to run. If it serves to obscure Amy's true identity a little further, it is a rumour that must be encouraged, don't you think?' She gave Trish a superior smile. 'After all, apart from the air of mystery, Amy deserves to have a personality that commands some respect. Correct?' She ran her eyes up and down Trish in a manner full of disdain and very different from the way that Akshay had looked at her.

Oh,' Trish said, ignoring Zee's question. 'I'm also curious about why you would tell Akshay I've come in for a job interview with you. That seems unnecessarily proactive. Or rather, a plain lie.' A part of Trish couldn't believe the bold words coming out of her own mouth. But Zee deserved it. Taking credit for her writing, explaining it was for the good of the column and attempting to put Trish down, all in one fell swoop. This was a business arrangement, she reminded herself, not a bloody fiefdom. She, for one, refused to fawn over this egomaniac.

Zee's nostrils visibly flared at this. She appeared to be exercising some self-control. 'Let us get down to the business at hand. I'm a busy person.'

'Oh, I'm a total vela,' Trish said gaily. 'Perhaps your Indian half knows what vela means? I could do this all day! But anyway, if you insist, let's start.'

Zee calmly said, 'So. The column continues to grow in readership.'

'Yes. Nivedita shared the numbers with me. It's by far the most read.'

'However,' Zee continued as if Trish hadn't spoken, 'Before we get too self-congratulatory, I think there is a need for us to examine the direction in which we're going.'

'Is there?' Trish was being deliberately flippant. 'I thought this paper was all about the numbers. As long as it's being read, it's right.'

'Print journalism is serious business,' Zee almost snarled. 'There's a certain thing called journalistic integrity which you would do well to try and imbibe now that you're calling yourself a journalist.'

'Integrity?' Trish was amazed. 'It's an anonymous column with a so-called *persona* manufactured from day one, and you're deliberately spreading false rumours about who's writing it.'

'Let's not digress,' Zee shot back. 'I'm talking about being clear about what we are doing, and maintaining consistency with our vision.'

'Our vision? You mean *your* vision?'

'The point is this. You have to stop sympathizing with your audience. The column is increasingly losing its clinical and sarcastic tone. This isn't bloody Ask Dr Phil, remember that. Your answer to that schoolkid was unprintable.'

'That kid deserved proper advice.' Trish was now getting angry. 'And sympathy. I took great exception to your not printing my reply.'

'We have the final call on what gets into the paper.'

'You could still have put it up online!'

'Also our prerogative. In the contract.'

'I know what the bloody contract says,' Trish said, not bothering to watch her words. 'But what would you have lost if you put that reply up? It might have helped that kid.'

'We didn't feel the need. It would have taken away from the ...'

'Persona. Right?' Trish finished sardonically. 'Right.' She took a deep breath and spoke earnestly. 'Zee. Why don't you make me the admin for online content? Let me manage it completely. It will mean less work for you and Nivedita, and I'll be able to provide real-time answers. It will be more efficient all around, and you'll still have complete control on the print part.'

'While you'll be in complete control of the online property, right?' Zee was examining her fingernails, sounding bored.

'I've done this before. And this is *my* column, damn it!' Trish was getting increasingly frustrated. 'You're anyway flooding me with so many queries. At least let *me* deal with the bulk of the questions online!'

'Efficiency isn't the key here,' Zee said smoothly, seemingly more at ease now that Trish was getting upset. 'It's about control. And please, don't labour under the impression that Ask Amy is your column. It's the *paper's* column. You're merely under contract to provide content. And you're being compensated handsomely for it.'

Trish wasn't denying the pay was good. But this had come to mean much more to her than just any writing assignment. She felt a certain connection with the people who wrote in. But who was going to explain that to a person like Zee?

Zee went on. 'And let's not forget the contract can be

terminated at any point of time if we feel the arrangement isn't working out or if your contribution is no longer up to standard.'

Trish clenched her fists. But then she remembered the situation she was in financially. There was still no other steady income on the horizon. And, unfortunately, this immensely successful column, while bringing in the cash for now, was doing nothing to her resumé because of the privacy clause. She was stuck. Her feet suddenly went cold.

Zee added, 'I hope you understand what I'm saying? Am I clear?'

Trish swallowed hard. 'Crystal.'

She stood up to go before Zee could dismiss her. She stalked out of the office without a word, brushing against and jangling the blue-beaded curtain roughly as she left. She stomped past Nivedita's desk without even turning her head to say bye, past the reception, turning away from the route leading to that cretin Akshay's office. That lech was probably waiting for her like he said he would. He probably wouldn't be able to believe she would pass up the opportunity to see him. Well, she could only hope he would keep waiting for a long time. It would be the only satisfying outcome for her from this visit to the damned office she hated so much but just couldn't get away from.

17

With Sahil

'Move, move, *move!*'

Bloody Mumbai traffic. Trish drummed her fingers impatiently on the wheel. She was just a few hundred metres from home, but this jam looked like it would take forever to clear. She took a deep breath and reminded herself this was hardly some official meeting that she had to rush for. Still, she really wanted to get home.

Her heartbeat quickened at the thought of Sahil waiting for her at home. She shook her head. It would be dumb of her to imagine there could ever be anything romantic between the two of them. They were too different from each other. It was just that he kept insisting there was a connection of some sort between them, and he clearly had some weird notions about what it all meant. Well, she would have to work hard to keep herself grounded about this. They were just hanging out. That was all.

By the time she finally reached home, it was half past five. She opened the door and let herself in. Immediately, her nose was assailed by the smell of ginger tea and … what was that – pakoras? Of course! Sahil was clearly here already, and Ma had gone ahead and had her way.

Ma didn't turn from the oily kadhai as Trish passed the kitchen. Trish walked into the drawing room, heartbeat quickening again. She stopped short when she saw there was no one there.

'In Ba's room,' called Ma. Trish whipped around and doubled back a couple of steps to peep into the kitchen. Ma still had her back to her. Trish hurried down the hall. What on earth was Sahil doing in *there*?

She stood in the doorway and watched with growing wonder. Ba and Sahil were sitting on Ba's bed, both tall men stooping over the chessboard placed upon the wooden breakfast table between them. They both appeared totally engrossed in the game, and neither noticed her. Trish's eyes widened when she saw that Ba was sitting up without back support – something he'd been struggling to do of late. She cleared her throat.

Sahil turned around and saw her. He scrambled to his feet and gave her a warm smile. 'Hey, Trish!' His eyes twinkled at her through his glasses and his voice was low and gentle and, for some reason, his attention made her skin go pink.

'Hello, Sahil,' she said, sounding more formal than she meant to. 'Sorry I kept you waiting.'

'Oh no, that's fine.' He laughed. 'I was just hanging out with your parents. They're so much fun!'

'They are?' Trish said, her tone incredulous.

'Will you shut that door, Trishna, the draught will blow all the pieces away,' Ba barked. She quickly stepped inside the room and closed the door behind her. The curtains had been billowing about at the open windows and they now settled down. Ba went on, grumbling, 'As it is, your friend over here has been cheating. He somehow beat me in the first game.' Sahil grinned at her and shook his head good-naturedly as Ba continued, 'But don't worry! We're doing two out of three.'

'Oh.' Trish came over and sat down on a chair near the bed as Sahil settled back into the game. Two out of three? That sounded like it would take some time. She frowned. She thought Sahil had come over to spend some time with *her*. Still, Ba was obviously happy right now, despite all his complaining. She sat in silence, observing their next few moves, both players being painstakingly careful.

Sahil was clearly a good player. Anyone who could beat her father was probably at near-professional levels. Ba, who had been lacking a serious challenger for the longest time, seemed eager to prove who was boss. Trish couldn't figure out how Sahil had managed to even get this far with her father. Ba was fiercely protective of his space. He never came out of his room, nor did he let anyone in, especially not a stranger. Most of the time, he wasn't lucid enough to hold a conversation with anyone. The few times that he was, he was ashamed of his disease, afraid that he would forget something or do something that he wasn't supposed to. So he usually avoided company like the plague.

And yet here he was, deeply involved in a game of chess with a stranger. Sahil clearly had a way with people. At least with weirdos like her parents, she thought. As if on cue, the door opened and Ma came in, balancing a large tray with cups of tea and steaming pakoras. 'Chai time! You boys can take a break from that silly game now.'

172

'The door! The door!' Ba pulled at his white hair in frustration as the room became windy and the curtains started flapping wildly again. As Ma pushed the door closed with her elbow, Ba's face broke into the broadest grin that Trish had seen on it for a while as he said, 'Aha!'

He triumphantly moved his queen into position and looked up at Sahil. 'Well, young Sabharwal? See what you just did?' He gave him a crafty, knowing smile and announced, 'Checkmate!'

Sahil looked down at the board and groaned before slapping his knee and laughing. 'Oh, no. I don't believe it. I should have seen that coming!'

Ma was still standing there with the tray and Sahil jumped up to say, 'Let me help you with that, aunty.' He took the tray carefully from her hands and placed it on the bed.

173

'Use that table only, beta Sahil.' Ma indicated the wooden meal table as Ba cleared the pieces from the board.

'No,' snapped Ba. 'We need it. We have one more game to go after this. The deciding game.'

'Have your tea first, Ba.' It felt odd for Trish to be siding with her mother. But when a guest came home, you offered him tea. Not endless chess sessions with a cranky old man. She whispered to Ba, 'And his name is *Aggarwal*. Sahil Aggarwal.'

'That's what I said,' grumbled Ba, helping himself to a pakora. As if remembering his manners, he looked at Sahil and gestured invitingly towards the tray.

Sahil grinned broadly and picked up a cup of tea and held it out towards Trish who took it. Then he picked up another cup. 'Aunty, for you?'

Ma shook her head and said, 'I only drink tea after my evening puja.'

Trish felt a familiar twinge of irritation at Ma's pious,

martyred tone. They sipped on their tea, and she realized she didn't like the fact that she was sharing Sahil with her parents today. How ridiculous was that? What difference did it make anyway? She turned to Sahil, about to ask him how he'd been. But Ma spoke first, looking fondly at him and saying, 'So what do you do, beta?'

Sahil cleared his throat and lowered his cup of tea. 'Well, aunty, actually, we have a family business. Er, Aggarwal Sweets and Namkeen.'

'Oh, Trish loves their stuff.' Ma's eyes gleamed. 'She's always buying the bhujia sev. And the gulab jamun, the laddoos and ...'

'Ma!' Trish hissed furiously.

Sahil was trying to hide a smile. 'Well, aunty, the thing is, I'm not really a part of that business right now. I think there's something else I'd rather be doing, but I'm still in the process of figuring it out.'

Trish thought that this would shut Ma up. After all, Sahil had pretty much confessed to being a confused jobless bum. But to her surprise, Ma continued to beam. 'That's perfectly all right, beta. It happens. After all, even our Trish is in the same situation. She's also trying to figure what to do ever since she got herself fired.' Trish bristled, but her mother continued happily. 'There comes a time in *everyone's* life when they must sit back and think about what is really important to them. Jobs and career and all that will follow if people are intelligent and qualified, which *you* clearly are.'

Trish rolled her eyes, wondering how Ma had assessed Sahil's qualifications – from his face?

Ma went on addressing an attentive Sahil. 'And, after all, jobs come and go; but at a certain age, finding the right life companion becomes far more important.' Sahil nodded sagely, and Ma seemed to be encouraged by this because she said, without a trace of tact, 'So what *is* your age, beta?'

Sahil was sipping his tea and he coughed a little and then manfully swallowed. Trish was mortified, but he smiled up at Ma and said, 'Er, thirty-five, aunty.'

'Oh!' Ma said. 'Well, an age gap between husband and wife is not a bad thing at all.' She looked over at Ba. 'We also have a seven-year age gap! After all, women mature faster. At least *some* of us.' Trish glared at her, willing her to shut up. But Ma didn't notice because she was looking to Ba for confirmation.

Ba didn't look at Ma. He was in the process of gulping down the last of his tea. He wiped his mouth with the back of his hand and then snapped, 'You talk too much. No one wants to hear what we oldies have to say. Now eat a pakora and stop your rubbish.' Ma looked stricken, but in another beat, her husband was smiling at her. 'For *those* pakoras, I might marry you all over again.'

175

What was this now? Trish stared. Ma was actually blushing and smiling. What was with Ba today? She had *never* seen him act like this, forget the last few years with Alzheimer's.

Sahil tactfully bit into his pakora, but Trish could see he was trying to hide his smile. Ba now turned keenly to Sahil with an 'Eh? Isn't it good stuff?' Even Trish had to laugh at the pretend-solemn way in which Sahil nodded, while Ma muttered for Ba to stop *his* nonsense.

She suddenly realized that there were four people enjoying tea with the fresh evening breeze blowing in from the ocean in this small room usually shrouded in gloom and hopelessness. On most days, there was a strange and uncomfortable distance between her and her parents which she never tried to dissect. But at least for now, it actually felt like all was well with the world.

For the first time in a long while, Trish felt like she was amongst family.

❦

Ba and Sahil were allowed to finish their third game. Ma cleared the tea tray out and Trish watched them play quietly. Ba eventually won the game, although Trish suspected that Sahil had let him win. But Sahil expressed the correct amount of dismay and then accepted defeat with a gracious shake of Ba's hand.

Trish then gave Ba his medicines and asked him if he'd like to lie down. It had been over an hour and a half of sitting up, which was quite a strain for him. Ba nodded, and soon he was lying on his side, looking content as they tiptoed out of the room.

176

'Come back for another round soon, Sabharwal!' he called after Sahil.

'I will, sir,' Sahil called back.

Trish stopped and hissed at her father through the door, 'Aggarwal! *Aggarwal!*'

'Aggarwal,' Ba repeated agreeably. 'Whatever. Both are welcome.'

Trish shook her head, wondering if Ba was losing it or trying to be funny. It was hard to tell these days. She shut the door behind her gently and followed Sahil into the drawing room.

'Sorry about that.' She kept looking at the floor as they sat next to each other on the sofa.

'Sorry for what?' Sahil laughed. 'It was great. I love chess.'

'Did you let him win?' Trish demanded, unable to contain her curiosity. 'You didn't have to do that.'

'I did not,' Sahil said with dignity. His face broke into a grin. 'Actually, he's *way* better than me. I think, in the first game, he was just a little thrown by having someone actually challenge him. I had the advantage of surprise.' His face took on a resolute expression. 'I'll beat him next time, though. You'll see.'

'Okay, then.' Trish rolled her eyes. He appeared to have enjoyed that session and was already planning a comeback. It was as if he hadn't missed the opportunity to talk to her at all, while she found that she had been hiding her impatience about getting him to herself again. What was wrong with her? She never felt that way about anyone. This guy confused her, but she couldn't help feeling that he also brought her alive in a way she hadn't known before. Okay. She was beginning to act foolish now, she had to control such thoughts. She still didn't fully know why this guy insisted on hanging around. But it had certainly helped Ba today, and she couldn't help smiling at the memory of his triumphant expression.

177

'What?' Sahil was watching her face closely, all his attention on her now. 'What's funny?'

'Funny?' Trish sighed. 'Nothing. More like ... strange.'

Sahil nodded and didn't press further, changing the subject instead. 'So my letter worked, huh?'

'Look, can we just forget about all that, you think?' Trish's cheeks were feeling hot again and she hoped fervently that he wouldn't notice the change in colour.

'Yes.' Sahil leaned over to her, making her feel even more self-conscious. 'But only after you accept my thanks for saving my ...'

'Please,' Trish begged. 'Don't, Sahil. It was just a random thing. Anyone would have done it.'

'You must be kidding.' Sahil ran his hand through his

brown hair in that distracted manner of his that she secretly found endearing. '*No one* else would have done it. No one else *did* do it. I even went back there a week later and checked. I heard the whole story from a bhutta-waala. He saw it all. So, anyway. Thank you for that.'

'Okay. You're welcome. *Now* can we get over it?'

'Okay, okay.' He laughed. He then added earnestly, 'Just one more thing, Trish. It's not something I've done before and it's certainly not something I'm proud of. I know my life is strange and I have these weird ... *issues,* but I'm still really, really lucky to be alive and I shouldn't have let myself get so disturbed that I almost threw it all away. It was really stupid of me. Please don't judge me for it.'

'I wasn't judging you for it.' Trish was surprised at the thought. 'I wouldn't judge anyone for being in that state of mind. I would only try to help.' She was speaking sincerely but broke off midway, thinking that it sounded foolish and trite.

Sahil didn't seem to think so. 'You know, you're a really goodhearted person, Trish.'

She felt her heart beat faster. He was sitting really close to her, and she was suddenly afraid that he would touch her. Or not touch her. Or something. But what could he possibly do right now? Ma and Ba were both in the house. Of course Ba was sleeping, and the low monotonous hum from the kitchen told her that Ma was in the middle of her evening prayers. It felt like anything could happen. A spark of electricity seemed to be passing through the space between them. For heaven's sake, she was hearing bells.

'You ... want me to get that?' Sahil asked politely.

Trish realized with a start that the doorbell was ringing. Ma's prayers from the kitchen had become louder now, as an indicator that she for one was certainly not going to get up and answer the door. Trish sprang up and away from Sahil and hurried over to the door.

Who could it possibly be but Akanksha, dressed in a short red summer dress with high-heeled sandals, crying, 'Hi, sweetie!'

What timing. Trish opened her mouth to say she had company right now, but Akanksha was even more caught up in herself than usual today. She just breezed in past Trish, saying, 'Listen, darling, I just don't know what to do with Lisa. She's becoming absolutely impossible to deal with. This is the problem when you have kids. You're so lucky, Trish. You don't have kids. Take my advice and don't *ever* have kids. They're just ...'

She had already reached the drawing room, with Trish in vain trying to quell her. Akanksha found herself face to face with Sahil, who was now standing near the entrance to the room.

179

'Oh,' she breathed. 'Sorry. I mean, hello. I'm Akanksha.'

She held out her hand towards Sahil, and Trish was surprised by the flash of jealousy she felt when Sahil took it. She suddenly felt out of place in her own home, dressed in her relatively simple skirt and blouse. Akanksha had her head of shiny hair tipped to the side flirtatiously, her demeanour having changed entirely from the distraught mother of a moment ago to a coquettish young woman. Sahil held her hand politely for a second and said, 'Sahil. Nice to meet you.' He then gently dropped her hand.

'Well.' Akanksha looked around at Trish. 'You didn't tell me I was interrupting.'

'You didn't *let* me tell you anything,' Trish reminded her dryly.

'I suppose I'll be on my way then.' Akanksha didn't move

towards the door, though. She just continued to gaze up at Sahil.

Sahil cleared his throat. 'Actually, it's getting a little late for *me*. I've got to make a move.' He looked at Trish over Akanksha's shoulder and said, 'So I'll be seeing you again soon?'

'Umm. Okay,' she said, trying to hide her disappointment. The evening had passed so quickly with tea with her parents and chess with Ba and now it had been ruined by her nosy, intrusive friend. She added, 'And I'm sorry we didn't really get to talk.'

They looked at each other over Akanksha's head for a long moment. Trish contemplated offering to walk him out to his car, when Akanksha said to him in a high-pitched voice, 'Bye-bye!', wiggling her fingers at him.

Trish glared at the back of her head disbelievingly, as Ma came out of the kitchen, saying, 'Is Sahil leaving already? Arrey, beta, stay for dinner, no?'

Sahil busied himself with fending off Ma's entreaties to stay. 'Next time, aunty,' he promised as he headed down the hall towards the front door, with Ma in close pursuit. With one last quick wave at Trish, he disappeared from view.

'And I don't know if you've noticed, but she's become so rude. I think perhaps a good whack is what she deserves. I've just been too lenient with her, you know?' Trish's attention came back into the living room, to her friend's complaining.

Akanksha had flopped herself down on the sofa in the exact spot where Sahil had been sitting. Trish looked at her, frowning.

Akanksha went on. 'I think the basic problem is that I've let her have her way for too long. She's even started being cheeky with Dad, and that's one thing I just won't stand from her.'

'You know what *I* think?' Trish interrupted. 'I think the basic problem is something very different.'

'Huh?' Akanksha looked up blankly. She clearly hadn't expected Trish to express a point of view on the subject. 'What?'

'I think the problem is that you've ignored your kid for too long,' Trish said firmly, in no mood to mince words right now. 'Pay more attention to her and try and find out what's bothering her. Maybe something's going on with her.'

'Yeah, something,' Akanksha said sarcastically. 'She's mutating into a monster.'

'She's just a little kid!' Trish protested. 'Maybe she just needs more time from you. Did you ask her why she doesn't actually want her guitar classes any more?'

'I *did* ask her that, and she doesn't give me a straight answer. And then she says I don't understand anything! I'm telling you, she's just doing it to drive me crazy. I even told her. I said, "Look, do you know how much that guitar and these lessons are costing us? You had better enjoy them like you said you would, or ..."'

'That's not what I meant by talking to her about it.' Trish was getting even more annoyed now. 'You've just been talking *at* her! You can't *force* her to enjoy something. She told me it's too difficult for her and she's getting the feeling ...' She stopped short of telling Akanksha what Lisa had said about feeling she wasn't wanted. She felt Akanksha should hear that from Lisa. She went on quickly, 'Anyway, as a mom, it's your job to first figure out what exactly is bothering her. But I'm telling you, Akanksha, something's up with that little girl, she deserves your attention.'

'Oh come on, Trish.' Akanksha rolled her eyes. 'What do *you* know about being a mom? It's different babysitting once

181

in a while. You don't have to deal with any real problems. This is hardly your area of expertise.'

'Yes. Sure,' Trish said, feeling a lump rise unexpectedly in her throat. 'I have no experience. I have no kids, so I have no right to advise you about yours. It's not like I could possibly care about Lisa as a mere babysitting "masi", right?' Akanksha looked up with a surprised frown, as if recognizing that this was a tone she hadn't heard from Trish before. But something inside Trish snapped, and before she could stop herself, she was saying, 'So from now on, while you're out gallivanting and having that frickin' affair of yours, just do me a favour and stop making me a part of the whole thing by leaving Lisa here.'

Akanksha's face went white. Trish instinctively knew that she had hit the nail on the head. But the words had come out harsher than she had meant. This wasn't the right way to deal with Akanksha. Now she had just succeeded in putting her on the defensive.

Without a word, Akanksha rose from the sofa. She breezed past Trish and called quietly over her shoulder to Ma, 'Bye, aunty.' She walked out of the house, her heels click-clacking and echoing in the hallway.

Ma came out of the kitchen again and called out after her. 'Arrey, even *you're* not staying for dinner? I was making choley-bhaturey.' There was no reply. Akanksha had already gone. Ma looked hurt. 'Why did she leave like that? What's the point now of making anything special if there's no one to eat it?'

Trish ignored Ma. She already felt sorry for talking to Akanksha like that. She had a strong feeling that she might just have lost the one person who had come closest to actually being her friend.

18

Flow

'Well, good riddance,' Trish thought to herself for the umpteenth time in the week. And yet, she remained unconvinced. Akanksha's stricken face came into her mind and she pushed it away again. She squared her shoulders. At least for the next sixty minutes, she knew she would be free.

She stood in front of the large mirrors, waiting for Raj to start the music up. She no longer felt self-conscious in the class; she loved the workout. In fact, these days, it was only during Zumba that she felt at peace. As soon as the music came on, Trish began to put even more energy into the moves, releasing all her pent up frustration and stress in vigorously dancing along with the pumping music.

After the class was over, she leaned against the wall, panting and feeling a sense of relief. But the unwanted thoughts were coming back already, damn it. She hurried over to pick up her bag and leave, but Raj called out to her, 'Hey, Trish!' She turned towards him. He said, 'Just a sec, wait up.' He finished disconnecting the music system. He then trotted up to her in his white t-shirt and fluorescent orange shorts – he was the only man she had ever seen who could carry off that colour – and said, 'Could you give me a ride to an auto? My car's out.'

'Sure.' Trish nodded. 'You ready?'

'Yup.' He took a big gulp of water from his bottle and swallowed. 'Let's go, let's go! Homeward ho!'

Trish rolled her eyes at his never-depleting enthusiasm. His energy levels amazed her. Just one class was enough to exhaust her, but she knew he took several classes a day. How on earth did he manage that? They headed out to her car and he trotted around to the passenger side as she unlocked it. He squeezed into the seat next to her, whistling a happy tune and looking for all the world like his day had only just begun.

'Where you headed?' he asked as she started up the car.

'I live on Bandstand.'

'Wow! Rich girrrl!' He whistled as she smiled, shaking her head at his teasing.

'Tiny apartment. But great view,' she admitted.

'So I'll get an auto from there only.'

'Sure?' She asked, frowning. 'It's a little out of the way for you, no?'

'Ah, it's five minutes! And I'm in no hurry. I'd love to ride with you.' He grinned at her so disarmingly that she laughed and shrugged and took the turn towards her home.

They drove along in companionable silence for a few minutes, broken only by Raj's occasional tuneless humming of some song playing in his head. She decided to go ahead and ask. 'So Raj. How do you do it? I mean, how do you have so much energy? What is it, three classes a day?'

'Four from today,' he replied cheerfully. 'We just added an

early morning batch.' He laughed at the wide-eyed glance that she threw him. He then added, 'I don't know. I don't think about it that much. If I did, I might not be able to manage it!'

'Yeah.' She smiled, scanning the side of the road for autos. 'When you're doing the impossible, better not to think about it, I guess.'

'It's not that.' Raj grinned back. 'I think I've finally just hit the sweet spot with my work. I'm doing something I enjoy, which pays me a decent amount, is good for me and gets to spread happiness and help other people too! So it energizes me more than it takes it out of me. It's like I'm in some sort of ... flow.'

Trish nodded along slowly. She'd never thought about work that way. 'Wow. You're lucky.'

'Lucky-shmucky,' Raj scoffed. 'I've struggled like anything to get this far. For three years, I was barely making ends meet. Mumbai's a tough city, and an expensive one, you know. And it's not like this is the best paying or most respectable profession in the world, either.' He stuck out his arm dramatically, showing off his muscles, and said, 'But you get a good body. No?'

'Ewww.' Trish laughed and pushed his arm away. 'You're sweaty.'

Raj looked at her and grinned appreciatively. 'It's working well for you, you're looking so good these days.'

Trish blushed, but managed to keep her head held high. 'Thanks, Raj.' She threw him a quick grateful smile.

'Oh, there's an auto, stop, stop.' As she pulled over, he bellowed, 'Thanks, girl. See you next class!' He gave her an impetuous hug which took her by surprise. Then he jumped out of the car almost before she completely stopped and bounded into the waiting auto. Trish watched as he even slapped the bemused auto-waala on the back with a cheery 'Chalo, boss! Malad West!'

Trish smiled after him as he took off with a wave at her. That guy was a bundle of pure energy. He had done her a lot of good. Perhaps more than he knew.

She pulled her car into her regular parking spot, still smiling as she got out, and slammed the door shut. She then noticed the car right next to hers. It was familiar, and even more familiar was the face of the person leaning against the hood, with the deep brown eyes that were amusedly watching her as he waited for her to register his presence. She immediately felt a little weak around the knees, and it certainly wasn't the aftermath of the Zumba.

❋

186

'Zumba, huh?'

'Yep.' Trish looked up from the menu at him. He was gazing intently at her.

'He didn't look like a ... Zumba teacher,' he commented lightly.

'Instructor,' she said matter-of-factly and then narrowed her eyes at him. 'Wait, you said you didn't even know what Zumba was until I just told you.'

'Yeah, yeah,' Sahil muttered. 'But now that you've told me, he didn't look like one.'

She frowned. 'Okayyy.' She thought of pursuing it, but decided to let it go. She looked down at the menu again.

'Too ... muscular, you know?' Sahil clearly didn't want to let it go just yet. Trish's head snapped up again, suddenly realizing what was going on. She didn't quite know how to react, although a part of her felt like laughing.

'He is very muscular,' she said non-committally. 'Quite fit.'

'Yes, but fit doesn't have to mean that muscular, right?'

He spoke so earnestly that she had to hide her smile as she cleared her throat and said, 'No, not at all. You can be fit and lean. Whatever makes you feel good, I guess.'

'Yes,' he said and then added, almost to himself, 'He also seemed very friendly. A little too friendly, but hey. Maybe that's what Zumba instructors are supposed to be like. How would I know?'

Trish felt the colour rising in her cheeks. He had obviously seen Raj hugging her. Not that she had to clarify anything to him, but this was all getting a little embarrassing. She racked her brains about how to change the subject and came up with a casual 'So how's it going at home?' as she looked around the café. They were back at Costa Coffee, where they had met the first time; or rather, the second time if you counted the time she attacked him for following her. Wait, the third, if you counted her saving him. Whatever!

She sensed that his home situation wasn't something he really felt like discussing much. But after a slight pause, he just gave her a small smile and said, 'It's going. It's going. I think Dad will start talking to me again soon.'

'And your mom?'

'Mummy dearest!' Sahil laughed bitterly. 'I think she's suffering the most in all this. She's still mortally afraid that I'll go and do something stupid again if Dad continues to pressurize me. She doesn't know it was the other thing bothering me. No one at home knows it's back, really. I can't bring myself to tell anyone about it.' He gave Trish a meaningful look. 'So anyway, Mom's after Dad to "forgive me", and he's annoyed with her for "taking my side" and so on. But hey, you know what?' He grinned. 'The other day, Dad and I bumped into each other on the way to the bathroom and he actually said, "Oh. It's you," before quickly walking away. So actually, he's sort of talking to me now!'

Trish couldn't help looking incredulous.

Sahil asked innocently, 'What? What is it?'

'Nothing,' she said. 'You're just being rather cheerful for a suicidal jobless psycho who's out of favour with his parents.'

'Hey, will you stop with that psycho thing?' he scolded, but he was being playful. She smiled. She always felt lighter and happier when she was out with him. '*You* tell me.' He took a big bite of his sandwich. Swallowing manfully, he went on, 'How're things at home. Is Uncle ready to be beaten by me at chess? Is Aunty already heating up the oil for the next batch of pakoras? How come you didn't invite me into the house today?'

188

'Just.' Trish pursed her lips. She didn't feel like admitting that she wanted to get time with him alone. Ma and Ba would have tried to hog him like last time, and he didn't seem to mind as much as she would have liked. 'Well, yeah, Ba has been asking about you, actually. Very strange. He usually hates talking to strangers. Makes up all sorts of excuses to avoid interacting with people. But he seems to like you a lot. And Ma … well …' She just waved her hand dismissively.

Sahil wisely refrained from saying anything about Ma. He instead remarked, 'So how's that friend of yours, the one I met the other day?'

Trish's guard was up immediately. His tone struck her as being a little too deliberately casual. 'Akanksha. Why are you so interested?'

'Arrey!' Sahil looked surprised. 'I'm not interested. I was just asking because …' He stopped short and shrugged. 'I was just asking.'

'Because what?' Trish prodded, sensing something was up.
'Nothing.'

Trish felt she could tell when this guy was keeping something from her, and she definitely got that feeling now. Did he know about their fight somehow? It was her turn to shrug. She stabbed her bagel with unnecessary force as she said, 'Well, I don't know how she is. And I don't care.'

His eyes were wide open in surprise. 'What happened?'

'Nothing.' She knew it sounded childish but she couldn't help it. She didn't want to talk about it.

He looked so bewildered that she couldn't keep it up. She sighed. 'Well, if you must know, we had a huge fight after you left that day, and now we're not talking. I think that's pretty much the end of that relationship. No biggie.' She shrugged and stuffed her mouth with her bagel, looking over his shoulder instead of into those clear brown all-seeing eyes. She couldn't avoid his eye for long, though, and when she next glanced at him, she saw his face looked disturbed. 'What?' she asked sharply.

'Nothing.' Again too quick, too casual.

'Sahil.' She put her fork down. 'Can you please stop with that?' She lowered her voice and asked, 'What is it that you're not telling me?'

He looked really uncomfortable now. Trish frowned as she thought back to that day. She recalled now, even though it had been brief, Akanksha clinging on to his hand and then Sahil dropping hers as quickly as possible. It was a subtle thing, but Trish had picked up on it, and something now clicked. She hissed, cocking her head to one side, 'You saw something, didn't you?'

He looked around the café, first to the left and then the right, as if making sure that no one else was listening. He bit

189

his lower lip once. 'Yes,' he said quietly. 'But I can't tell you what it is.'

Trish's nostrils flared for a second, but she showed no emotion. 'Look. That's fine. I'm not interested anyway. That friendship is down the drain. So whatever you saw is none of my business.' Sahil appeared to be struggling with something, but Trish didn't want him to think that she was curious about Akanksha. She went on lightly, 'So is this why you don't have a girlfriend? Because you're scared that every time you touch her, you'll see something ominous?'

He made a face. 'I guess so. Imagine getting intimate with someone and then suddenly getting a flash of something horrible, right in the middle of it. That would really kill the mood, huh?'

190

Her cheeks pinked up at the visions this conjured up in her mind. She cleared her throat and changed the subject again. 'Er, so. What are you planning to do next? I mean, in terms of work and stuff?'

He looked thoughtful. 'So I was thinking of going back to my corporate job, you know? I was doing pretty well there before I caved in to Dad's pressure to answer my calling as the namkeen baron of Mumbai.' He rolled his eyes heavenward and Trish couldn't help smiling. 'And you know what else? I was thinking I'll just go back to some volunteer work. I used to teach at this school for underprivileged kids a few years back. Weekends. I don't know why I dropped that. It made me really happy.'

'Really? What did you teach?'

'Music.'

Trish raised her eyebrows at this. 'You taught music?'

'Yeah, a little bit of guitar, the keyboard, some drums, dash of the flute. I learnt a bunch of instruments as a kid. I was part of a band in college, actually. I'm probably really rusty now, though.'

'You're being modest,' Trish guessed. 'You're probably this major musical genius who's just being self-deprecating.'

'Self-deprecating. Well, you'd know about that, right?' he shot back. 'Only a writer would use a word like that in real life.'

'Whatever.' She took another sip of her coffee and smiled at him. It was unusual for her, but it felt nice and natural, this good-natured banter. She enjoyed volleying with him. Her voice became sincere. 'I'd like to hear you play some time.'

'Okay,' he said, grinning. He had begun to look more and more handsome to her, albeit still in a nerdy way. The way his eyes lit up when he grinned at her always caused her to feel a little flutter somewhere inside.

'So today when I was talking to Raj,' Trish said, trying to distract herself from the effect of that easy grin. '*He* said he'd found his calling – he called it his sweet spot – by chancing upon the intersection of what he loves doing and what helps others and what pays him enough to make a living.'

'Wow. Lucky dog.' Sahil whistled and then asked, with mock-seriousness, eyes twinkling. 'So ... You saying I should become a Zumba instructor?'

'Why not?' Trish smiled at the thought of bespectacled gangly Sahil in orange fluorescent shorts leading a dance-fitness class. 'Anyway, I kind of thought he had something there. He found something where it all came together for him and he's kind of in flow. At least that's what he said.' Her voice trailed off and she bit her lip.

Sahil waited patiently and then, when it looked like nothing else was forthcoming from Trish, he ventured, 'Trish? Are you not *liking* writing the column?'

'Not liking?' she scoffed, fingering her coffee cup and staring into the warm brown liquid. 'Hah! Actively *despising* is more like it.'

'Why? Come on, you like writing, right?' She nodded slowly at this, and he went on. 'You're helping a lot of people. I read your column every single day and I think what you say makes so much sense.' He grinned. 'Hey! How come you're so good at sorting out *other* people's lives?'

'What does that mean?' she demanded. '*Other* people's lives. Are you saying my life is messed up?'

'No, no. I didn't mean that.' Sahil hesitated and then said, 'But it's not ...'

'What?' she snapped.

'Flowing.' He made a sweeping gesture with his hands and then added craftily, 'To use your own words. Or rather, the words of the great Zumba-muscleman, Raj.'

192

She ignored his jibe. 'Well, I think my life is flowing just fine.' She didn't know why she was getting so defensive. She looked at her watch and said a little curtly, 'I guess we should be getting back now.'

'Hey,' he said gently. 'All okay?'

'All fine. Just fine.' She turned and signalled to the waiter and then fumbled in her purse to pull out her wallet. She swept aside Sahil's protests about letting him pay the bill. He gave up and just sat back and watched her. She studiously ignored him as she counted out the money.

So what if she had a slightly weird relationship with her parents and hated her job and had just lost her best friend? That didn't mean that her life was messed up. Did it? Well, she didn't want him to judge her for it. He still probably thought there was something to that stupid thing he'd said to her before about feeling some sense of loss or something.

Well, he was wrong about that. It was nonsense. Stuff and nonsense. She'd always been fine by herself and didn't need to be thrown off track by anybody, not even him.

He was still quiet as she gathered up her things. He was staring at the table as she stood up, but then said, so quietly that she almost missed it in the buzz of the café, 'Trish.'

She turned towards him impatiently, hovering and, for some reason, itching to get to the door and get away.

He didn't move, saying, in a tone that was dead serious, 'When Akanksha calls you, pick up the phone. It's just a feeling I have. Okay?'

Trish stared at him for a long moment.

She didn't even say goodbye as she turned on her heel and walked away.

193

19

The Call

'I don't believe it!' Trish groaned as she scanned the letters for the day. What was going on here?

This was getting to be some serious shit.

A letter where a woman talked about how she had been suffering marital rape for the last eight years. It made Trish's stomach churn to read it. These letters were anonymous, so she couldn't even call the cops. She quickly moved on to the next one. It was from a teenager who had got his girlfriend pregnant and felt guilty about asking her to get an abortion. Another one was from a kid from a broken home, fifteen years old, and being manipulated by her parents, both of whom were resorting to bribing her to trying to get her to live with them.

This was getting increasingly difficult. Only one in about four letters was of the type that Trish used to savour writing her sarcastic responses to earlier. It put her in a major dilemma.

She found herself having to wade past and deliberately ignore the more dire problems in search of the frivolous ones which were answerable. All in the name of maintaining the god-damned tone of the god-damned column. But each letter that she ignored went ahead and settled down somewhere in her consciousness. She felt heavy-hearted at the end of the couple of hours that she had been at her computer.

'Trishna ... Trishna ...' His voice rang out plaintively from the other room.

She sighed and snapped her laptop shut and got up to hurry inside and see what Ba wanted. She thought he seemed to be getting weaker each week. She kept exhorting him to exercise his muscles, but he still refused to get up and walk except for when he needed to go to the bathroom. Maybe he needed help standing up, she thought, quickening her step near the door. It was her mortal fear that he would fall one of these days and break a bone.

Ba wasn't trying to get up, though. He was just lying in bed, dressed in his usual white kurta-pajama. He scowled when she came and sat down beside him. 'You don't listen. I called for you ten times!'

'Ba,' she said patiently. 'Use the bell, no?' She pointed to the untouched little button that she had installed on the side of his bed weeks ago. 'Your voice is getting softer and it's not always easy for me to hear you.'

'Bell!' he scoffed. 'You people have turned me into a lifelong patient and this room into a hospital.'

'Look here, Ba,' Trish said with a sigh. 'We're the ones who are always telling you to get *out* of this room. Get some exercise. Start physiotherapy. Interact more with people.'

'Interact with whom?' Ba grumbled. 'That one decent chess player you brought here, Sabharwal, he's not come again. You

195

two ladies are the only ones here, and your mother doesn't even make sense half the time.'

Ma's voice rang out from the adjoining room immediately. 'I can *hear* you. And look who's talking. Most of the time, you're just babbling incoherently.'

Trish quickly called out, interrupting her mother, 'It's okay, Ma. Let it be.' The grumbling from outside continued. She whispered to her father, 'Shhh. Talk softly, Ba.'

Ba immediately raised his voice. 'First you say my voice is too soft for you to hear and then you say that I should talk softer! Make up your mind, girl! See? You're becoming just like your mother, making no sense.'

Trish narrowed her eyes at him. '*Don't* say I'm like her, Ba.'

Even though she had been very quiet, her mother's voice snapped immediately. 'That's right. Now *you* also start to insult me.' To Trish's surprise, Ma appeared at the doorway, quivering with anger. 'All you two have ever done is gang up on me exactly like this. My whole life I've been dealing with this. You two have each other, who do I have?'

'Whose fault is that?' Ba shouted back. 'Not my fault. Not Trishna's!'

'Oh, I see. It's my fault?' Ma's eyes were wild. '*Mine*? Have I not suffered?'

'We *all* suffer,' barked Ba. 'Only you make your suffering an object of worship!' Ma gasped at this, her face turning visibly white.

'What is *wrong* with you guys?' Trish said, swivelling her head to glare in turn at her parents.

Ba opened his mouth, but Ma raised her hand and pointed a trembling finger at him, saying in a quiet, deadly tone, 'You're going too far, Vikram.' Trish was shocked. Ma was actually using Ba's name to his face. She was clearly over the edge now. Ba seemed to somehow sense this too, because he just withdrew into stony silence.

Ma glared through reddening eyes at the two of them and then swept away. Trish looked at Ba, who was now studying the scenery outside the window. His breathing was a little uneven. She thought about asking him what that had been about, but suppressed her curiosity for the sake of his health and peace of mind. She just reached out and took his skinny hand. It felt clammy, and she gave it a gentle, comforting squeeze.

He didn't respond for a while, but then he turned his head to look at her face and, with a wan smile, said, 'So. When is that Sabharwal coming again?'

'He'll come, Ba. He'll come soon, okay?' She patted his hand reassuringly. 'You just get stronger so that you can make sure he doesn't actually beat you next time.'

'Hah!' said Ba and coughed weakly. 'You said something about calling some physiotherapy chappie home? What happened to that? Forgot about it?'

'*Forgot?*' Trish said incredulously and then checked herself. Deliberately casual, she said, 'No. I'll check with him again. He can come tomorrow, perhaps. Three days a week in the evenings, he said his schedule is free.' She tried to hide the thrill that she was feeling. She'd been after him for months and now Ba was bringing up the physiotherapy himself? He was actually ready to give it a try! This was great.

Ba just grunted at her and she took it as a sign of dismissal. She didn't want to push her luck right now in case he did another turnabout and changed his mind about the physiotherapy after all. She left him lying in bed, half turned on his side, with his eyes closed.

She figured Ma needed some more time to cool down after

197

the strange fight. They bickered often, but she had never seen her parents this angry with each other. It actually looked like they hated each other for a moment there. In spite of their differences, they had always stood by each other. What could have caused them to react like that? She tried to shrug it off, it was between them, after all. It bothered her, but she would just have to deal with that herself.

She heard her phone ringing as she reached the drawing room and hurried toward it. Maybe it was Sahil. Hopefully not Nivedita. She reached for her phone and saw the name flashing on the screen.

Akanksha, of all people. Trish bit her lip. It had been three weeks since she had heard from her. Trish had to admit to herself that she missed Akanksha, and she missed Lisa too. In fact, she was worried about Lisa. Besides, Akanksha wasn't really all *that* bad, she'd come through at times that Trish really needed her. It was just that she wasn't sure she really felt up to a conversation with her right now.

It was only on what must have been the seventh or eighth ring that she remembered what Sahil had told her. She pressed the answer button and said in a cordial manner, 'Hello, Akanksha.' Maybe things were going to get better.

'Trish!' Akanksha wailed, sounding so distraught that Trish's blood ran cold. Akanksha let out a loud sob and then choked out, 'It's my dad, he's fallen from the terrace!' Another sob while Trish clutched at the side of her table to steady herself. Then Akanksha's voice, shocked and anguished, finished with an incredulous note that suggested she didn't quite believe what she was saying herself: 'He's ... *dead*.'

❦

The next few hours passed by in a blur. Trish was only dimly aware of the crowd of curious and morbidly fascinated onlookers and the futile blaring of the ambulance siren as it got louder. She saw and then quickly averted her eyes from the cream-kurta-clad body, twisted up at an impossible angle, lifeless eyes staring upwards in a surprised manner, blood still spreading out from behind the white-haired head. The thought flashed through her mind that the papers would report the body being found in a pool of blood, as they always did. The camera flashes all around right now could only be courtesy the media bloodhounds. She felt a vague sense of shame for being associated with the industry.

The building was fourteen floors high. There had never been any chance of survival. The only reason Trish got close enough to even get a glimpse of the body was because she had made her way right up to Akanksha near the front of the crowd. Akanksha was wailing hysterically, inconsolable. Trish looked around and saw to her shock that Lisa was there too, pale-faced with fright, with a dull-eyed maid holding on to her arm.

'What are you doing?' Trish shouted at the maid. 'Take her *away* from here, for god's sake!' The maid started into action and tugged at Lisa's arm unsuccessfully. The child remained rooted to the spot. Trish went up to Lisa and enveloped her in a hug. Lisa went limp against her. Trish held her by the shoulders and knelt down to face her. 'Listen. Lisa. You go to my place right now, okay? Ma is at home.'

Lisa seemed to register this and nodded, still looking frightened. Trish repeated the instruction to the maid, who nodded and managed to lead Lisa away. Trish fervently hoped that Ma would take care of Lisa properly. She hadn't had much time to tell her anything after the call except that there had been an accident and Akanksha's father had passed away. Her mother's jaw had dropped open in shock, but Trish was already halfway out the door before Ma could say anything. Trish had called over her shoulder, 'Don't say anything to Ba.'

She made her way back to Akanksha. The body was now being lifted on to a stretcher, covered in a white sheet which immediately turned red in various places. Akanksha sensed Trish's presence and clung weakly to her. Trish put her arm around her friend's trembling shoulders and squeezed tight. As the body was lifted up into the ambulance, Akanksha collapsed sobbing against Trish's shoulder.

Trish asked gently, 'Where's Vinay? Is he away?'

Akanksha continued to sob, but another sari-clad lady, whom Trish vaguely recognized as Akanksha's next-door neighbour, nodded. Trish felt Akanksha's unceasing tears against her shirt and felt her sense of loss acutely. Akanksha had truly loved her father, and Trish could completely relate to the feeling. She made an effort to steady herself. She stroked Akanksha's back repeatedly, comfortingly, murmuring platitudes without meaning, words that made no sense, even to herself, even as she said them. 'It's okay ... it's going to be okay.'

❋

'And where were you at the exact time of the incident?' the fat, khaki-clad policeman droned.

'She already told you twice,' Trish snapped, losing her temper. 'She was heading back from a meeting and had almost reached home when her neighbour called and told her ...'

The policeman who had introduced himself proudly as the investigating officer, gave Trish a long, pained look that silenced her. Akanksha just sat in her chair, staring at the ground, shaking her head. The thin, short policewoman who was clearly the IO's sidekick had been hovering in the corner of Akanksha's drawing room. She now stepped forward and said in her reedy voice to Trish, 'Perhaps, madam, you had better step out if you will keep interrupting like this.'

'I won't interrupt,' Trish growled, pressing her lips together. The jerk had been interrogating Akanksha for the last forty-five minutes. He had so far demonstrated all the sensitivity of a bull. Couldn't he see she was in shock? Trish thought about protesting yet again, but kept mum for fear of being escorted off the premises. She exhaled, keeping her focus on Akanksha's face.

Akanksha was white as a ghost, and her mascara was running wild. The rest of her makeup had already been rubbed off her face. She looked vulnerable and unsure, even haggard.

201

'If necessary, we will be able to confirm the time of meeting with the person you were meeting?'

Akanksha did not look up from the floor.

'Please can you give us details of your meeting?'

She responded so softly that Trish had to strain to hear her. 'Give me that sheet of paper, I'll write his details down.'

The policeman hesitated and then tore out a sheet of paper from his notebook and handed it over with a pen. Akanksha scribbled something on it for a few seconds.

The policeman looked down at what she had written and then coughed. 'Okay, madam. We will be in touch. Please do not leave the city any time during the course of this investigation.'

Akanksha nodded mutely. Trish had to bite back a comment about her friend hardly planning a holiday any time soon. She stood up impatiently, waiting for the policeman to get up too. He looked at her disdainfully, as if disapproving of her manners, and hoisted himself up off Akanksha's expensive white sofa. He walked past Trish towards the door and the lady officer followed him out.

Trish went over and lowered herself gingerly on to the arm of the sofa where Akanksha was sitting. She put an arm around her and said gently, 'Hey. You okay?'

'Yes,' she replied. 'Am glad they've gone.'

Trish called out to Akanksha's maid, 'Mohini.' The maid appeared in the doorway. 'Can you please make a cup of tea for Akku?'

When Trish turned back, Akanksha's face was twisted into a humourless smile. 'I think those two also expected a cup of tea.'

202

'I don't know what they expected, and I don't think we should care,' Trish said firmly. 'You need to just look out for yourself right now, and Lisa.'

'Lisa.' Akanksha started. 'Is she okay?'

'She's fine,' said Trish. 'I called Ma. She said she refused to eat anything, but has now fallen asleep.'

'Did she say anything?' Akanksha looked worried. 'I don't even know what she saw, what she's thinking ...'

'I don't know, Akku. She looked shocked and scared when I saw her. We'll keep an eye on her, okay?' She sighed, rubbing her eyes. 'When will Vinay be back from Delhi?'

'He's rushing to get the earliest possible flight back tonight,' Akanksha said. Her lower lip quivered and she burst into tears again, putting her hands over her face. Trish felt helpless as she stroked her friend's hair wordlessly. 'Why did I go?' Akanksha groaned, rocking back and forth like a child. 'Why did I have to go?'

'Hey,' Trish protested. 'Listen. You couldn't have known. It was an accident. He shouldn't have been up there alone on the terrace, the ledges are too low, no one ever goes there. Why was he even there?'

'But I shouldn't have *gone*.' Akanksha looked up, and the remnants of the mascara were running down her cheek, giving her face a hollowed skeletal look. 'You were right, Trish. I've been screwing around. With Vinay's friend, his business partner!' She squeezed her eyes shut and more tears sprang out. 'I shouldn't have done it. You warned me, and this is my punishment. Divine retribution in the most horrible way. And my poor dad had to suffer for it!'

'Akku. Akku.' Trish shook her by her shoulders. 'Stop it. What are you talking about? There is no such thing as divine retribution. That doesn't even make sense. Why would your *dad* have to pay for something you did?'

203

'It wouldn't have happened if I'd been home, I know it!' Akanksha's voice was full of anguish. She then drew in a deep staggering breath and went on quietly. 'Vinay will know. They will all know now. I've had to give the details of his name and address to the police. It will all come out into the open. Vinay will be shattered. He's such a good, trusting man.' She turned towards Trish, and her face crumpled again. 'Everything is *broken*, Trish.'

Trish just reached out and hugged her friend. 'Akku, what's done is done. You have to be strong now.'

'I'll never cheat again. It was so pointless, so *low* of me. Just thinking about myself. Vinay never deserved this from me.'

'Okay, listen, Akku,' Trish said, firmly. 'Let's just pick one line of thinking and stay with it, okay? So let's say *everyone* gets what they deserve eventually. This is a phase, and it will pass. So now, please just be as strong as you can and deal with it. For your own sake and your family's.'

Akanksha took a long shuddering breath and tried to steady herself. The maid walked in carrying a tray with two steaming cups of tea on it.

Trish picked up one cup from the tray and handed it to Akanksha, who just stared at it for a moment. She then looked up at Trish and said, in a dazed manner, with all the wondering innocence of a child, 'But Trish, if everyone gets what they deserve, what did my dad do to deserve an end like that?'

Trish had no answer and so she chose to say nothing.

She indicated with a gentle lift of her chin that Akanksha should drink her tea. Like a zombie, Akanksha finally raised the cup to her lips.

20

Music

'Now wait, where was I?' Trish stared at her computer screen. She had blanked out yet again, right in the middle of reading a letter. They continued to flow in faster than she could manage, and she now had a major problem concentrating, to boot. The words on the screen often just blurred together and made no sense, and she had to shake herself to try and get her focus back.

She was looking in every day on Akanksha and Lisa, and was still worried about them. It especially bothered her how pale and withdrawn Lisa had become. She was like a shadow of her former self. Trish knew that she had shared a special bond with her grandfather at a time when her mother was neglecting her, and he was gone already from her life. Akanksha herself was a changed person, only showing signs of animation when expressing worry about Lisa, but the little girl wasn't responding to her attention now. Vinay too seemed very subdued the last couple of times Trish had seen him. She knew Akanksha had talked to him and confessed her secret to him. However, he also looked steady and calm as always, and Trish fervently hoped that things would eventually be all right between him and Akanksha.

It was even tougher for Trish to write with sarcasm now; she wasn't in the right frame of mind for it. Her mind was still playing on the strange and sudden death of Akanksha's father, the speculation about whether it was suicide or just an accident, and the family's pain and confusion. Lisa appeared to be on the verge of giving up speaking altogether. She seemed to be in a constant daze, staring into space and not responding to questions directed at her. Akanksha had told Trish that Lisa probably felt the void even more than she did. This was the first time she was dealing with the idea of death. Trish urged Akanksha to start some form of counselling for Lisa. Akanksha agreed, resolving that as soon as the twelfth-day ceremony for her father was over, they would get some professional help.

'Until then.' She had squeezed Trish's hand. 'Please, Trish, spend some time with Lisa, try to get her to talk. She's not saying anything, how she's feeling, what she thinks. No matter how hard I try to get her to open up. I've lost the ability to connect with her.' Her eyes had filled with tears again. 'She needs something I can't give her right now.'

Trish had promised her that she would try her best. Today, Lisa was to come and spend some time at home. Trish kept glancing at the clock anxiously, expecting the bell to ring any moment.

She went back to the letters, deciding to just try *something* out, even if she didn't feel like it. She felt more and more like a fake and she composed her answers listlessly. She stopped in the middle of writing a sentence. She would have to try and channel her inner bitch, but it didn't look like she was in touch with her any more.

I'll try channeling Nivedita instead, or even better, Zee, she thought. Inspired a little by this, she began writing again, and this carried her through for the next couple of letters, although she still found herself cringing at some parts she wrote.

She started reading another new letter listlessly. As her mind slowly registered what the words were saying, her blood froze. All other thoughts went out of the window and her heartbeat quickened as she read.

Dear Amy,

I don't know if you'll read this or whether I'll still be around if and when you choose to reply. My head is all messed up and I think I'm depressed. I'm twenty-three years old and I've known I was homosexual for the last six years. But my parents are old-fashioned and I know it would absolutely break them to know this about me. They're trying to fix me up for an arranged marriage with a family friend's daughter. I've known the girl for years too and I'm fond of her. I couldn't possibly ruin her life like this. I'm sick of the lies, of pretending to be someone that I'm not.

I love my parents dearly, but I don't think I'm ever going to be able to be the son they want me to be. It's easier for me to just end it. I've thought about suicide a couple of times in the past, but I always chickened out. This time I'm not going to.

I don't even know why I'm bothering to write this. There's nothing you or anyone can do to fix this. I hope you tear into me for all my bullshit. I deserve it. I'm a loser and a coward. It's better this way.

Hopeless

Trish inhaled sharply and then read the letter again. This one definitely deserved a genuine response. And she didn't care what Nivedita or Zee had to say about it, there was someone's life at stake. Biting her lip, she began to type.

❋

'Sounds like it's been a really horrible week for you ...'

Sahil's voice was soft as he sat next to Trish on the sofa. When the bell had rung, she had thought it would be Lisa, but her heart had lifted when she saw Sahil standing at the door. The conversation hadn't ended on a good note the last time they met, but she was so glad he was back again. His smile had faded immediately when he saw her face, though, and had been replaced by an expression of concern. He could clearly tell something had happened.

She had told him the whole story, haltingly. He now looked searchingly at Trish's face and she felt conscious about the dark circles under her eyes. She felt like she hadn't slept in days. He went on, 'I'm sorry I wasn't around. I wish you'd called. I don't know why I didn't ...'

She just shook her head gently to quell him from going down that path. She hadn't even thought of reaching out for help. Besides, things had been too crazy. She suddenly felt exhausted. She closed her eyes. The nightmares had been waking her up almost every night. The sight of the body lying lifeless on the ground, the grotesquely twisted limbs, the blood – it was all etched into her mind, and the harder she tried not to think about it, the more insistently the image seemed to float back in when she least expected it.

The incident had also awakened a new sort of fear in her – for Ba. Seeing Akanksha mourning for her father, she realized

208

how scared she was herself about losing Ba. The medication was clearly not working. Maybe it was too late now for the physiotherapy to make any difference. He was impatient with the physiotherapist and complained incessantly about being pushed and feeling too tired. No matter what she did, she couldn't stop his deterioration. She couldn't stop time for Ba. Even though she was so much older than Lisa, for her too, it would be the first time she would have to face death so close to home. And death was so ... final.

She opened her eyes and smiled wanly at Sahil. 'Now that you're here, I'm kind of hoping you might be able to do something to cheer Lisa up today. I have this feeling I won't be able to handle it too well myself.'

'Sure,' said Sahil. 'She's seven, right?'

'Yes. She got a guitar recently, it was bought for her by her grandpa.'

'They were really close, huh?' Sahil's voice was soft.

'Yes.' Trish sighed. 'Lisa was being moody before, constantly fighting with Akanksha. She was much better around her grandpa. Now she's in absolute shock.'

Sahil nodded. He reached out and took Trish's hand. 'How are *you*?'

Trish felt the usual slight jolt of electricity when he touched her but didn't remove her hand. She hesitated and then asked quietly, 'Sahil. Do you see something when you touch me?'

'Really want to know?'

She nodded.

He thought about it and then said slowly, 'You're the only person with whom I never get a clear vision. Just ... feelings.' She frowned. She hoped he wasn't going to start up about those supposed feelings of hers again. She opened her mouth to warn him, but his face was already breaking into a broad smile, as he finished, 'And I can't tell you how fabulous that is for me. Such a relief!'

She looked at him suspiciously. 'Okay. If you say so. Just don't start thinking we'll be experimenting any further with this ... touching thing.'

He threw his head back and laughed and said. 'You want to bet?'

She smiled after what felt like the longest time, her cheeks reddening again. To cover up, she withdrew her hand and said lightly, 'So. Ba has also been waiting to play chess with you again. When he wakes up, maybe you can say hello to him?'

'You bet.' Sahil grinned. 'But no mercy today on the old man.'

'He wouldn't have it any other way,' Trish countered loyally.

'I know.' Sahil laughed. 'You're a lot like each other, you two.'

'Two peas in a pod, that's us. I'm nothing like my *mother*.' She made a face as she said it, automatically lowering her voice, remembering the last time she had made this statement within earshot of Ma. After all, she might be hovering nearby, although if she had, she would have probably come in to see Sahil by now.

Sahil gave her a long look but wisely refrained from saying anything. Trish ran her hand through her curly thick hair, pulling at it in an attempt to get some relief from the throbbing headache that was just starting up. Sahil asked, 'And how's the letter-answering business going?'

'Sucks,' she replied. She hesitated and then figured there was no harm telling him. Especially since he was the only person who knew about the column. 'Actually, today I got something that read a lot like ... a suicide note.'

Sahil let out a low whistle. 'Heavy. I've never understood people who can contemplate suicide.'

He looked at her innocently but the twinkle in his eye gave him away. She stopped glaring at him. 'Yes. It's "heavy". Actually, it's a huge burden. I have no idea if it's just someone trying to get attention, but I can hardly take a chance with something like that, you know?'

'No,' he agreed, serious this time. 'You can't.'

'It's getting too difficult.' Trish couldn't hide her frustration. 'I don't know if I can go on this way.'

'Well, you know, you sound like you should actually become a counsellor,' he said. 'I mean, you know, train properly to be one and then deal with people's issues individually. You'd be good at that, you know. You love helping people.'

'I do?' Trish sounded doubtful.

'Er. *Yeah*.' Sahil raised his eyebrows. 'You helped me; you've been taking care of your dad; you're helping a friend out and her little daughter; and there are loads of people out there who've benefited from your words, I'm sure of it.' He had a sudden gleam of excitement in his eyes. 'Hey! I'm telling you, that's it! That's your *flow* thing! I mean ...' He paused, seemingly checking himself now. 'That is, if you want to, of course.'

'Well,' Trish said thoughtfully. 'I always thought if I were to invest in any form of study, it should be something like an MBA. That's what seems to be the biggest gap in my resumé.'

'Oh, come on,' Sahil rolled his eyes. 'An MBA? I've done an MBA myself. Highly overrated. You'd be wasting your time.'

'Yeah.' Trish looked at him with tired eyes. 'But you're out of a job because of your own choice. It wasn't mine to be stuck writing a column I hate. I'm out of options.'

Sahil looked like he was going to say something in response

211

to this, but he appeared to change his mind and just looked at her silently.

The bell rang and Trish stood up. 'That's Lisa.'

It was indeed Lisa, with Akanksha. Lisa still looked pale and wan, but Akanksha looked better to Trish. She had even remembered to put a little light lipstick on and looked more like herself than she had in days.

'Hey,' Akanksha said to Trish with a small smile and hugged her. 'Thanks for having her over today.'

'My pleasure.' Trish bent down to Lisa. 'Hey, Leez. What do you feel like doing today?'

Lisa didn't answer, she just stared at the floor. Trish glanced up at Akanksha, who was now dragging in Lisa's guitar case. 'We've got her guitar today. Just in case she feels like it.'

Trish wasn't so sure about this. But before she could say anything, Sahil's voice rang out from behind Trish, making Akanksha jump: 'A guitar? Really?' Lisa looked up to see who this stranger was. He walked up to them and greeted Akanksha quietly. 'Hi, Akanksha. Sorry for your loss.'

Akanksha nodded with the same little brave smile that Trish had seen her use whenever anyone brought up her father's death.

Sahil bent down, putting his hands on his knees. 'This must be Lisa.' Lisa gave a small nod, not taking her eyes off the floor. He continued, 'You're the guitarist?' After a long pause, there was another tiny nod, barely perceptible.

'Sahil plays guitar too!' Trish said brightly. 'Come in and sit, Akanksha, have a cup of tea.'

'I'd love to,' Akanksha said, 'But I've been called in for questioning again. I don't know why they're treating me as a suspect. It's not as if Dad's left any major inheritance behind or something. It was just an accident, not murder!' Trish noticed Lisa's head snapped up with a shocked expression. Trish frowned at Akanksha, indicating the little girl with a tilt of her head. Akanksha said, 'Sorry. Didn't mean to upset you, Lisa.' She squeezed Lisa's thin shoulders. Trish saw that for once Lisa wasn't squirming away from Akanksha's touch.

'You go on ahead,' Trish told Akanksha. 'We'll take care of her.'

'Thanks, Trish.' Akanksha gave her a grateful hug. She gave Sahil a small wave and turned to leave, saying, 'I'll be back in a couple of hours.'

They were now alone with stony-faced little Lisa. She walked in past them to the drawing room and they followed her. Lisa sat down on her usual place on the sofa, and proceeded to stare listlessly at her shoes.

'Okay,' said Sahil, 'So I'm going to go and get that guitar.' And he trotted off down the hall.

213

❋

Trish was spellbound.

Sahil turned out to be an amazing musician. He had a deep, melodious singing voice and his fingers moved lightly and skillfully over Lisa's guitar as he sang and played for them. He was very versatile, playing rock, and pop, mostly old songs and even a fabulously haunting instrumental piece that turned out to be his own composition. Trish couldn't help but think it made him incredibly sexy. This guy was just full of surprises.

To Trish's delight, Lisa was listening intently too and she seemed to be moved by the music. She had flatly refused to touch the guitar to play anything herself, but now Trish saw that there was a light in her eyes.

'Uncle,' Trish was startled to hear Lisa's voice, small as it was. 'Can you maybe play that song, "*Jamaican farewell*"?'

'Okay.' Sahil grinned at the request. 'Can you maybe just call me Sahil?'

Lisa shook her head shyly, which made Sahil laugh. Trish was too surprised to do anything but gape. Lisa was smiling!

Sahil started strumming again. They spent most of the next hour listening to him play. After a while, Ma also came into the room and quietly sat down on a chair in the corner to listen. Her face was withdrawn, but Trish noted that her features relaxed a little as the music went on.

A cool breeze floated in from the windows into the drawing room filled with the sound of Sahil's music. Trish looked over again and again at Lisa, with the fervent hope that this evening would mark the beginning of her healing.

But now she saw that Lisa had suddenly shrunk back into the sofa, drawing her knees up against her chest. Trish glanced up to see what had startled her and then began to laugh incredulously. Sahil stopped playing and turned to follow her gaze.

'It's okay, Lisa.' Trish reached out to pat Lisa on the arm, still barely able to believe her eyes. 'It's only Ba!'

Ba. Who, for almost a whole year, had refused to leave his room except for the times when he had to be rushed to the hospital now stood leaning against the door weakly in his long white kurta-pajama. Ma was out of her chair and beside him in an instant, scolding, 'Arrey, why didn't you call me to help? What do you think you're doing?'

'Ma, it's okay,' Trish called. 'Ba, you wanted to join us? To hear Sahil play?' She marvelled at this. Sahil's playing was magic.

Ba spoke gruffly. 'None of you were listening to me as

usual. I just wanted to tell Sabharwal to stop fooling around with that ukulele of his and come and have a game with me. Rude young fellow, comes and doesn't even bother to say hello to the man of the house.'

'Uncle!' Sahil protested. 'I fully intended to have a game with you, but Trish said you were sleeping.'

'Who could sleep with that racket you were making?' Ba grumbled, but Trish could tell that he didn't really mean it.

'Oh come in and sit down with us, Ba.' Trish indicated the chair next to the sofa. 'A couple of songs more and we promise Sahil and you can bore us with your chess after that.'

Still grumbling, Ba slowly made his way into the room, brushing aside Ma's attempts to help him. 'Leave it, I *can* walk, you know.' Somewhat unsteadily he made it to the nearest chair and sat down heavily.

Trish felt ludicrously happy. She looked over at Lisa, who seemed to have calmed down now, her attention back on Sahil as he strummed her guitar lightly again. Lisa hadn't seen Ba before, so she had just been startled, Trish supposed, but she couldn't help wondering briefly: why on earth had she looked so *scared*?

215

❀

'Trish, I've got to get going now.'

Trish looked up from answering her letters. She was almost done for the day. Lisa was now watching cartoons. Trish was very relieved, the kid was behaving almost normal today.

'Ba's asleep?' Trish asked Sahil.

'Your mother's giving him his medicines. He's tired. I gave him a tough game today. He still won though.'

'Okay.' Trish smiled gratefully at him. 'Thanks so much for being around, Sahil.'

'No problem.' Sahil smiled back. He went over to Lisa and said, 'Okay, young lady. I'll see you another time, all right?' He held out his hand to her formally. She hesitated for a second and then, with her shy smile, she reached out and took it.

If Trish hadn't been watching closely, she wouldn't have noticed the change in Sahil's expression. He let go of her hand and straightened up, muttering something that sounded like 'sorry', and then, louder, 'Catch you soon, take care of that guitar. It needs constant playing or it'll get warped and we don't want that, right?'

His voice was cheerful. Something in it rang false to Trish. He waved and walked out, calling back, 'I'll let myself out.'

But Trish was on her feet and following him. 'Wait, Sahil.'

He was already at the door now, and he turned and hovered. 'Getting a little late ...'

'What is it?'

Sahil slumped against the door, suddenly looking more tired than she had seen him. He shook his head determinedly. 'I can't tell you.'

'Why not?' Trish was frustrated.

'I just can't, okay?' Sahil sounded frustrated too. 'I'm not going to use this stupid *thing* of mine any more.'

'Even if you think you could be helping someone else out? A little girl?' Trish hissed. 'We've been trying to get into her head for the last week, and you just got in there. Now you tell me what you saw.'

'She'll be all right,' Sahil said even though he didn't sound too convinced. 'She's going to be okay.' He seemed to be in two minds about this. He drew himself up and squared his shoulders. 'She was better today, right?'

Trish couldn't deny that. She just nodded stonily. She felt like kicking Sahil for not sharing whatever he knew with her.

'You know, too, Trish,' Sahil added. He suddenly leaned in close to her so that his lips were almost touching her ear. 'There's so much you know that you just don't *know* you know.'

He drew away from her and gave her a significant look. Trish realized that she had been holding her breath. Her heart was beating fast and she tried to calm it down.

'Fine,' she said, trying not to sound snappy. 'Fine. If that's the way you want it. Play games all you like. If you really think that's what's needed right now.'

He said evenly, 'I'm not supposed to tell you what you can figure out for yourself.'

With that, he gave her a tight smile and his brown eyes flashed at her before he turned around and walked away.

21

Breakdown

'Where the hell is it?' Trish shouted into the phone, unable to keep her voice down. She didn't even know whether Ba was awake or asleep, but she couldn't help it. This was the limit.

'Calm down, darling,' Nivedita's voice floated into her ear.

'Don't you fucking calm-down-darling *me*. Where. Is. That. Letter?'

'Language, dear,' said Nivedita, who herself had the foulest mouth Trish had ever heard.

'Listen.' Trish took a deep breath. 'Try and wrap your little mind around this fact. That guy was on the verge of *suicide*. I specifically told you that there was no way that we could ignore that letter and that the response should be printed on priority. Do you understand there's maybe someone's *life* at stake here?'

'Well yes, your suggestion was considered, but at the end of the day, it was an editorial call.'

'Are you frickin' *nuts*?' Trish's voice rose again. 'An editorial call? What if that guy actually *does* something to himself? Do you people not understand this?'

'Oh, don't worry.' Nivedita was quick to soothe. 'I checked with the legal team. We have the disclaimer at the bottom of the column with more detailed terms and conditions on the website. There's no way we would be held responsible even if the guy actually does go ahead and ...'

Trish had already hung up. This wasn't going to be possible on the phone. Much as she hated her, she would have to meet with Zee and explain this to her in person. She picked up her bag and was already on her way out when she almost collided with Ma in the hallway.

'What is it now?' Ma said sharply. 'Who were you fighting with? I hope it wasn't Sahil.'

Trish couldn't deal with her mother right now. She didn't bother to answer, and just sidestepped her and continued towards the door. Ma must have been in an even fouler mood than usual because she growled at Trish's retreating back, 'Would be just like you to throw away the only good thing to ever happen to you.'

Trish froze for just a second and then turned around. 'Ma,' she said carefully, 'You don't know what you're talking about.'

'Oh yes I do!' cried Ma. 'For whatever reason, a perfectly nice boy seems to actually like you. And every time I see you, you're just pushing him away. You seem to think that Ba and I just don't matter and your decisions won't affect us.'

Trish struggled to formulate a response. 'Oh, I see,' she managed. 'Well, forgive me for thinking that my personal relationship decisions don't actually have to centre around *other* people.'

'Yes, yes, be sarcastic,' her mother shot back. 'Why would

we care about you getting married? We are only your parents, after all. We don't deserve a thought. We don't long for grandchildren or a man in the house who can take care of all of us.'

Trish was on the verge of losing it. 'When has your care ever been compromised, Ma? I've been there for you, always. But it'll never be good enough for you, will it? What's the point of all your pretending to be open-minded and hippie, with your love marriage in the seventies and all, when all you've ever wished is that you had a *boy* and not good-for-nothing *me!*'

She spat out the words, even though they were more than she had meant to say. She'd had enough put-downs from her mother; all those subtle taunts since *forever* that suggested that she was not good enough and never would be.

220

Her mother went white and stood very still, but Trish saw that her small frame was quivering with emotion and anger. When she spoke next through gritted teeth, her voice was deathly quiet. 'And you say *I* have no idea what I'm talking about.'

Trish frowned in confusion, but Ma had already turned away. She walked off, her back stiff, still quivering slightly and, for a change, looking every bit her age.

Trish stood staring after her for several seconds and then shook herself out of it. Shoving the exchange to the back of her mind, she hurried out. She couldn't afford to lose any more time.

❋

'I need to speak to you, Zee.'

The entire roomful of editors and designers buzzing around Zee stopped in their tracks and gazed at Trish, giving her a strange sense of déjà vu. But she wasn't going to bother with niceties today.

Zee, on her throne behind the desk, coolly surveyed Trish as if she were an insect. 'You do not have an appointment. You will have to wait until we finish this.'

She held up a large sheet of paper and eyed it critically. A short balding man standing behind her chair bent low and said in a grovelling manner, 'Zee, we were just trying something different for the monsoon special edition, so these colours ...'

Trish stepped in closer and said in a loud voice, 'No, Zee. It *can't* wait. It's urgent.' The balding man froze midsentence and looked at her open-mouthed, seemingly amazed at her audacity. Trish looked around at the shocked expressions of the others in the room. She addressed the crowd. 'Look, could you all just give us a few minutes, it's something important.'

The folks looked at each other and a couple of them uncertainly picked up their notepads, but Zee's voice rang out, freezing everyone cold again, with one imperious word: 'Stay.'

'Stay?' Trish repeated. She couldn't help it. She looked around at the others. 'What are you guys, her pets?' She could see several offended expressions, but knew instinctively that the resentment was directed more at Zee than at her.

'You have no *right*,' Zee said through gritted teeth, nostrils flaring, 'to interrupt me like this.'

'Okay, fine,' Trish snapped, the remnants of her patience dissipating. 'You want them to stay and listen? No problem. It's about that email I sent you yesterday, which you seem to have missed. That letter ...'

Zee stood up suddenly and looked around at her team. 'We will resume in exactly thirty minutes from now.' For a

221

change, no one snapped to attention. Zee shot wild glances around the room. 'Well? Leave!'

Then, in a disgruntled manner, they picked up their things and started to leave the room, a lot more slowly and reluctantly than the last time they had cleared off. In spite of herself, Trish had to hide a small smile. It seemed that her standing up to Zee was making the others collectively feel that they didn't actually need to be treated like animals who could be herded out at the snap of a whip.

Only the small bald guy still looked nervous as he tried to make his way to the front of the dispersing crowd and escape first. Trish waited till the last of them was out and then whirled towards Zee.

'How could you ignore that letter? Anything could happen to that guy. We owed him a response, and I wrote that in the ...'

'We owe him nothing,' said Zee cuttingly. 'And more importantly, you should know that what you just did was unacceptable. Don't you dare ever try and undermine my position here with a stunt like that.'

'A stunt?' Trish laughed but it rang hollow. 'And, *that's* more important, you said? You're playing with the life of a guy who's unstable, going through hell and has reached out to our publication for help. He's desperate. And you choose to ignore him? Why?'

'Not that I owe *you* an explanation.' Zee sounded bored as she turned away from Trish to look into her computer. 'But since you're so insistent, let me tell you. I decided that his letter didn't have merit and wasn't in line with the direction of the column. And neither was your answer. Keep that sort of soppy sentimental thing up, and you might actually find yourself only cut out for some average friendly neighbourhood agony aunt column.' She turned to look at Trish, the dislike evident on her face. 'Now that's actually not a bad idea. We could then just fire you and be done with it.'

'You don't employ me,' Trish said through gritted teeth. 'So you can't fire me. We have a contract.'

'And the contract says that it's an editorial call as to whether the publication actually prints the response received from the party of the first part,' Zee rattled off as if she were reading directly from the legal document. Her voice became dismissive again. 'So let's not keep going on and on about something which is a non-issue.'

'It *is* an issue.' Trish's voice rang loud in her own head, over the sound of the pounding of her blood. 'We can't be so *irresponsible,* there's a reader out there who needs to get some proper counselling.'

'And we are not the ones to provide it,' Zee cut in. 'Do I have to remind you that you're not actually a real counsellor? Please. Don't get caught up in your own image. And do try to remember, it's not even your own! Amy belongs to the paper, and will continue to do so long after you're gone.'

'Who cares about Amy and her bloody image?' Trish was shouting now. 'That guy needs help. Won't you feel sick about yourself if he actually hurts himself?'

'We're not liable,' Zee said smugly. 'Our terms and conditions cover that. You must think we're novices in this game. We happen to have one of the best legal teams in the country. As a media house, we need to cover ourselves against any eventuality. But then what do *you* know about the way things work?'

'It's not about whether you're liable in court. How will you be able to sleep at night if something happens to him?' Trish shook her head slowly. She could see she wasn't getting through to Zee, but went on desperately. 'This is wrong. Zee, listen to me and print that letter tomorrow. Or we'll all be reading the news of yet another suicide and wondering if we could have done something to prevent it.'

'*Or*.' Zee's black eyes had a strange gleam in them. 'If that actually does happen, we'll have a fabulous story on our hands about how we got that letter just one day too late, how we were the first to hear about it, but despite our best efforts, we couldn't get to the poor fellow on time.'

It took effort for Trish to understand what Zee was actually talking about. What kind of a monster was she dealing with? She found her voice somehow. 'The dates would give you away – I would too – and then you'd probably go to jail for abetting suicide.'

Zee threw her head back and roared with laughter. It rang out rich and sonorous and made Trish's skin crawl. Every passing second made her want to throw something at Zee. She stood there, clenching and unclenching her fist. When Zee recovered, she heaved a sigh and looked at Trish with distinct amusement. 'You really *do* have no idea how things work, do you, dear little Trish? Who do you think holds more clout with any authority figure that matters? The leading editor of one of the most powerful media houses of the country?' She made a wide sweeping gesture around her office. 'Or someone like ...' She didn't complete her sentence and the disdain on her face, as she raised one finger towards Trish in a lazy gesture, ensured that she didn't have to.

Trish realized that she was breathing heavily. Her head was spinning and she could feel every hair on her body standing on end. She would have to keep herself calm somehow, or she would fly at and physically attack this bitch. She swallowed hard and tried a different tack.

'Look, Zee. If you're not going to print the response anywhere, not even online, at least help me understand if we can identify the sender somehow. Was it over email or was it transcribed from a physical letter? Which part of Mumbai was it from, do we know anything?'

'Sorry,' Zee purred in a manner that suggested she was anything but. 'That's privileged information and we are not allowed to give that out.' She narrowed her eyes. 'Besides, you might just mess everything up with your poking around and give things away, and that's hardly good for the future of the column. Or you, right?'

Trish's shoulder's slumped in defeat. She had tried everything. She knew she couldn't get anything more out of Zee.

She turned away slowly to leave and Zee's voice rang out, 'A last word of advice for you. You should work a little harder at knowing your place.' Trish didn't turn back to see Zee's expression but she knew she was sneering at her. 'You don't seem to have the least idea of who you really are.' Trish heard the sound of some papers being shuffled, and then Zee concluded, 'Nobody.'

Trish closed her eyes for a second and pressed her lips together to keep from responding. She somehow made it to the door. The important thing now was for her to keep walking, and she did just that.

By the time she made it home, her mind was a complete mess. Ma was giving her the silent treatment, but she barely registered it. Thankfully, Ba was already asleep, so she was spared having to pretend to be cheerful for his sake.

She felt tempted to call Sahil, and felt a little irritated with herself. She had always been independent, she had never needed anyone's help to figure anything out. And Sahil had been so reticent the last time about the Lisa thing. At one level, she respected his decision to keep his visions to himself. But at the same time, when it was possible for him to actually help someone out by sharing it, why wouldn't he? Trish had briefly considered pulling out the 'I saved your life and you owe me' card, but emotional blackmail of any sort just wasn't in her nature.

She lay in bed, her mind racing in a hundred different directions. She didn't feel like eating even though her stomach was rumbling. She felt sick with helplessness about that unpublished letter. She would never forgive Zee if something happened to that guy. More importantly, she would never forgive herself.

She tossed and turned, sleep eluding her completely till well past midnight. When she finally did drift off, it was only into fitful dozes with strange, unconnected images and thoughts making their way into her dreams.

She saw the words of the unanswered letter; Ma's face quivering with anger; Sahil's eyes flashing as he told her that there was so much that she already knew; Zee's cruel, cackling laugh as she held out a newspaper with the bold headline, 'Media house first to receive copy of suicide letter'; and the most uncomfortable image of them all, the sight of Akanksha's father, grotesquely twisted in death, the exact same sight she had seen the night of his fall, only this time the view was from far above, as if she were seeing it from the sky. It looked even more frightening like that and she felt like crying. As she dreamt, she felt tears running down her face, and she was dimly aware that this was strange because Trish didn't cry.

She awoke with a start and sat up straight in bed, her heart beating fast. Her mouth was dry and she felt like she couldn't breathe at all. To her surprise, her cheeks were actually wet. She wiped her face with trembling hands. She couldn't remember the last time a dream had left her feeling so shaken and scared. There was a strange undercurrent of emotion that she couldn't put her finger on immediately, even though it felt vaguely familiar to her. She thought it resembled the sensation of guilt.

She reached out to switch on her bedside lamp. A bottle of water was lying on the table next to her and she grabbed it and raised it to her lips, the cool liquid soothing her parched throat. She put the bottle down and stared out of her window at the still-dark sky for a long time.

Just because the letter wasn't published by *DNX*, it didn't mean that there was no way to get it out there. It was an online, interconnected world. It was best to just do it now before she was tempted to change her mind. She'd had enough of this anyway. It wasn't worth it, no matter how much it paid.

She got up and tiptoed down the hall to the living room where her laptop was. Switching it on, she sat down, her mind racing. She would need the help of the most connected person she knew. She wrote for a while and then sat back, rubbing her throbbing temple. There. Hopefully Akanksha would be able to help, even though it was a difficult time for her with everything going on, especially Lisa.

At the thought of Lisa, a blinding flash of pain went through her head, like a knife. She winced. With the pain had come sudden clarity that cut through the shadows in her mind.

The view of the dead body seen through frightened, guilty eyes hadn't been from the sky.

It had been from the terrace of the building.

Lisa had been up there.

22

Destiny-shestiny

'Sahil! You *have* to tell me, what exactly was it you saw?' The voice on the other end of the line slurred something inaudible.

Trish snapped impatiently, 'What?'

'I *said*,' Sahil's voice was thick with sleep and yet warm. 'Most people say good morning when they phone someone at such an ungodly hour.'

Trish looked over at the clock and bit her lip. Only five-thirty? She had been unable to sleep for hours and had only been waiting for the sun to come up so that she could talk to him. 'Sorry,' she mumbled and then added, 'So are you going to tell me?'

'Trish, we talked about this.' He yawned, sounding like he was indulging in a long slow stretch. 'I'm *not* going to interfere. If this thing has to be a part of my life, it's going to affect only me from now on.'

'Why, Sahil?' Trish said sharply. 'And please don't give

me some bullshit about not interfering with destiny and all that jazz.'

'Why not?' he countered. 'What if that's what I believe? That whatever is meant to happen will happen and just because I have some weird mental disease, that ...'

'Will you stop calling it a disease? For all you know, it's a gift and you've always just been bloody ungrateful about it, ' Trish growled. She then said in a lower voice, 'I had a ... strange dream last night.'

'Really?' Sahil sounded interested. 'Was I in it?'

'No, idiot.' Trish rolled her eyes even though Sahil couldn't see her. 'It was about Lisa. I had this strange idea that maybe she actually saw her grandpa fall.' She bit her lip and then said in a rush, 'Is that what you saw too?'

'Trish.' Sahil sounded warily amused. 'Is this a ploy to get me to tell you? Some kind of twenty-questions game so that I end up giving you the information?'

229

'Do I sound like I'm playing a game right now?' Trish asked, her voice cold.

'No,' he admitted. 'But it's not just that.'

'Not just what?' Trish asked sharply.

But Sahil seemed to want to change the subject now and his voice came through, deliberately light and nonchalant. 'So hey, are you suggesting that my disease is actually contagious? You're becoming some kind of psychic too? Cool! Maybe I'll go around spreading it to more people. I could become famous, like some kind of Baba.'

'Will you stop babbling?' Trish's head was pounding now and she felt weak from the lack of sleep. For a while there, she had thought she might have figured it all out, but Sahil wasn't helping her confirm anything. She pressed her hand against her temple and tried to think.

'Look.' Sahil's voice became serious. 'I really do think you should let this be. You're going to drive yourself crazy like this. Lisa deserves all the help that she can get. But you're *not* her mom.'

'I'm her aunt. Well, kind of.' Trish paused. 'I care about her.'

'I know you do, and that's great.' Sahil sounded earnest. 'And I care about *you*. And you have to know where to draw the line. She's not *your* responsibility, and she's going through whatever she's meant to go through; her fate is linked with that of her parents and it has nothing to do with you. So can't you just let it go?'

Trish was silent as she thought about what he was saying. When she spoke, it was slowly and carefully. 'You know what, Sahil? I've drawn boundaries my whole life. I've tried hard not to let anyone in, given everybody their space. And it didn't get me anywhere.' She exhaled, feeling more certain with every word that came out of her mouth. 'I don't regret interfering with your fate either. It brought you into my life, and that means ... a lot to me.' He said nothing but she knew he was listening intently. It was the first time she was actually admitting how she really felt about him. She went on. 'So you're wrong about this. I may be *just* Lisa's fake-masi or whatever. But if your so-called fate has any plans for her, it had also better factor in an interfering aunt.'

There was silence at the other end. Then, Sahil said, very quietly, 'Maybe you should go and talk to Akanksha and Lisa again.'

❀

'Hey.' Akanksha gave Trish a surprised smile and then opened the door fully to let her in. 'Come on in. What's up?'

Trish walked in past her, into the large, luxurious living room. 'How are you, Akku?' She sat down on the white sofa and looked around. 'Where's Lisa?'

'In her room.' Akanksha sat down next to her. 'She's still really quiet. I thought she was better after that day with you guys, but she just clammed up again. We took her for her first counselling session yesterday. She didn't say a word.' Her face took on a haunted look as she said quietly, 'I don't think it's going to work, Trish. So,' she added with a note of false brightness. 'I got your mail and put it up on Facebook, if that's what you wanted to ask about. Don't worry, I tagged all my socialite friends too.'

'No,' Trish interrupted. 'I mean, thanks for that. But that's not what I came to talk to you about right now.' Akanksha looked at her expectantly. Trish bit her lip nervously and went on. 'I had this weird feeling. About Lisa.' Akanksha frowned in confusion at this, but Trish swallowed and continued valiantly. 'Do you know exactly *where* she was when the fall happened?'

Akanksha nodded. 'They found her in her room, the maids, after the neighbours rang. I wasn't home, but they said she was just lying in bed. She and Dad had just returned from her guitar lessons a little while before it happened.' Her eyes welled up suddenly. 'It must have been such a shock for her to hear about him. I wish they hadn't told her till I got back.'

Trish asked gently, 'Do you think we can talk to her about it?'

Akanksha looked uncertain. 'The counsellor said that we have to work on erasing the bad memories associated with the incident.' She pursed her lips and then went on. 'On the other hand, he also said that we first have to get her to open up about it since she still hasn't expressed *any* feelings.' She

231

seemed to come to a decision. 'Okay. Let's do it. God knows I've tried, but maybe she'll speak to you.' She rose from her seat. 'I'll go and call her. I'm not sure if it'll be better for me to be around, though.'

'You hang around. Let's see.' Trish remembered what Sahil had said.

Akanksha nodded and went out of the room. Several minutes passed and when she came back with Lisa, the little girl looked lost and dazed. Trish thought she looked thinner than ever now.

'Hi, Lisa,' said Trish kindly. Lisa mumbled something that sounded like hello. 'Come and sit with me?' Trish patted the sofa next to her. Lisa uncertainly went over and sat beside her, drawing her knees up to her chest. 'Lisa.' Trish remembered the no-nonsense seven-year-old Lisa had been just a few weeks ago and decided to go straight to the point. 'There's something I wanted to talk to you about. Please listen, and feel free to say whatever you want to say, okay?'

Lisa nodded ever so slightly.

Taking a deep breath, Trish said, 'The maids say that you were in your room when your nanu fell.' Lisa's face froze but she gave another tiny nod. Trish looked her right in the eye and spoke softly. 'Leez. Were you up on the terrace any time that evening?'

No explicit reaction. But Trish saw the sudden fright and panic in her eyes.

She said quickly, 'It's perfectly okay, you don't have to feel scared, Lisa, we're just trying to understand.'

Suddenly, Lisa closed her eyes tight and two large tears rolled down her cheeks. Trish watched, too shocked to do anything as Lisa began to sob, rocking back and forth as if trying to comfort herself. Akanksha was by her side in an instant. Trish panicked and was about to withdraw when she saw the look that Akanksha was giving her. She was nodding in encouragement at Trish, even as she put her arms around Lisa. 'There, there, sweetie, it's okay, you can tell us.' She nodded once again at Trish, this time with urgency.

Trish recovered enough to find her voice again. In a low, soothing tone, she said, 'Lisa. You know your mom loves you, and so do I. You can trust us completely. You can tell us what happened.'

'You *won't* love me.' Lisa's voice came out muffled, her hands pressed tightly against her face, the tears overflowing anyway. 'No one will love me ever again. It was my fault. My fault!'

'Why do you say that, darling?' Akanksha whispered, her face distraught. 'Why?'

'Because it was my idea!' Lisa screamed. 'Nanu was tired after picking me up from guitar class, but I said I wanted to go up on the terrace again. He even said to me it was getting too dark, but I said I wanted to see the lights from up there!'

'What?' Akanksha looked totally confused. 'You were up there before too?' She glanced over at Trish helplessly. Trish said nothing and just watched Lisa cry.

'It was our secret. I made him promise not to tell you because I thought you would scold me for going up there.' Lisa's words came out in a rush, tears streaming down her face again. 'And then, when we went up, I ran and hid behind the water tank for a really, really long time and didn't come out. And he kept calling for me and I thought it was funny, so I kept quiet. He said, "Lisa, Lisa," and then he sounded really worried and so I was about to come out but then he slipped near the edge and shouted "Lisa!" loudly and he *fell because of me*, Mom!' Her voice ended up in an anguished wail. The sound was muffled when she buried her face into Akanksha's shoulder. Trish closed her eyes, trying to keep her head from spinning.

The child, sick in the heart for so many days, had been fighting not just the trauma of watching her grandfather slip and fall to his death, but also the relentless guilt that resulted from her blaming herself for the accident. Guilt and loss. Loss and guilt. Why did that combination feel so familiar to her, something she could relate to so well? But Lisa was just a child, she couldn't have known better. Akanksha had been right. Her father hadn't deserved an end like that. But he was gone now, and what was left behind was a small, broken spirit, sobbing inconsolably into her mother's shoulder.

Akanksha slowly registered what Lisa had just told her. Trish watched her expression change as it all sank in. The shock and disbelief were first, but they passed, and tears ran down her face as she hugged Lisa tightly and determinedly, saying, 'Lisa. I love you and always will. And I'm so sorry for what happened. But it was just an accident. That's all. *It wasn't your fault.*'

Trish saw that this was a different Akanksha from the one she had known before. Some sort of wall between the mother and daughter had been broken and they both hugged each other tightly, rocking back and forth together. They were both weeping quietly now and it looked like they wouldn't stop for a while, but something lifted in Trish's heart and she knew instinctively that they were going to be okay.

By the time Trish finally got back home, it was late evening. She had spent most of the day with Akanksha, trying to help her figure out what was to be done for little Lisa. She had been through a lot and needed the best possible professional help. They had spent a significant portion of the day researching profiles of child psychologists and calling friends and acquaintances, mostly Akanksha's, to get recommendations. They'd also spent hours researching the topic, and found that guilt after the loss of a loved one was potentially a cause for depression and other serious issues. And in Lisa's case, she directly blamed herself due to the way events had unfolded that day. There was going to be a lot of work to do, but the grit that Akanksha was showing made Trish see her in a new light, and with new respect.

Trish had realized only several hours into the day that she didn't have her phone with her. She had left it at home in her hurry to get to Akanksha's and talk to her. It hadn't seemed worth it to leave Lisa and Akanksha to go and pick it up, so she had just called Ma and informed her about where she was and that she could be reached on Akanksha's number. Ma, who was clearly still upset with her, had answered shortly that Ba was fine and that there was no need for Trish to rush back home.

By the time she got back into her room, she was feeling completely knocked out and ready to crash. She had dully noted that Ma was making it obvious that she still wasn't speaking to her. She didn't even remember what was making her so mad, and she didn't have the energy to ask. She picked up her phone from where it lay on the bedside table. Fifteen missed calls, all from Nivedita.

Oh. Okay. She knew what this was about. No point in putting it off. She dialled.

'Trish!' The phone was answered in the middle of the second ring and Nivedita's voice was more hysterical than

Trish had ever heard before. She screeched, 'What did you *do*? How *could* you?'

'What's up, Nivs?' Trish said casually, as if Nivedita weren't on the verge of an apoplectic fit. A part of her wished that she weren't enjoying this. 'You sound a little upset.'

'A little *upset*?' Nivedita screamed. 'You blew it completely! It's all over the place.'

'It went viral?' Trish couldn't help feeling a sense of excitement at this news.

Her enthusiasm was clearly not shared by Nivedita. 'You're going to really get it now. Look, Zee's here, and she's ...'

'Give me that, you imbecile.' The grim voice rang out over the line and it sounded like the phone was being wrenched right out of Nivedita's hands. Now the voice talking at Trish rapidly was Zee's. She could make out from the accent although it was a lot more high-pitched than her usual sonorous, rich tone. 'If you think you're going to get away with this, you'd better think again.'

'Zee!' Trish exclaimed happily. 'Is that really *you* on the line? What a nice surprise. I was always under the impression that you didn't "do" phone calls. I feel so special.'

'Feel special while you can, you little bitch.' Trish's smile only widened at Zee's suddenly uncultured language. Zee went on, now in a low hiss. 'Because we're going to sue you for every miserable last penny that you're worth.'

'Zee, darling. It's paisa here, not penny. And you're welcome to try suing me,' Trish purred into the phone. 'I'm sorry, but I don't think you have too much of a clue as to how things work over here.'

She was talking through her hat, of course, but she wasn't going to get bullied by Zee any more. There was silence at the other end of the line, and then Zee said coldly, 'You are, of course, fired.'

'Told you before,' Trish said gaily. 'Don't work for you, so you can't fire me.'

'The contract is *over*. Amy's dead, and by the time I get through with you, you'll wish you were too. It's all over, do you hear me?' Zee's voice was getting louder and shriller now.

'You bet your big queenly butt it's over, lady,' Trish said, her tone still pleasant. 'But allow me to just say what a pleasure it's been working with you.'

'Will you just FUCK OFF?' Zee was shouting in frustration.

Trish tsk-tsk-ed, not without sympathy, and said, recalling a conversation from earlier in the day, 'Zee, darling, most people who call this late usually end the conversation with good night.'

She was treated to the sound of a frustrated stifled scream and then there was nothing. Zee had hung up. Trish tossed her phone aside and snuggled into bed. All in all, a fairly productive day, she decided. Within less than a minute, she was fast asleep.

237

23

Resignation Letter

Dear Hopeless,

You wrote a letter to 'Ask Amy' on 3 July. You talked about how difficult it was for you to live with your secret of being homosexual, how your parents would never 'forgive you' for it and, therefore, how you were planning to end it all by committing suicide.

Well, I'm sorry your letter never got published in the column, and neither did my reply. However, I thought I'd try and reach out to you anyway, even if I fail in the endeavour, it's important for me to try.

You know, it must be difficult feeling you're keeping a secret from people you care about; when you think you won't be accepted once they find out who you really are. It sounds like a terrible way to live. Sucks.

But since I have no experience in being dead, I can't vouch for that possibly being a better state to be in. I mean, the pain is over, but then so is everything else, right?

Now, when you're not being who you really are, when you're suppressing yourself all the time, that's not being fair to yourself, that's not living, really. Right now, you're sacrificing your own self, your own identity, for the sake of pleasing others. Newsflash: 'Others' are never going to be happy because of you anyway.

I can't say how your parents or others who love you are going to react to your homosexuality. All I can say is that it's your business and those who really love you will, by definition, need to overcome their own prejudices enough to decide they're going to stick by you. If they don't, their loss.

Be who you are, and make a decision to go ahead and live your life to the fullest. And please, please know that I must confess to this – I'm just a regular person like you. I'm not a trained psychologist and I can only urge you to get professional help regarding your suicidal thoughts. They're not to be taken lightly. I don't know enough about this, but I do know one person who failed in his suicide attempt and is glad for it every day. And so am I.

Finally, since you've got me thinking and inspired me to stop being a fake version of myself, I want to let you know this is my last letter as Amy. I've had it with pretending to be an expert on these matters, which I'm not. I don't know it all. I'm still figuring life out, just like everyone else.

Therefore: I quit the column. You quit the suicide plan. Deal?

Trish (Not Amy) Saxena

Trish scanned through the now familiar words. The letter was up on yet another popular Mumbai blog. She went straight to the comments section, hoping to find the response she was looking for. It was everywhere now, re-posted on at least 150 blogs so far, the links tweeted and shared everywhere. A lot of newspapers were already doing features about it, journalists unable to hide their glee at the downfall of the most popular column of their rival paper, whose readership numbers were apparently already falling at a fast pace.

There were over two hundred comments on this one, and Trish gave up after scanning through the first three pages. She would just have to continue to hope that the person she wanted most to find it would eventually find it. At least it had been made hard to miss, and she tried once again not to let negative thoughts enter her mind.

The doorbell rang and she got up hurriedly to answer it, grateful for the distraction. It was Sahil.

'Hi there!' He grinned. He then cocked his head to the side and lowered his voice. 'Not still mad at me, are you?'

Trish laughed. 'I'm supposed to be mad at you? I didn't know.'

240

'Oh good.' Sahil took a step forward. 'You know, I thought you might still be wondering why I didn't tell you.'

She smiled and reached up to put her arms around him in an impetuous hug. 'It's okay. We figured it out. Thank you.' Suddenly realizing what she was doing, she dropped her arms from around his neck and stepped aside, cleared her throat and said, 'Er, come on in.'

Sahil was staring at her with a wondering smile. 'Wow. Now we're getting welcome hugs at the door? Maybe I'll just take a quick walk around the block and come back again in five minutes?'

'Very funny.' Trish was embarrassed. 'Get your skinny butt in here.' She had to suppress her smile and turned away from him to hide her blushing cheeks, quickly walking down the hall. 'It's hot. You want some lemonade or something?'

'Water would be great. My throat is parched.'

She brought in a glass of water and found him settled comfortably on the sofa.

He took a long sip and then put the glass aside. 'So. I saw your letter online. It's all over the place!' He smiled at her admiringly. 'Well done.'

'Yeah.' Trish sat next to him and sighed heavily. 'I just hope he gets to read it.'

He nodded and then ventured, 'It was a risky move, though. What are you going to do about the job?'

'Oh, *that*.' Trish grinned. 'Yeah. I lost the column. For about seven hours. After that, *DNX* was apparently flooded with letters and calls from readers asking them to put the column back up, with me back in charge. Apparently, the anonymity thing that Zee talked about wasn't that big a deal after all. They seem to really just want to read it.' She smiled. 'So the lady who had threatened to sue me for breaking the contract is now pretending that it was all one big joke and has offered me the column back – for more money!'

'Hey.' Sahil sat up straighter. 'Are you serious? That's great. Are you going to do it?'

Trish shook her head firmly. 'No way. I'm done with that. I'm not going to work with an egomaniac like her ever again. And she's still insisting on maintaining that damned "signature tone" in the column which I don't want to do any more.'

'Good.' Sahil hesitated for a second. 'I never liked that.'

'You didn't?' Trish narrowed her eyes 'You said you enjoyed reading the column.'

'I mean, I enjoyed reading it because it was you writing it, that's all. But you know what they say, sarcasm is the lowest form of wit.'

'Yeah.' Trish blushed. 'I don't know why I've always been like that. Kind of an automatic defence reaction or something.'

241

'You're doing less of it now, though.'

'Thanks.' She laughed. 'I'll keep a check on it.'

'So what *are* you going to do then?' he pressed.

'You know what? I have some savings now, so I'm thinking of actually investing in training for psychotherapy or counselling. I've looked them up, there are some decent courses here in Mumbai. And there are also international certifications which I can do online, and I'm thinking of actually trying both if I can afford it. I've also got a bunch of other writing assignment offers already from other publications, so I will probably pick up a couple of those, that should help with funds for a while.'

'That's great!' Sahil was grinning ear to ear. 'Counselling. It sounds like something you'll be fabulous at. I don't know why *I* never thought of that.'

242

'Very funny,' Trish said, recalling fully well whose idea it had been in the first place. 'And what about you?'

'Well, actually, I've cut a deal with Dad. I'm going to be consulting for his business. I know I can do a lot to professionalize it. But I've told him I'm not going to operate as an owner, and will do it only part-time. In the meantime, I'm getting together with a friend of mine to launch something. It's a low-cost, high-fidelity recording studio for use by small-time musicians who want to launch their own albums.'

'That sounds right up your alley!' Trish said. 'Is there enough of a market for it, you think?'

'We live in Mumbai. Everyone wants to make it big.' He smiled broadly. 'We've already got a couple of bands to sign up for it. My friend is well connected in the industry. I'm just the brains of the outfit.'

'I'm sure.' Trish rolled her eyes, but she couldn't stop grinning in her excitement. 'I'm so glad it's working out for you.'

'You bet,' Sahil said. 'Dad's insisting on paying me this fat salary, but I've negotiated it down to about half now. It's still more than I need. But I think it's going to be all right.'

'Negotiated it down to half, eh?' Trish repeated and shook her head. 'You really are one of a kind, Sahil.' She privately added to herself that was just why she liked him so much.

'Likewise.' Sahil bent his head towards her, drawing in so close that their faces were almost touching. Her heart skipped a beat as the scent of his aftershave gave her a heady feeling.

'So we're all sorted now?' she murmured. 'No more secrets that you're keeping from me?' She had been half joking, but the fleeting guilty expression on his face didn't escape her sharp eyes. 'Sahil,' she said, a warning tone in her voice. 'There's something else?'

He looked defiant. 'Nothing that you can't find out for yourself.'

243

She growled at him, a sudden thought hitting her. 'Was it you who wrote that suicide letter? Was that some kind of sick joke?'

'Calm down, Trish.' Sahil held his hands up. 'It wasn't me, I swear.' He looked completely sincere. Trish unclenched her fists. Good. Then she realized that it meant there was still an unhappy suicidal man at large whom she hadn't heard back from.

Trying to put that thought out of her head, she said, 'You know, Sahil, I always know when you're not telling me something.'

'I know. It's almost like, with you, you're the one who's reading my mind instead of the other way around. We make a funny couple, right?'

'Funny *couple*?' Trish reddened. 'We're not a couple.'

'That's what you think,' Sahil said confidently.

'Sahil. I … don't think I can handle a relationship.'

'I know you don't think that.' He grinned flirtatiously. 'But seeing as I'm so much older and wiser, you can leave the handling to me.'

'Older, yes,' Trish quipped. 'Wiser, not so sure.' She smacked his arm lightly. 'Don't patronize me.' She tried to change the subject. 'Um, so what were you talking about, the thing I'm still supposed to figure out for myself?'

Sahil sighed, as if contemplating whether to give in or not. 'I can't figure it out, really,' he murmured. 'It's a whole family thing. I think it's something you all block out collectively.' He looked at her appraisingly, one eyebrow raised. She tried to ignore how cute it made him look.

'Ma's not speaking to me, for some obscure reason. And Ba, he barely knows what's going on most times.'

As if on cue, Baba's voice floated in. 'Trishna … Trishna?'

Sahil stood up. 'You know what? I'm leaving now.'

'You don't have to rush off,' Trish said quickly, also standing up.

'I'll be back later,' Sahil said. 'Your dad needs you. Go.'

'You know,' Trish narrowed her eyes at him. 'You can be really irritating at times.'

'Thank you.'

'Trishna!' Ba's voice was more insistent now.

Trish scurried towards the door past Sahil, who called after her, 'Don't worry, I'll let myself out.'

She trotted into Ba's room and said, 'What is it, Ba? Are you okay?'

'I thought I heard that Sabharwal fellow's voice,' Ba said gruffly. 'Is he coming in here?'

'He had to go,' Trish said, sitting down next to Ba, relieved that he seemed all right. 'He said he'll be back again soon, though.'

Ba grumbled. 'Who does he think he is, popping in and out as he pleases? If he thinks I'm going to agree to let you marry him with this kind of casual behaviour, he's got another think coming.'

'Ba!' Trish interrupted. 'Who said anything about our getting *married*?'

Ba looked surprised. 'I just assumed you would. Aren't you almost thirty?'

'Oh god.' Trish groaned. 'I finally managed to get Ma to stop, and *you* start off on me?'

This seemed to remind Ba. 'Your mother is upset with you,' he informed her.

'She's always upset with me. I don't even know why this time. What did I say, anyway?' She turned to Ba. 'Did she say something to you?'

'No,' Ba said.

Trish gazed at him for a long moment. And finally decided to ask. 'Ba.' She hesitated. 'Is there something you guys haven't been telling me?'

The expression on Ba's face lasted only a split second, but it was enough to confirm Trish's suspicion. It was as if he'd been expecting this and had feared it. He grunted, 'Why do you ask?'

'Why do you answer with a question?' Trish countered swiftly.

Ba didn't reply, he just turned away to look out of the window. His eyes began to cloud over, but Trish was determined not to let him slip away this time.

She headed over to the other side of the bed, blocking his view of the window, and said, 'Ba. There *is* something. And I think it's time you stopped lying to me.'

'We haven't lied about anything,' Ba barked the words out.

'Okay.' Trish sighed. She continued to look at his face. Ba averted his eyes again, this time staring at the far wall. Trish took hold of his hand and squeezed gently. 'Ba,' she said quietly. '*Please*.'

Ba glowered stonily at the wall for a long time. She noticed his jaw was working and he seemed to be going through a major internal struggle. He then took a deep shuddering breath and said, 'You'll blame me. She has, always, always.' He turned towards Trish and she was shocked to see the pain in his eyes. He gripped her hand tightly now with both his hands. 'It was my idea,' he said, with the air of a man getting something heavy off his chest. 'I wanted to protect you. I didn't think you had to know.'

'Know what?' Trish asked, suddenly afraid, and getting the strong feeling she didn't want to hear this. 'Ba, listen, you don't have to do this if you're going to ...'

But Ba was just shaking his head from side to side, the words tumbling out, and he didn't seem to hear her. 'You were so small, so tiny, so helpless. I was afraid something might happen to you too. I made her promise. And by the time you grew up, I really thought it was better for all of us to just forget. But *we* didn't forget. Even with this wretched old-timer's disease.' His face was screwed up in anguish. 'I can't forget. It's all I think about.'

'Ba, you're not making sense.' Trish was half convinced that he was losing it all over again. But something told her that this outburst was different from his previous spells.

His voice dropped low. 'She never forgave me for it. It ruined everything, everything. And now you'll never forgive me either.' He looked up at her with reddened eyes. 'But no matter what happens, Trishna, you've been everything to us, always. A daughter, a son, everything. No one could have taken better care of us in our old age.'

'That's not true, Ba,' Trish said, thinking about how she spoke to Ma at times. 'But what does this have to do with Ma being upset?'

And then, the sudden realization struck her. Ba had said it too. And she remembered Ma's face when she had thrown those words at her, about wishing she'd had a son instead of Trish.

'A brother?' Trish whispered, unable to believe what she already knew to be true.

Ba's eyes were closed, screwed tightly together. He nodded slowly and then looked up at her. 'You wouldn't remember him.' His grey eyes were sorrowful and then his face crumpled. 'He died before he turned two. Before *you* turned two.' He drew a deep, shuddering breath and then added, barely audible, 'Twins.'

24

Sunset

Trish felt numb. At one level, she was aware that she was in shock. It had only been a few minutes, but time seemed to be moving in slow motion. Ba was still speaking, alternating between explaining the circumstances to her, justifying his viewpoint and profusely apologizing. She could barely understand what he was saying any more.

All her life, almost three decades, they had kept it from her. Her parents had decided – or rather, Ba had decided – that it was irrelevant for her to know. After all, he had rationalized as part of his explanations, it would be impossible for her to miss something that she never knew she'd had.

Except that he was just so wrong about that. There *had* always been something missing. She'd just never known what it was, or rather who. And so she'd been dismissive about it; even defensive when it came to what Sahil had been telling her. She remembered clearly how he had tried to describe the feeling of loss that he sensed with her. He had been firm on this even though he hadn't been able to pinpoint it down to anything specific. How could he possibly have? Even for her, she realized only now, it had always remained just a vague feeling of incompleteness. And it was a feeling she had accepted long ago without realizing what kind of an impact it would have on everything.

That feeling of not being good enough, of never being enough for her parents – or anyone. The inexplicable sense of guilt that she had always carried around inside. Strangely intensified around her birthday, always a depressing time for her, and one that she hated even the slightest fuss about. Was it possible for her to have actually known at a subconscious level? These weren't things that Trish had ever believed in. Hers had always been such a practical approach towards life. But then, she also knew without a doubt that she now believed in Sahil's strange extrasensory perception. She was being forced to reevaluate almost everything about the way she looked at life.

A brother. Not just a brother. A twin. They had shared a womb together. Nine months plus almost two years in the outside world, probably always at close quarters. Through the rest of Ba's ramblings, she had deciphered that they had shared the same crib. What had happened? Ba was almost completely incoherent about this, but she gathered it was a bout of pneumonia that both of them had contracted. It had been serious, but then Trish had made a sudden recovery, while her brother had not. How had that happened? Trish had once watched a documentary about twin foetuses, where one tended to consume more of the mother's bodily resources at the cost of the other. It had strangely fascinated her at the time. Oh god. Had she been born stronger than him for that reason?

Her head was spinning with all sorts of thoughts now. Her stubborn determination to always prove she didn't need anyone; her tendency to push people away. Did all of it stem from this kind of beginning, even though she had never been in a position to understand what had happened? For so many years, she'd had all that excess weight, she knew that a part of her always felt protected by the extra layer of fat, and served to deepen the feeling of guilt and worthlessness and alienation. And what about the discomfort she felt when she was in a lift or any enclosed space with anyone else? Was *this* why? She closed her eyes. It was all too much to take at one go.

She dully realized that Ba was still weeping. She squeezed his hand automatically. 'Shhh, Ba, it's okay, you've told me now. Don't. It's going to be all right.' She didn't quite know what she was saying, but she knew she didn't feel angry at Ba. She was still too shocked to feel anything. Even in her numb confusion now, she was aware that it wasn't good for Ba to be so emotionally wrought. She shook herself a little to try and snap out of it, and noted that it was time for his medicine.

'Here, Ba. Take these.' She handed him his pills, along with a glass of water. He swallowed the medicine and then lay back on his bed, staring at her with watery grey frightened eyes.

'Trishna,' he said softly. 'Are you angry?'

'No, Ba. I'm think I'm just disappointed.' She sighed. 'I'm trying to understand where you were coming from. It's just that I really *would* rather have known. I didn't need that kind of protection. It didn't help.'

She couldn't put it any better than that, but the look of understanding on Ba's face as he nodded made it clear that she didn't need to. 'I'm sorry. Your mother was right all along. She *wanted* to tell you, but I stopped her. It put up walls

250

between all of us.' He shook his head and said, 'She deserved better. She went through so much.'

Ma. Trish realized with a start. What she had been through. The loss of a child. Trish could only imagine what it would have meant to lose a baby. A devastating illness and the survival of one child only. What kind of bittersweet victory would that have been for a bereaved mother? The initial relief that at least one of them had made it, but the everlasting awareness that it was meant to have been two children?

And then, to not be allowed to talk about it, to express her grief, to always have to keep it a secret from her own offspring. Trish suddenly let out a bitter laugh. No wonder they had always kept a 'healthy' distance from all their relatives. She barely knew which of them existed and where they lived. It had been necessary to maintain the secret.

Ba shut his eyes tight as if he could read her mind and she instinctively knew that this had been his idea too. She saw it all now. After all, what if some relative in the know had actually given it away to Trish at some point? So much had been sacrificed. All in the name of 'protection.'

Ba didn't open his eyes. She waited till she was sure that he was asleep. He fidgeted for a while, but then drifted off. He seemed to be more at peace now. She quietly extracted her hand from his, stood up and switched off the light before she went out of the room.

❀

'Ma.'

It was only one word, but said more tenderly than ever before. Ma had her back to her as she sat in the living room, writing something on a piece of paper. Her thin shoulders stiffened at the sound of Trish's voice. She said nothing, but half turned, and Trish saw tears glistening in her eyes.

Trish knew she had heard. The walls weren't thick enough in this tiny house to keep out the softest conversation. It was impossible to keep a secret here. Although Ma and Ba had managed for the longest time.

Ma was speaking in a voice so low that Trish might not have heard her the first time, were it not for the fact that she was holding her own breath. 'Did your father tell you his name?'

'No,' breathed Trish. She realized she hadn't even thought to ask.

Ma turned around fully to face Trish. 'Would you like to know?'

252

It took only a moment for Trish to decide. 'No.' She could read the confusion on her mother's face, and went on. 'Not yet, I mean.' Trish paused. 'When you're ready to tell me everything else about him too.'

Ma's face crumpled and she reached up to cover her face with her hands. Without another word, Trish went over to her mother and put her arms around her. Ma's shoulders were shaking silently as she wept. Trish held her until Ma finally reached up to her tentatively and returned the embrace, somewhat awkwardly.

A single tear ran down Trish's left cheek. She didn't bother to reach up and wipe it. She knew it wouldn't be easy for her to forgive either of her parents for what they had done, but at least a part of her was able to understand how difficult it had been for them. It wasn't going to be easy for them to get past this, but she knew with certainty that they were all in it together, and the silence was broken. Her mother tightened her grip around her and Trish realized, awkward or not, it was their first true embrace ever.

❋

'You're still really irritating,' Trish informed Sahil.

They both sat on Bandstand, staring out together at the orange glow of the setting sun over the water. Sahil had bought two bhuttas and they were both savouring the taste of the corn with its spicy masala and nimbu. He finished swallowing another bite. 'Mmm. I know.'

She had told him everything. He had listened quietly to the whole story without interruption. There had been no judgement, no comment. Just listening with empathy. She loved that about him, she realized. Amongst other things.

She went back to staring at the waves, and he ventured, 'So why exactly am I so irritating this time?'

'I don't know,' Trish sighed. 'I'm just used to saying that, I guess. Sure you're not going to be telling me stuff you see any more?'

'You know what, Trish?' Sahil said thoughtfully. 'The more time I spend with you, the fewer visions I've been getting. Or maybe it's just that I'm feeling more sorted. Whatever it is. It seems to be going away, and I prefer it that way. See? You're my doctor and you're curing me without even knowing it.'

'Hah.' Trish laughed. 'Well, maybe you're right. Maybe it's better not to know stuff. Maybe you just find out what you're supposed to when you're supposed to.'

'Wow.' He put his arm around her. 'My darling Trish's getting philosophical. So not like her.'

'Careful, mister. Ba might be watching us right now.' But she didn't shake his arm off. It felt nice.

253

'So now that your family secret's all out,' Sahil continued teasingly, 'I might even tell Mom about mine some day soon. Who knows? Except that first, there'll hopefully be more important news to give her.' He gave Trish's shoulder a warm squeeze, turning to look closely into her face. 'That's right, that's your cue to become Miss Tomato Face. Oh, excellent. Delicate pink. Very kissable shade.'

Sure enough, Trish felt the colour rising in her cheeks, but this time she held his gaze challengingly. He leaned in to move his face closer to hers. She spoke up, exactly then. 'Sahil. Can I ask you a question?'

He gave a mock sigh and rolled his eyes heavenward. 'Okayyy. What?'

She nestled against his shoulder and said, 'Are we going to live happily ever after?'

She could sense he felt the same thing that she did. Quiet contentment with the beauty of the sun setting over the waves in front of them. Peace. An overwhelming sense of gratitude for somehow having found each other.

'Honestly, Trish. I don't know.' He moved his mouth closer to her ear. 'But I'm willing to wait and find out.'

Good, she thought, smiling to herself. So was she.

Unmindful of who might be watching now, she raised her face to his.

Epilogue

From: adsuri
To: trish.saxena
Subject: I saw it!

Dear Trish,
Just a note to let you know I saw your letter addressed to me on Facebook. All over Facebook, actually, and everywhere else. I really valued your response. I'm still around, and I intend to stay that way for as long as I can. You'll be happy to know I've broken off the engagement and I'm going to be telling my parents why this weekend. If they get it, great. If not, I'll figure things out anyway.

You're a wonderful person and I hope you know what a difference you've made to me. I owe you everything. Wish me luck.

Not so hopeless any more,
Akash Dev Suri

p.s. I know you said you're not a trained psychologist, but have you got any experience in the area of family skeletons? Maybe I could buy you a drink some time to talk?

p.p.s. Actually, hey, you think getting my parents really drunk first is a good idea?

Acknowledgements

My heartfelt thanks go out to:

My wonderful family, for putting up with cantankerous me, as I attempted to find snatches of time to write and edit this book.

The city of Mumbai, where I lived for only a year, but which has left a lasting enough impression on me to set a whole story there.

And to the team at HarperCollins, especially:

Karthika V.K. and Manasi Subramaniam, for helping craft this book into its final form. They added significant value in the process, arguing relentlessly with good intentions about what to name the book and the main character.

Sameer and Amrita from sales and marketing respectively, for all their tremendous support and good-humoured jabs at me.

A final special mention for my bright-eyed little eight-year-old, Anoushka, who has already finished reading my first book, *Just Married, Please Excuse*, and now fully intends to have her own book(s) published some day. She's clearly inspired by me, but if only she knew how much I'm inspired by her. Every single day.

'A beacon to all couples contemplating marriage'
—Hindustan Times Brunch

BEST-SELLER

Just Married, Please Excuse

Yashodhara, a quick-tempered gal from the big city, is hitched to Vijay, a laidback desi boy from a small town. In one word: Trouble! The young couple must learn to adjust to married life and to each other, whether it is Yashodhara's 'tamper tentrums' or Vijay's foot-in-mouth syndrome. With the unexpected arrival of baby Anoushka a.k.a. Peanut, the battles escalate, fuelled by their vastly divergent views on raising a child. Will their many differences – so endearing at the start of their romance – actually turn out to mean that they are just incompatible?

A fresh and honest take on marriage, parenthood and all the chaos that comes with them, this is a story of self-discovery that will have you laughing out loud ... and sympathizing wholeheartedly with its quirky and likeable cast of characters.

Sorting Out
SiD
FROM THE BESTSELLING AUTHOR OF JUST MARRIED, PLEASE EXCUSE
CAUTION: MAN IN PROGRESS
YASHODHARA LAL

Sorting Out Sid

Meet Sid, a master at the art of denial, in this hilarious, insightful tale of modern-day living and relationships. Siddharth Agarwal a.k.a. Sid has it all: a fifteen-year-long marriage, devoted friends and the chance to be the company's youngest ever VP – all at the age of thirty-six. But behind the scenes, his life is slowly falling apart, what with his marriage on the rocks, parents who treat him like a delinquent child, and overly-interfering, backstabbing friends. And that's not even counting the manipulative HR vixen and the obnoxious boss he must tackle in office. So, when lovely, spunky single mom Neha materializes in his life, she brings into it a ray of hope. But will she cause the brewing storm to finally erupt?

Who said it would be easy sorting out Sid?